The Gentlemen's Conspiracy

The Gentlemen's Conspiracy

A novel

NICK DANIELS

Risen Books
Portland, Oregon

Risen Books is an imprint of D&D Books, LLC
Beaverton, Oregon

Edited by Renni Browne

Scripture quotations are taken from the Holy Bible, King James
Version.

ISBN-13: 978-0-9840931-1-3
ISBN-10: 0-9840931-1-7

Printed in the United States of America

To my awesome wife,
my number one fan.

Paris, 1744

Voltaire's late-night note had better be worth it.

Georges-Louis Leclerc swore as his horse galloped through every puddle on the narrow cobblestone street. Mud splattered his white trousers, and a chilly wind tore at him. He longed for the cozy fireside, for the half-empty glass of wine he'd left at home.

The fourth house on the right from the corner of Rue Droit. There. He pulled on the reins to halt the horse and dismounted. The horse nickered, a plume of steamy breath billowing into the darkness. Georges-Louis patted the horse's neck.

"Attends, Naudin." He tied the reins to a post and turned toward the house. The dwelling looked slovenly. Certainly not a place for a man of George-Louis's social standing.

He lifted a hand to knock, but the door swung open. A hunched old woman with bad teeth peered around the heavy black wood. Georges-Louis swiped at his trousers.

"Je cherche pour Monsieur Voltaire."

The woman pointed over her shoulder and disappeared into the house.

He walked in.

A flickering light slipped through the few inches of open door at the end of the hallway.

He could hear voices.

Georges-Louis passed a hand over his fine coat. Why would Voltaire choose this filthy place?

Voltaire's voice escalated to an audible tenor as Georges-Louis pushed the door open with one finger. The room was larger than he'd imagined. Two servants scurried around the dozen or so men gathered around a massive table. At

7

the opposite end sat the famous Voltaire, despite the official word that he was not in France. Perhaps that explained all the secrecy. The man had powerful enemies.

Voltaire's fist came down hard on the table. "The despots claiming divine rulership of our land are criminals and traitors, religious bigots who mock our intelligence by asserting to have a book written by the hand of God. While their church coffers are filled, our people starve in the streets. And is that shameless behavior enough for them? No. They try to silence those of us who denounce injustice and superstition. If only we had the liberty they have in England. We would be the heroes restoring the glory to our fatherland!"

Georges-Louis rolled his eyes. What foolish and blind love for all things English. He detested King Louis XV and the church as much as he detested Voltaire's idealism. And Voltaire knew it. So why invite him? What did Voltaire see in him that could be advantageous for his cause? Was he interested in his scientific achievements or in his social influence?

"My friends." Voltaire narrowed his eyes. "These wretched times prompt our immediate action. We are the writers of freedom. Let us create a secret society that enlightens the minds of the French people. Let us write pamphlets, epigrams, poems, and plays that shake the foundations of tyranny and ignorance."

A low murmur spread through the room. Georges-Louis saw a few heads shake, but Voltaire continued.

"And if they come against us, threatening to burn us along with our pamphlets, we will deny them. Anonymous truths flying from hand to hand, while we deny our authorship and run free to our pen and paper to write even more poems and plays."

The men on the table nodded as one, but Georges-Louis sneered. Poems and plays? *Quel imbecile!* Only the wealthy king-lovers read that stuff—and for entertainment solely.

Yes, a secret society would be needed to achieve anything in France and still avoid going to the Bastille. But rhymes would change nothing. Plays would not. Pamphlets would not.

But he knew what would.

The idea forming in his mind brought a grin. This idea made it all worthy. This idea would change the world.

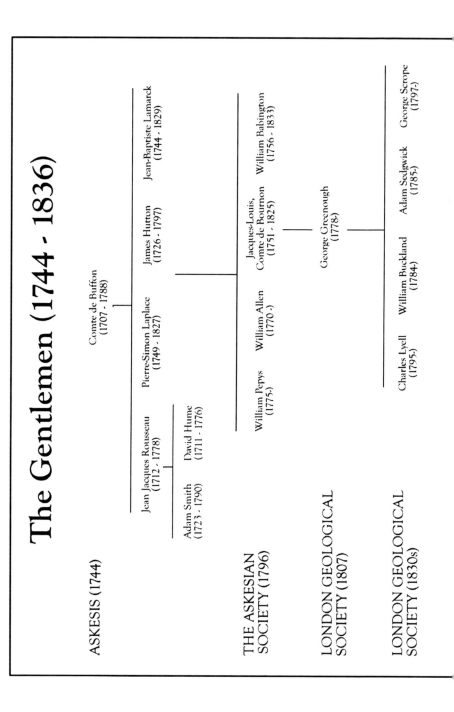

The Gentlemen (1744 - 1836)

ASKESIS (1744)

Comte de Buffon
(1707 - 1788)

Jean Jacques Rousseau
(1712 - 1778)

David Hume
(1711 - 1776)

Adam Smith
(1723 - 1790)

Pierre-Simon Laplace
(1749 - 1827)

James Hutton
(1726 - 1797)

Jean-Baptiste Lamarck
(1744 - 1829)

THE ASKESIAN
SOCIETY (1796)

William Pepys
(1775-)

William Allen
(1770-)

Jacques-Louis,
Comte de Bournon
(1751 - 1825)

William Babington
(1756 - 1833)

LONDON GEOLOGICAL
SOCIETY (1807)

George Greenough
(1778)

LONDON GEOLOGICAL
SOCIETY (1830s)

Charles Lyell
(1795-)

William Buckland
(1784)

Adam Sedgwick
(1785-)

George Scrope
(1797-)

PART I

"First of all, you must understand that in the last days scoffers will come, scoffing and following their own evil desires. They will say, "Where is this 'coming' he promised? Ever since our fathers died, everything goes on as it has since the beginning of creation." But they deliberately forget that long ago by God's word the heavens existed and the earth was formed out of water and by water. By these waters also the world of that time was deluged and destroyed."

2 Peter 3:3-6 NIV

ONE

LONDON ⁃ TUESDAY, 16 FEBRUARY, 1836

5:12 P.M.

A hand on his arm yanked Daniel out of his thoughts. He spun and saw Alexander emerge from the shadows of the half-closed entrance of the Geological Society's museum.

"What are you doing? I was about to go to the library to meet you. Did you finish your work for the day? We—"

"Let's go," Alexander said.

"You're all covered in sweat. What have you been doing?"

Alexander trotted down the stairs and Daniel followed, wondering what had gotten into his friend this time. He exited the society's apartments on the north wing of Somerset House and crossed the courtyard toward the street, walking fast.

"Alex! Would you wait for me?"

A cool fog had begun to set down on the city along with the sun. Merchants bundled in down coats roamed The Strand.

"There's Francois." Alexander sighed. "Me and my luck."

Daniel glanced east and saw the familiar Bold family carriage moving in their direction. Alexander pulled him back toward the building.

"I can't believe my father sent for me."

"What's the problem?" Daniel freed himself from his friend's grasp. "Just tell him you don't want to go home."

"Come, it will be dark soon. We can sneak out from the

13

terrace onto the bridge." Alexander ran across the courtyard and into the terrace overlooking the Thames.

Daniel grumbled and ran after him. He was used to foolish adventures when in Alexander's company, like that time at Oxford when he cut a hole in the bottom of everyone's uniforms in their row team. But today his friend's mood seemed far from adventurous. He actually looked scared.

Daniel reached the terrace and put a hand on Alexander's shoulder.

"Will you tell me what's going on?"

Alexander stopped and turned. "Well, it's complicated. I'll tell you more, but not so close to the society's apartments."

"What are you talking about? Is this one of your games?"

Alexander's face turned somber. "What would you say if I told you that you and the other members of the Geological Society are being misled by the leaders?"

"What?"

"They're covering up a rotten thing."

"The leaders? Please, Alex. They're scientists and respected gentlemen. You work here, you know that. Nobody's being misled. At the society we deal with facts, with the truth."

"What if it isn't true?"

"You're worrying me, seriously."

Alexander stared at his feet and then back at him. The last sun ray dissolved.

"You'll understand when you see the letters," Alexander said.

"What letters?"

"Not here." Alexander walked to the west corner of the terrace, facing the Waterloo Bridge. "Let's go somewhere else."

Daniel sensed somebody behind him—then a blow on the back of his skull knocked him to the ground. For a moment, everything faded into a painful black haze. He pushed against the dirt and lifted his head as a rush of adrenaline momentarily cleared his vision. A few feet away, Alexander struggled with a man at the edge of the terrace.

Daniel felt his arms starting to give way. "Al—" His mouth wasn't working right.

Alexander fell to his knees and cried out. An asphyxiating hollow formed in Daniel's chest. How could he help him? Blood ran down his face, and his legs wouldn't respond.

The attacker raised his weapon, a rock or a knife perhaps, and struck Alexander hard. This couldn't be happening. It couldn't—

Daniel collapsed back into the dirt and his vision blurred. The last thing he heard was a faint splash and François, the coachman, swearing in French.

8:06 P.M.

"He'll be just fine." A man's voice woke Daniel from a thick fog. He saw a grave face staring at him.

"Thank God, doctor," a soft voice said.

"You have a hard skull, young man," the doctor said. "It's the reason you're still alive."

Where was he? Warmth and brightness surrounded him—thick blankets and a soft mattress. What about Alex? All he could remember was lying on his stomach in a carriage while the trotting horses jerked his blood-spattered body in and out of consciousness. His lips trembled with the memory of the cracking blow he saw Alex receive.

He tried to sit but a bolt of pain struck the back of his head and ran through his spine, making him moan.

"Now be careful." The doctor's hands reached to help him settle back on the bed.

Thin brown curls came into view behind the doctor, framing a lovely face. Susan. Sweet Susan. She stared at him with teary eyes. How he wished to hold her.

Susan aligned the pillow with Daniel's head while the doctor lowered him onto it. He felt a sharp tingling when his head touched the pillow but said nothing. The sensation passed after a few seconds. The pain seemed to have shaken awake every dormant sense. Weakness embraced each limb, dryness parched his throat, and stiffness pinched his face—he reached with one hand and fingered bandages.

"Do you know where you are, Mr. Young?"

Daniel looked around. Thick purple draperies descended from a high ceiling, and ornamented side tables sat beside a magnificent bed. He had seen this room once before, just a few weeks ago. Alex had been striding down the hall, and Daniel rushed to catch up when he glanced into one of the many guest rooms and saw a maid dusting the table now at his right.

"Where's Alex?" Daniel said.

"You are in Lord Bold's home." The doctor sat on the bed. "Do you understand?"

But Daniel locked his eyes on Susan, who stood three feet away fidgeting with a scarf in her hands. Her rounded cheeks were flushed, but the sharp contrast of the brown curls against her white forehead soothed him nonetheless. Her sea-blue eyes reminded him of Alex—anyone could see they were siblings.

How he longed to be close to her. She diverted her glossy eyes for a second and pulled the scarf to her face to wipe new tears away.

The doctor blocked his view of her. "Do you remember what happened to you, Mr. Young?"

"Barely." Anxiety tickled Daniel's guts. "Where is Alex? Is he alive? Did you find him? The river, he fell into—"

Susan started to cry.

"Let's take care of you first, shall we?" the doctor said.

"What? How do you expect me not to worry about my friend?"

"You must keep still for a few days until I change the bandages."

Daniel stared at the doctor, incredulous. The medical babble continued, but he didn't hear a word of it. The man would not answer his questions, Alex was probably dead. The only person in the world he wanted to be with was Susan, alone. Would the doctor ever finish and leave? The last link in this chain of thoughts audibly slipped out of his mouth.

The doctor frowned. "Very well, then." He stood, took his ditty bag, bowed to Susan, and left.

Susan sighed and drifted closer. She would not look into his eyes.

"Susan," Daniel said.

Her shoulders sagged and she knelt by his side, sobbing. He caressed her hair for a moment, struggling to contain his own tears. At last she spoke.

"I was so afraid I would lose you, too."

"How did I get here? I can't remember—"

She straightened up and wiped her face. "Father sent François to pick up Alexander from work, but then he comes in carrying you, all covered in blood, oh Lord! The servants gathered to see everything, my father rushed to help. François said Alexander had been beaten and thrown into the Thames—oh, heavens, that filthy river!—and that he found you hurt but alive." Susan closed her eyes, releasing a dozen tears. "Then Father ordered the butler and his son to bring you up here and to go fetch Dr. Gray."

Half-wiped tears smeared her reddened face and her chest rose up and down as she choked out the words.

"Father took François to the library. I believe he didn't want the servants to listen."

"Where are they? Did François tell you anything?"

"After a while, Father and François just left. They didn't say where they were going."

"Hmmm."

"Oh, Daniel, is it true? Is my brother really dead? "

Daniel shook his head. How could he know for sure? It all felt so unreal, so dream-like.

"I only saw a figure in the dark. I know I was attacked first and Alex—Alex fought with this figure, this man." He closed his eyes to recreate everything in his mind but only managed to increase the already unbearable headache. He winced.

Susan covered her face with the scarf in her hands. It looked like Alex's. Daniel could not bear watching her grieve. Why had this happened?

"Why?" Daniel muttered. He clenched his fists and swallowed more questions he knew Susan couldn't answer. He shouldn't upset her more.

Tap-tap-tap. Steps in the hallway.

Susan leaned towards him and whispered in his ear.

"I think Alexander knew his life was in danger."

Daniel tensed. "How do you…"

A puffy-eyed woman stood at the door, her stare lost somewhere. Susan's mother.

"You are awake."

"Mother!" Susan sounded surprised, but Daniel could see from her expression that she wasn't.

"I am sure they will find him," Lady Bold said. "My boy will come home soon." She looked hard at Daniel. "Don't you agree, Mr. Young? Lord Bold and the coachman are surely on their way with my boy."

Lady Bold's face was pale and her eyes bloodshot, but she regained her characteristic rigidity and strode into the room.

"Susan, my dear, you must let Mr. Young rest." Her voice sounded casual now. "Mr. Young, you must spend the night here. Doctor's orders. Susan, come with me."

"Yes, my lady," Daniel said.

"Have a good evening, Mr. Young. I hope you will feel better in the morning." As the two women walked out of the room, Daniel heard Lady Bold's gruff whisper. "Why were you kneeling by his bed? Improper."

Daniel's eyes lingered on the door for a long time after Susan left, the splash of his friend's bloody mass reeling in his head like an endless thread.

Alone. Daniel didn't want to be alone. He wanted to talk to Susan. He wanted to talk to Alex. But Alex was gone.

Had Alex really known his life was in danger? Is that why he'd behaved so oddly that afternoon?

8:11 P.M.

George Scrope felt bile rise in his throat as the Duke of Wellington dumped his customary Tory speech in the House of Commons. He ground his teeth—truth be, he wished he could ram the duke out of Parliament. He searched the faces of his fellow Whigs, but none of them seemed eager to defy the former prime minister. He had to say something.

Scrope looked up and spotted Charles Lyell, the president of the London Geological Society, in the audience balcony. Lyell met his gaze with the hint of a smile. Scrope smiled back.

"We must put to rest the issue of political representation," the duke said from the middle of the room, "and focus on the matters most important to the king. Enough power was yielded in the Great Reform of '32."

Scrope's smile vanished and he looked at the duke with contempt. How dare he say that? The Whigs had labored hard to bring forth the Reform Act of 1832, which Wellington's party opposed from the beginning. Scrope remembered well the public riots when the Act was first rejected, forcing the king to intervene. The Act passed. One had only to look at the MPs on the floor to see its effects: large industrial cities with no political representation now held seats in Parliament, the corrupt representatives of ghost towns thrown out of the House of Commons. The Act doubled the number of people in the kingdom that could vote.

Most Whigs around Scrope were as content as they could be with the Act of 1832. But for Scrope the Act was only the first step in a transformation far nobler—and less bloody— than the recent French Revolution.

The duke continued. "Forget not what Reverend Paley taught us: Sovereignty descends from God to the king. Parliament exists only to advise the king. As long as the king is pleased with its advice, no further reform is needed. Whether Parliament is representative of the distribution of the people in England or not is irrelevant, because power does not stem from the people."

The duke's words were like a whip to the Whigs who jumped from their seats, flapping their hands and arguing incoherently.

Scrope arose. Enough was enough.

He lifted his hands and motioned his party members to sit. He remained by his seat, leaving the floor to the duke but defying him with a penetrating gaze. The duke could not meet Scrope's eyes and looked away. He would teach him a lesson.

"Honorable Duke Wellington," Scrope said, "Paley was a magnificent clergyman and a respectable thinker indeed, but his interpretations of the scriptures were wrong, having rendered the mythical story of the Deluge as factual history. Paley would have us believe that monarchy is the most natural form of government because that is the way

THE GENTLEMEN'S CONSPIRACY

God governs the world—as revealed in his judgment of sin with Noah's flood."

He looked around, drinking in with pride the emotional uproar he was causing in the Tories, and then continued.

"You are a man of arms, Duke of Wellington, and a man of state. I am a man of reason. A man of science. And science now speaks, revealing that the forces of erosion and volcanic uplift are so perfect, so clear to explain the geology of the earth, that we no longer need to ascribe to the biblical flood to understand the features of the continents. As Mr. Lyell rightly says in his writings, such myths only impede the progress of science."

He glanced at Lyell in the balcony, who nodded. Scrope fixed his eyes on the duke again.

"And so perfect are those forces God set in motion millions of years ago that we have not seen any more of him since, nor have we any need of him to rule the forces of nature. Why then should we need the king to hamper the natural laws of society? The fact is, honorable members, that sovereignty emanates from the people to Parliament, not from the heavens to the king."

A deafening debate erupted in the room.

TWO

LONDON - WEDNESDAY, 17 FEBRUARY, 1836

7:14 A.M.

Morning light spilled into the room, waking Daniel to a throbbing headache. He had fallen asleep half propped by a pile of purple-red cushions with fur balls hanging from them. Back and neck pain now accompanied his headache in a tortuous parade.

Sunbeams poured through a line between the window drapes and reflected off a wall mirror into his face. He squinted and leaned forward to get out of bed. The sudden movement made him dizzy. Grabbing the post, he waited for the swirling to abate.

When it did, he faced the blinding mirror: bloodshot eyes and messy hair; a bandage around his head down to his chin. He turned slightly to the left to see if he could peer at the wound, but the light shone into his eyes again. What an unusual London sky.

Tilting his head to the right, he saw that the dried blood had turned the cloth—and his light brown hair—into a sticky red and black mess. He passed his fingers over the cloth. It still hurt.

Alex.

He should go find Lord Bold and ask what he had learned about Alex. Surely his friend was dead. He had seen the force of the blow and heard the splash. Lady Bold was deluded. It would be foolish to think Alex would be back home safe.

He headed for the door but stopped at the second step, glancing down at his body. Was he dressed properly? Blood stained his shirt, but his trousers were in an acceptable condition. At the far corner of the room, he saw a stack of men's clothes on a table. Perhaps a servant had brought some of Alex's clothes for him.

Daniel put on a clean linen shirt and stuffed it into his trousers. The shirt's high collar touched the bottom edge of the bloody bandage. Nothing he could do about that. He then tried on the boots. Another pair of trousers, a dark blue cravat, and a single-breasted morning coat remained on the table. A black armband for mourning lay on top of the coat. It hurt just seeing it.

He heard a faint knock on the door. "Daniel," someone whispered.

Daniel walked to the door and placed his hand on the knob. A few seconds passed.

"Daniel, open the door."

Susan.

He flung the door open. Susan jerked and straightened.

"I heard you moving around, and—"

"Good morning."

"Come with me, Daniel, I have to show you something."

"But I haven't finished dress—"

Susan grabbed his arm and pulled him down the hallway. He stumbled and almost fell. "Agh!"

"Shush!" She pressed a finger over her lips.

What was she going to show him?

Once before, at her family's country house, Susan's father had promised her a new Arabian horse and she had chattered and looked out the window every two minutes, waiting for the servants to bring the beast from the stable. She was excited now, too, although he could sense her fear.

She led him up the stairs to the third story. "Hurry."

24

Daniel lagged behind. "Where are we going?" he whispered.

"To my brother's bedroom."

"Did they find him?"

"I haven't talked to father yet, but last night they returned without him. Father went out again this morning."

They walked down the red and gold carpet in the ancestral hallway—dozens of portraits of deceased Bolds covered both walls. At the far end, Daniel noticed the door to Alex's room, usually shut, was wide open. They entered and Daniel smelled his friend's characteristic scent, faint salty mix of sweat and nuts. Shirts and trousers lay scattered over the floor around the carved bed and wardrobe on one side of the room. He felt something amiss in the place—but the ash-filled fireplace, the modest library with the walnut sofa, the coffee table and the desk seemed as always. What had changed? No, what was missing? Alex. This was his first time in the room without Alex.

Daniel watched Susan walk to the desk stacked with papers, dip pens, pencils, and inkwells. The room brought a flood of memories. His gaze went past the shelves of untouched books to an undetermined place in the past.

"Alex wasn't fond of books but he loved to read and write letters." He turned to Susan. "He said letters glowed with an authenticity lacking in books."

She nodded. "I know." Sorrow enveloped her face. "And some letters may have led to his death."

"What letters?"

She opened a small chest on top of the writing table and extracted a bundle of sealed and loose yellowish papers. She walked toward him and offered him the bundle.

"These let—" Approaching steps in the hallway—quick steps—cut off the words. Her eyes widened and she hid the bundle behind her back.

"Oh," a voice said from the door. "I did not expect to see you two in here."

Daniel turned and saw Charles Bold walking toward him.

"Glad to see you up and well," he said, extending a hand to Daniel.

Daniel shook the long, pale hand, surprised at the strength in such a delicate-looking man. But that was the character of Charles Bold, Earl of Devon. A thin, tall man, always exquisitely dressed, respected by both foes and friends in the House of Lords.

"Yes, sir, thank you." Daniel, often awkward in front of Susan's father, felt even more so as his damp fingers trembled. "And thank you for your care."

Lord Bold's probing eyes made Daniel blink and look away. His right shoulder twitched, and Lord Bold released his hand.

"Alexander's clothes were found early this morning on the riverbank," Lord Bold said in a detached tone, as though it were trivial news. "His body must have been carried away by the current."

Daniel and Susan both gasped. A sting-like sensation cut through his chest. He'd really lost Alex, all hope gone.

Lord Bold half turned and extended an arm toward the door. "Let me introduce you to Superintendent Michael Oatts from the Metropolitan Police. He is in charge of the investigations."

Through watery eyes Daniel saw a short, stocky man in a black frock coat emerge as Lord Bold stepped aside. Oatts stood in the doorway, twirling his mustache. He looked more like a dandy than a policeman. But then Daniel noted the mud on Oatts's boots and a dark stripe at the base of the coat's skirts—a watermark. A true dandy, a clothes-wearing man as people called them, would never enter an aristocrat's house with dirt on his clothes.

Oatts stepped forward. Daniel kept looking at the man's boots—in a moment, they were right in front of him.

"Very pleased to meet you, Mr. Young." Oatts's Irish accent lilted his words.

They shook hands.

"I'm sorry for your ould friend. Me job here is to find the killer. And that I will do." He emphasized the 'I will' both with his voice and with his eyes fixed on Daniel.

Daniel bit his upper lip. He had long ago ceased to trust the police, ever since the incident with his brother.

Oatts stared at the bandages on Daniel's head. He seemed to hesitate and then said, "We need to have a little conversation, so try to remember all you can about the crime, will you?"

"I will," Daniel said.

Oatts looked over to Susan, who was still leaning against the table, both hands behind her back. Color had abandoned her face and she stared at the floor.

"Susan, dear," Lord Bold said, "would you please go to your mother? She needs all the comfort you can furnish."

"Of course, Father." Her voice quivered.

She took a deep breath before looking at the men around her and grabbing the bundle of letters and a pair of pens from the table. How brave of her! She passed between them in the middle of the room and gazed back at Daniel. Her sweet eyes focused away from him as she stumbled and flailed her arms to keep from falling. The bundle of letters flew to one side and landed not far from Oatts's boots.

Lord Bold grabbed Susan's elbow. "Are you all right, dear?"

Seeing the letters on the floor, Daniel froze. Should he trust Oatts with the information in the letters or should he find out first what they said? He still had many unanswered questions. And he was disinclined to trust the police anyway.

Oatts bent to pick up the bundle, still held together by a double cord around it. He frowned at the yellowish sheets.

"What's this paper for, ma'am?"

Susan shrugged. "To write, of course."

"Maybe you could get some new," he said, holding the bundle up.

"I like this kind."

"Please, Superintendent," Lord Bold said. "My daughter should go now."

Oatts nodded and offered the bundle of papers to Susan, who thanked him and walked out of the room.

Oatts kept his eyes on her while she left. He looked at the pens on the floor and raised his brows.

"Well, I'll just get to me work," he said. "Maybe I'll find some clues around here, don't you think, Mr. Young?" He went to search Alex's table without waiting for Daniel to respond.

Lord Bold pressed his hand against Daniel's elbow and hustled him away from the superintendent. "This is all so very unfortunate, a tragedy of great sorts, because you know Alexander was my only son, my first-born."

Daniel nodded. What was Lord Bold leading up to?

"Now who will pass on the family name? Worse, who will replace me in Parliament?" He let the question linger in the air for a few seconds. "I ascended to the House of Lords after my father's death, and Alexander was next in line. My daughters may not aspire to that post." Lord Bold stared at the ceiling, shaking his head. He still had that detached tone in his voice. Alex had never been close to his father, but shouldn't Lord Bold express at least some grief?

"Nevertheless," Lord Bold said, "we are still here and life goes on." He shifted in front of Daniel and looked down at him, at his bandages. "Do you feel all right?"

Daniel grimaced. "Well enough, sir."

"Good." Lord Bold straightened himself. "Now, you are obliged to not tell anybody what happened last night except Superintendent Oatts. We must keep these terrible events veiled from the newspapers and from the liberals in Parliament. No one should know about this until the case is solved. We will hold a funeral for my son and tell everybody it was an unfortunate accident."

Daniel blinked.

"And you will help me, Daniel. A murder in the family will only cast suspicions over my political career. It could destroy it. And I will never let that happen."

8:44 A.M.

Invoking the sudden return of a headache, Daniel slipped out of Alex's room and went searching for Susan, who was waiting for him with red eyes at the top of the stairs.

"How are you?" Daniel said.

"I believe I have no more tears left." She sighed. "Come. I must show you this."

She led the way to a small study on the second floor, the bundle of letters still in her hands.

"Won't your father find us?" Daniel said.

"He never comes here."

Daniel shut the double doors and leaned his back against them. He closed his eyes and rubbed his temples with his thumb and index finger.

"We must read the letters," Susan said.

"You said some of them are related to Alex's murder?"

"One day I found him poring over these papers. He didn't hear me coming and jerked when I touched his shoulder. I asked him what he was doing and he said he was just reading some letters he brought from the library—"

29

"From the Geological Society's library?"

She shrugged. "I suppose."

"So? What happened?"

"I tried to reach for one of the letters but he yelled, 'Don't touch them, they'd kill me if something happens to these letters!'"

"For heaven's sake, Susan, that could mean almost anything. You know Alex. He could even have been joking."

"He wasn't, Daniel. He really sounded scared."

That's what Daniel had thought right before their attack, that he sounded scared. Then he remembered.

"Alex did mention some letters. He must have meant these."

"Then you already knew about them." She spread the papers over the desk.

What had Alex said? That he would understand when he saw the letters.

"Look," she said. "Some of them have a symbol but others don't. Perhaps Alexander labeled them."

Daniel bent over the desk. "It looks like an 'X' but it could be well be an 'A'. The ink of the symbol looks newer than the original ink." He compared several letters with the markings and without them. Holding a marked letter in his hand, he said, "Perhaps Alex thought these were more important than the others."

He opened the letter in his hand and began to read aloud:

London, 17 July 1809

Dear Mr. Buckland,

I was pleased to hear of your geological tour of South Devon and your observations on the granite of Dartmoor. Time permitting I will reply to each one of your questions in a later letter.

Regarding your inquiries about my opinion of the newly formed Geological Society of London, I send you this brief note.

One year ago, George Greenough, Sir James Hall, and other members of the Geological Society came to my house in Buckingham Street to look at my fossil collection and my strata maps. Evidently, neither my collection nor my work pleased them and as of now I have been excluded from the society's membership. I was well aware of the social distinctions between the gentlemen in the society and myself but nonetheless was inclined to believe my geological insights would breach that gap. I now realize that the theory of geology is in the possession of one class of men, the practice in another. Neither that coxcomb Greenough nor the gentlemen in his dining club has ever practiced this science, which has been my whole life. From what I have heard, they are keen to discuss in their meetings all sorts of political and theological matters, and to debate such fruitless issues as the competing virtues of Plutonism and Neptunism. The society, I am afraid, would sooner study fossils for their beauty and form than attempt to discern their usefulness in determining the age of the rocks in which they are found.

Perhaps your efforts and influence at Oxford will someday illuminate the Geological Society, if that happens to be your inclination.

Wm Smith

"I know Buckland," Susan said. "He's come to visit Father. But who is Greenough? And who is Smith?"

Daniel glanced back over the flowing script. "George Bellas Greenough is one of the founders of the Geological Society. He was its first president, as a matter of fact. William Smith is 'the father of English Geology,' as Sedgwick called him a few years ago when the society gave Smith the Wollaston Medal. That all happened before I became a member."

"The society gave him a medal? From the letter it appears he would rather not be associated with the society."

"True," Daniel said, pointing to the date. "But the letter was written more than twenty years ago. Things change. People change."

"Alex was only the assistant librarian at the society. I don't see how this concerns him."

Daniel rubbed his chin. "Neither do I. Let me read another letter."

Susan grabbed a letter with Alex's marking from the desk and handed it to Daniel. When he loosened the seal, a white sheet fell to the floor from within the folded letter. She knelt to pick up the sheet.

"This one's in French," Daniel said, examining the letter. "Dated *le 14 janvier, 1796* and addressed to Jacques-Louis, Comte de Bournon. You will have to translate this for me."

"A list of names," Susan whispered. "I believe this is my brother's handwriting."

Daniel looked up from his letter and read the list Susan suspended before his eyes.

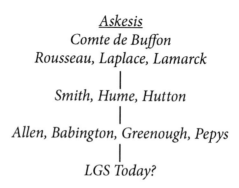

Askesis
Comte de Buffon
Rousseau, Laplace, Lamarck

Smith, Hume, Hutton

Allen, Babington, Greenough, Pepys

LGS Today?

"Askesis?" Daniel skimmed the names several times, shaking his head. "Naturalists, philosophers, astronomers, geologists—this is like a reading list for a physical sciences degree. This makes no sense whatsoever."

Susan pointed to the letter in his hands. "Perhaps that one holds an explanation."

1:02 P.M.

All the way to Somerset House Daniel thought about the names. Where had Alex got them? Why sneak the letters out in the first place?

A chilly wind blew through the cab's window. Daniel closed tight the flaps of his borrowed morning coat and crossed his arms around his chest. The wind carried a familiar odor—a mix of dust, horse manure, and the stench of the Thames. He looked out and saw Waterloo Bridge to the south. They had arrived.

He wanted nothing more than to go home but it was imperative he stop by Somerset House. He stepped out and glanced up and down the Strand. Carriages emerged from both sides of St. Mary-le-Strand church. Daniel hesitated— he'd seen many people run down in these streets that had no rules or limits.

It felt odd to visit Somerset House now: the place where Alex was killed, the place where he himself escaped death. He passed a hand through his hair but his fingers got stuck in the bandages. For a moment he'd forgotten about his wound. The doctor said he was supposed to remain still, but there'd be time to rest later. How could he stay at home with the killer loose?

As he crossed the north entrance Daniel glanced across the courtyard toward the terrace on the south. He stood there a few seconds, cold and alone, before entering the society's apartments on the north wing, accessible only from the courtyard.

The library's front desk was empty. No patrons in sight. A chill danced over Daniel's shoulders.

A cough sounded from the back.

Daniel turned and found Mr. Shaw, the librarian, hunched over unshelved books.

Shaw wiped his nose with the back of his hand. As if suddenly aware of Daniel's presence, he looked up, then back to the stack of books.

"May I speak to you, Mr. Shaw?" Daniel asked, stopping two feet from the librarian.

Shaw grunted, lifted three massive books, and walked past Daniel.

"How may I help you, Mr. Young?"

Daniel rushed behind him. "Well, you know about Alex's death—"

"Yes, unfortunate matter," Shaw said, "a terrible loss. I liked Mr. Bold, despite his eccentricities."

Alex was known for constantly irritating the poor old Shaw, but that was just who he was—a reckless bachelor who loved to gamble and make people laugh.

The librarian shifted the books to his right arm and placed them one by one on a shelf. He had to be used to carrying heavy books after all those years working at the library. He coughed again. A wrinkled, scarred face—probably from smallpox—hid deep, bitter eyes that now turned to Daniel.

Daniel found himself at a loss. He had been so focused on the mysterious list he hadn't considered what to say. What if Shaw opened his mouth and word reached the killer that Daniel was inquiring about the murder? He considered this for a moment and decided he had to take that risk.

"Hm, last week Reverend Buckland asked me to, um—"

"Does it hurt?" Shaw said.

"What?"

"Your head, Mr. Young."

"Oh, yes," Daniel passed a hand over the bandages. "The headaches are terrible but I'm, well, it's nothing, really. I'm wondering—"

"Excuse me, gentlemen…" Out of nowhere an ancient man stuck his head between Shaw and Daniel. "I am in need of assistance to… find a volume of the most important nature."

"Yes, sir," Shaw said. "What book is it?"

The old man opened his mouth but no words came out. His brows wrinkled and he shook his head.

"Oh, my… my memory has failed me…"

After two or three minutes of memory search during which annoyance crept up Daniel's throat, the man decided he wanted to read Scrope's *Memoir on the Geology of Central France*. Shaw found the book and the old man sat at a table by one of the windows.

The librarian returned to his desk.

"Mr. Shaw, please."

Daniel grabbed his shoulder. Shaw recoiled and faced him.

"I'm sorry, Mr. Shaw. But Reverend Buckland asked me to give some things to a member of the society, George Greenough."

Shaw raised one brow. Daniel could tell he wasn't buying it—especially the "some things" part. He should have come up with something better.

Daniel smiled. "Do you know where I can find him?"

Shaw smiled back. "Indeed. Let me see…"

He flipped through a thick book of handwritten pages, the text organized in three columns. An identical book remained closed on the desk. Membership records.

"Greenough, here it is," Shaw said, jotting the address on a piece of paper he handed to Daniel. "Interesting fellow, that Greenough. Be sure to make a good first impression."

"Thank you, Mr. Shaw," Daniel said, wondering what the librarian meant. In any case, Shaw was cooperating. "Mr. Shaw, I'm…interested in knowing more about the history of the society. Would you have some documents I could read?"

Shaw tilted his head to the left, still sitting on his desk. "Of course, we have a very extensive archive. Does anything interest you in particular?"

"I'm curious as to how it all began," Daniel said. "Perhaps read about the founders of the Geological Society."

"If that's the case, you can ask Greenough. He was one of the founders."

Daniel nodded.

"Come back tomorrow, Mr. Young," Shaw said. "I'll have some material ready for you."

2:22 P.M.

Henry Cole fumed as he wrote, anger the steam that moved his dip pen. Holy anger he would call it, the same anger Jesus felt when he whipped the merchants out of the temple in Jerusalem.

He took a deep breath, dipped his pen in the ink, and set on to finish his book on geology—his long treatise refuting the claims of geologist Adam Sedgwick.

Rev Sedgwick's position is a palpable evasion of the God's Verity, for the Scriptures do not, indeed, pretend to be a Revelation, or a rule, of all the pursuits and experiments of all natural science and philosophy; but, Sir, deeply and sacredly remember, that

36

they do pretend to be, and are designed to be A REV-
ELATION OF THE CREATION OF THE WORLD!
With that Revelation the Book of God opens; and
there is no other record of the World's Creation but
that Revelation: and it is the express design of the
Creator that there never should be any other.

Cole stopped and lifted his hands. "Heavenly Father, you
know I lack all knowledge of the science of geology but am
a faithful student of your Holy Word. Bestow your wisdom
upon me to defend the faith."
The sunlight shining through the window illuminated
his hands and writing but could not penetrate the rest of the
cramped quarters. The old sleeping cot, the water basin, and
the bag with his only spare shirt remained in the shadows.
Cole sat in silence for ten minutes before resuming.

Another position assumed by the graceless ad-
vocates of science is this: that none are qualified to
judge of the conclusions and deductions of any science but those who are fully acquainted with the
nature and details of the science on which they pro-
fess to pass their judgment. How manifestly absurd
a doctrine. How marvelous that men whose whole
lives have been spent in amassing data and making
speculative conclusions should arrive at such a conclusion as this. A person to whom God has given
natural vision cannot see whether he is in the light
or in the dark without the physical knowledge of
all the properties of light and darkness! An unlet-
tered traveler cannot judge whether he is standing
in a torrent of rain or under a serene sky, because
he knows not the physical causes of rain, nor of the
serenity of the air of heaven. A father cannot know

his children, nor a man his friends, because neither of them has studied the physical constitution of their bodies and souls. The absurdity of such a doctrine is monstrous.

No, men and brethren. An existence devoted to scientific speculations is not required here. The meanest and most illiterate member of the family of heaven, who has, by the Volume of inspiration, been made "wise unto salvation," will, in one moment and with one word from that Volume, confute and expose the most profound philosopher on earth, when his speculations, though the labor of a century, shall terminate in his drawing one conclusion, from his vain researches, which shall stand adverse to "the law and the testimony" of truth eternal. The Bible is not only "the law and the testimony" of all doctrine, and duty, and science; but it is also the inspired and literal history of the creation of this world; and not only so, but the inspired, literal and only source of all preprofane history of men, nations, and things. The Bible's preprofane history is either the literal and eternal truth, as Moses was inspired of God to write it, or it is the mightiest and most solemn imposture the world ever witnessed!

He paused and took a breath.

Thump, thump, thump, thump, thump, thump.

Cole hastened to the door before it cracked off its hinges.

"Pastor Cole, please," the short man at the door said. "My daughter. She's very sick." He was panting. His black, disheveled hair hung dirty and oily over his face. He had just a few teeth left in his mouth and no shoes. "Would ya see 'er, pastor? We have no chink for the crow."

No money for the doctor—of course: nobody in this parish would. Cole's muscles relaxed and his fiery mood dissipated. *It is time to tend my flock.*

"Yes. I'll go with you."

Having been a lifetime cleric in the Church of England, Cole was still getting accustomed to his new role as the pastor of the Islington Green Chapel, a Methodist church north of London. He'd never met the former pastor, who had died during a cholera outbreak the year before, but the members of the confederation of Methodist chapels who offered Cole the position assured him the former pastor had left behind a trouble-free and loving congregation. An unlikely feat in this borough.

They rushed across the crowded streets. A black drizzle of smoke drifted from the chimneys above. Cole's eyes lingered on two children—a boy and girl thin as toothpicks, extracting a brownish liquid from a street water pump. When he looked back to his path, he had to twist to avoid two mongrels fighting over a piece of meat in front of a butcher's shop.

"'Ere," the man said.

Cole glanced at the place and closed his eyes for a moment. *Dear Lord, grant me the grace and wisdom to minister to this family.*

The man led Cole to an old building where several families lived in the company of as many rats. They reached the third level. The girl lay sprawled on empty sacks spread on the floor. Cole looked at her and then at her mother. They were totally unalike.

The girl's face was white as foam, her mouth opened and closed in desperate gasps for air.

"When was the last time she had a meal?" Cole asked the father.

"We're very poor, pastor, you know."

"When?"

The man shrugged. "Monday. Maybe Sunday."

Cole stood a head taller than the girl's parents. He reached for his purse, emptying its contents into their hands—only a few silver shillings.

"She has the green sickness," Cole said. "Buy some liver and give it to her and your other children. I will pray she becomes whole again." He crouched at the girl's side and stroked her hair. He had seen worse cases. The girl would probably make it. "You'll be all right, chavy." Then he turned to the father. "Go, now!"

The father ran out the room towards the street and Cole followed behind, eager to get back home. He felt the lightness of his empty purse on the way back.

"The Lord shall provide," he said.

His mind drifted towards his book. The holy anger was returning. Was this flame the gift of God that burned in his heart?

"What wouldn't I do for you, Lord? Use me to silence the enemies of the truth."

Sedgwick. *I must silence Sedgwick.*

6:11 P.M.

Adam Sedgwick walked past Westminster Hall. He'd had a wreck of a day but he intended to let it go and rest. As he walked, he noted some beams still exposed by the 1834 fire that had destroyed most of the Parliament building. A few workmen were busy among the brick and mortar over the northern tower.

He stepped out into the cold night and searched for his carriage—it was on the other side of the courtyard. A policeman at the gate nodded at him. As he came down the stairs and onto the street, he saw a dark figure emerging from behind a boarded wall.

Sedgwick felt a chill of fear run through his body—he couldn't even feel safe outside Parliament. He quickened his pace. His carriage was only fifty feet away, but he could sense the pursuer. Sedgwick turned to face him.

"You!" Sedgwick said. What did he want this time?

The man lifted a pipe, took a step forward and swung the pipe at his head. Sedgwick ducked, the pipe hitting his left forearm. He fell to the ground.

"Help!"

The policeman at the gate began to run toward them. "Stop right there!"

The attacker dropped the pipe and bolted away. From the ground, Sedgwick saw two more policemen joining the chase. Sudden dread burst in his chest. *What if they seize him now?*

But the attacker reached the Thames, jumped to the riverbank, and vanished into the shadows. Relief settled on Sedgwick as the three policemen halted by the bank, apparently undecided about venturing down the attacker's path. One of them ran back to Sedgwick.

"Are you hurt, sir?" The policeman helped him to his feet.

"I'm not, thank you," Sedgwick said, dusting his clothes.

Soon the coachman returned with the other policemen.

"You must catch him!" the coachman told them.

Sedgwick rubbed his arm and gazed at the escape trail. "Let him go. He's just a drunken tramp."

7:05 P.M.

Daniel set down the empty bottle of laudanum and waited. The apothecary had said the remedy would kill the pain and help him sleep, but his sleep seemed to be receding along with the pain.

He sat on his bed staring at the stained bandages spread on the floor. No matter what the doctor said, he would not wear them any longer. He felt as if the tight bloody straps had deformed his face. At least he was alive, while Alex—

Who would kill him because of some old letters?

He reviewed Alex's last words for something that would shed some light on the attack. *What if it's not true?*

Those words had a deeper meaning. Because at the heart of the matter lay the possibility that Daniel had denied his faith for a lie.

He had been a good Anglican all his life—well, not lately, but most of his life. How could he not, living in the same house as his father, the most revered pastor in Norwich? Three times a day Daniel would hear from his father that the Bible was the word of God and that it was to be believed from cover to cover, literally. But outside his home, a swarm of theories and sermons reinterpreted the words between the Bible's covers, explained and gave them meaning other than what was literal. All thanks to discoveries in the new field of geology. It seemed ironic to Daniel that preachers now took their cue from geologists before teaching about the days of Creation and Noah's flood.

Daniel plunged his hand into a drawer, searching for his old Bible. It wasn't there. Then he remembered. He walked across the room and reached up to the top shelf on his library. Dust had settled on the cover. He flipped it open to Genesis 1.

> In the beginning God created the heaven and the earth.

A note on the margin carried a date: 4004 B.C.

Daniel chuckled. Even when he'd entered Oxford he still believed that James Ussher's date for the creation of the world, almost six thousand years ago, was true. He knew better now: the earth was millions of years old.

What if it's not true?

What if old-earth geology isn't true?

Undoubtedly Alex was misguided. The most respected geologists in Europe could not be wrong.

So, who's wrong? The Bible? Is God wrong?

"Agh!" Daniel hit the bed with closed fists. He had left God in Norwich for a good reason. Far from home, God didn't feel real any more. The world didn't turn out to be like his father painted it in his sermons.

Thump. "Mr. Young," a man's voice said.

Daniel opened the door and saw Mr. Welsh, the butler.

"Mr. Michael Oatts is here to see you, sir," he said. "He is waiting in the drawing room."

Daniel frowned. "Superintendent Oatts? Tell him I'll be there in a few moments."

"Very well, sir."

Daniel put the Bible in a drawer and trotted down the stairs. He felt sweat in his hands as he gripped the rail. Why was he nervous? There was no reason to fear. He took a deep breath and entered the drawing room.

Oatts examined a wall painting, his hands behind his back. He seemed to hear Daniel approaching and turned.

"A fine painting, Mr. Young," Oatts said. He looked around the room. "And a fine home, too."

"Thank you," Daniel said.

"Is this your estate or your father's—if you pardon me askin'?"

"Actually, it belongs to my cousin. He's on holiday in Switzerland and has left me as master of his house while he's away."

"I see." Oatts began fiddling with his mustache. "Is your cousin a titled gentleman?"

Daniel managed not to chuckle. "My cousin made his fortune with several factories he owns. I take care of his business, collecting the profits and the like." Daniel paused for just a moment. "But my real passion is science."

"I see."

An odd silence stretched between them.

"Please take a seat," Daniel said finally. Oatts sat by the fire and took out a notebook. "Tell me everything you remember from the night of the murder, Mr. Young."

Daniel told him how he found Alexander in the entrance to the museum and how they ended up hiding in the terrace but omitted the details about their conversation. He would not trust this policeman so soon.

"Why the terrace?" Oatts said.

"Alex thought we could sneak out from the terrace without François seeing us."

"Was 'e afraid of François?"

"Oh, no. That's just the way Alex behaved. He treated everything as a game. I think he intended to cross to Waterloo Bridge over some planks workers had put between the bridge and the west side of the terrace."

"What happened then?"

"I remember the sound of steps behind me, but a second later I felt this ringing pain…" Daniel touched his temples. "I was hit first, from the back. We were both looking west and didn't see the attacker coming."

"Did you see the killer afterwards, Mr. Young?"

"Not really. It was dark already. I saw their silhouettes in the dim light."

Oatts rested his chin on his hand. "Aye. Lucky killer, to attack on a moonless evening."

Daniel sat back on his chair and stared at the crackling logs in the fireplace.

"As I said, I saw only shadows. My vision was clouded

THE GENTLEMEN'S CONSPIRACY

from the blow. But I remember François's voice before losing consciousness."

"Could this François be the killer?" Oatts said.

"I don't think so," Daniel said, shaking his head. "I heard his voice coming from the entrance of the terrace. The attacker was fighting with Alex in front of me."

"But 'ow do you know it was from the entrance, Mr. Young? You just told me you were out of your senses."

Daniel thought about it for several seconds. "You're right. But the killer was a big man, and François is rather short. Have you met him?"

"Aye." Oatts scribbled on his notebook. "You ever heard the name of Martin Honecker?"

"No, sir."

"Mr. Bold had a gamblin' debt with Honecker. And a big fellow he is. Didn't your friend tell you about this?"

"Alex wouldn't talk to me about his gambling debts, knows I'd give him a sermon about it. I don't like gambling."

"Turns out this Honecker 'as an alibi, but I'll have to confirm—"

"I don't think Honecker killed Alex."

"Why, Mr. Young?" Oatts leaned forward and narrowed his black eyes. "Is there something you know but haven't told me about, then?"

THREE

MONTBARD, FRANCE, 1761

Rousseau shifted in his chair and yawned into his mani-cured hand. He seemed eager to leave, but Georges-Louis didn't care. Sleep was a waste of precious time.

"I don't care about the finer points," Georges-Louis said. "What is the heart of this social contract of yours?"

Rousseau rolled his eyes. "That each citizen places him-self under the supreme direction of the general will. Thus, we have free men yielding their authority to the group un-der a social contract."

"So you do away with the king?"

"*Oui*," Rousseau said.

Now they were getting somewhere. "What about reli-gion?"

"You know I'm a Calvinist—"

"Mere appearances. You must say something against religion, do you not?"

Rousseau gave him a wary look. Or was it weary? Hard to tell when the man was falling asleep in his chair.

"I restrict the dogmas of faith to those that do not col-lide with the general will of the people. I believe the follow-ers of Jesus would never be good citizens."

"Bravo!" George-Louis tapped on his own leg and jumped off his seat. Rousseau popped his half-closed eyes open and let out a feminine cry.

"You must publish this at once, Jean-Jacques!"

"In due time, *mon ami*," Rousseau said, regaining his composure.

47

"The time is now!"

"But in France, *il est très difficile!* Even in Geneva. The church and the king would put a price on my head." Rousseau looked Georges-Louis in the eyes. "Unless I do it Voltaire's way."

"Forget Voltaire! Forget France. We'll reach France eventually. Publish it in Amsterdam, Berlin, even Lond— no. Anyway, I must read it."

Rousseau shrugged. "*Pas problème.* It's only that I'm writing a novel on education that will—"

"A *novel?*" Georges-Louis felt like shoving him out the door.

"It is the story of—" Rousseau's voice quivered. He wet his lips with his tongue and stared at Georges-Louis like an accused before a judge. "The story of Emile and her tutor, where I deal with the very nature of man. I believe it to be a beautiful and important novel, *mon ami.*"

Rousseau's words stung his ears like a noisy thorn. Georges-Louis swung a hand in the air, stopping inches away from Rousseau's recoiling face.

He should not do this. Rousseau was useful and malleable, despite his depressive manias. He would eventually do whatever he was told—pity that wits and courage didn't come in the same package. Perhaps it would be better not to intimidate him. In Georges-Louis's experience, fear could make philosophers somewhat unpredictable.

He patted Rousseau on his shoulder. "You may tell me about your novel tomorrow, Jean-Jacques. You look tired."

Rousseau's face relaxed. He sighed and nodded.

"But promise me something before you go to bed. Promise me you'll finish your Social Contract before the spring."

Rousseau stood with a theatrical dignity and stretched his hand towards Georges-Louis. "Of course, *mon ami.* I will do it for the good of the society."

A malicious grin brushed Rousseau's face, and Georges-Louis wondered which society he was referring to.

Georges-Louis stepped out into the cool night. Silence pervaded within the late breeze. The countryside beyond his estate lay shrouded in darkness. The eeriness he felt now was not unlike the mood that night sixteen years ago, when he stood outside Voltaire's hideout in Paris.

Voltaire and his writers were still wasting their time. True, Georges-Louis lacked the membership of Voltaire's secret society. But patience would be rewarded. He sought out bright minds capable of overpowering centuries-old dogmas—like Rousseau's. But now the Genevan seemed to have fallen into the same idiocy as Voltaire, writing a novel instead of a political manifesto.

Georges-Louis filled his lungs with cool air, hoping it would soothe his anxiety. He must assume a stoic attitude towards Rousseau: a single harsh word could result in emotional havoc. But Rousseau would not disappoint him. If Georges-Louis hadn't told the Academy of Arts in Dijon to award him the prize for best essay in their 1750 competition, Rousseau would still be living in impoverished oblivion. Rousseau was well aware of that—his veneration sometimes became insufferable.

Be that as it may, George-Louis's plan was working. He just needed a few others to set his entire scheme in motion.

ꬵꙨꙋꙄ

9:30 A.M.

Susan took her mother's hand and leaned in close.

"We should go for a stroll in the countryside this weekend, mother. You've always enjoyed walks."

Lady Bold's puffy eyes stared away. Her rounded body trembled in the chair.

"What do you say, mother?"

No response. Susan sighed and caressed her mother's hair.

"Miss?"

Susan turned and saw Mary, the housekeeper, at the door of Lady Bold's room.

"No sleep and no food," Mary said. "You'll come down ill if you keep on like this, miss."

"I really don't feel like eating."

"But you must. You need your strength."

Susan thought about breakfast, and something stirred in her stomach.

"Perhaps I could have a little."

She turned to her mother and saw she'd fallen asleep on the chair.

"Go down and eat, miss. I'll stay with my lady."

Susan hesitated, then let Mary take her place by her mother's side. Downstairs she halted at the sound of her father's voice in the drawing room.

51

"Do you really think Daniel had something to do with what happened to my son, Superintendent?"

"I think he's hiding something. And I'll find out what soon enough."

A sudden weight fell upon her chest. Daniel would never hurt her brother.

10:00 A.M.

Daniel jumped out of the cab, wondering whether Shaw could give him something Alex hadn't taken already. He'd managed to keep Oatts ignorant of the letters, but sooner or later he'd have to share his findings with the superintendent.

A poster near the entrance to the society's apartments greeted him:

THE GEOLOGICAL SOCIETY OF LONDON
INVITES ITS MEMBERS TO
Mr. Charles Lyell's
Presidential Address to the Geological Society
To be delivered at the Anniversary,
On the evening of the 19th of February, 1836

Daniel tapped his forehead. The anniversary, of course. He'd forgotten. For weeks he'd been looking forward to hearing Lyell's report on the progress of geology. The society's members would travel from all over England to hear him.

He found that the doors of the library were shut.

"Closed for today, sir," said the clerk, a bone-thin man with a beak-like nose commanding his face.

"Why?" Daniel said.

"No one to open it, sir. The librarian is sick and his assistant died in an accident a few days ago."

So the rumor of an accident was already in circulation. "Is that so?" Daniel said. "What kind of accident?"

"I'm not sure, sir." The clerk pointed to the south. "I think he slipped off the terrace and into the river. Nasty thing, sir, if you ask me."

Daniel nodded and looked as somber as he could. The clerk looked to both sides and started walking away.

"G'day, sir."

"Good day," Daniel waited until the man was out of sight, then tried the doorknob. It was unlocked.

Perhaps Shaw had left something on his desk. And if not he could try and find the names himself. A drop of sweat ran down his face despite the cold weather. He turned the knob and stepped in.

The only light came from the windows, and when Daniel walked to Shaw's desk he saw nothing. Maybe Shaw hadn't had time to look for the documents. He had been coughing badly yesterday.

A few feet from the desk, ceiling-high shelves separated the common space from the realm of the librarian—exactly the place he needed to look.

Thud.

Someone was here.

Daniel dropped behind the desk and peered through the space between the shelves. A man reached for some papers on his right but dropped them. When the man turned, he exposed a box and the profile of his face.

Daniel covered his mouth and ducked down.

Thud.

He closed his eyes, trying to put a name to the familiar face. Last year, at Somerset House. The society's members were arriving for a meeting and Daniel stood outside with Alex, watching them come in. Alex was making fun of the bald and hairy alike. He'd turned somber when a stocky man descended from a carriage. That's where Daniel had seen the intruder here in the library.

Lloyd. George Scrope's aide, Stephen Lloyd. What could prompt Scrope to send him sneaking into the library? Perhaps the same thing as Daniel? Or was Lloyd here without his master's knowledge?

When Alex had told Daniel who Scrope and Lloyd were, in very few words, Daniel could sense his friend's fear. Of course, minutes later, Alex was mocking again.

That look of fear in Alex's eyes was unprecedented. Macabre. Could Lloyd be the killer?

Daniel peered again over the desk. Lloyd seemed big enough to be the tall figure at the terrace. He felt a tingling on his back and a burning sensation on his wound right where the bandages used to be. He rubbed his forehead, feeling the onset of a headache.

Out. He had to get out of here.

He crawled to the exit, following the low path beneath chairs and tables. He stood with caution and waited for the next thud to turn the knob.

Thud.

As Daniel slipped out the door, he saw a man in the hallway staring at him.

"Reverend Buckland!" Daniel felt the blood rush to his face.

"My lad, what are you up to?" Buckland said.

"I was… looking for the librarian, sir."

"I see." Buckland walked toward him. "I heard he's ill. Perhaps the news of his assistant's death worsened any condition he may have had. I'm sure he was very fond of Mr. Bold."

Daniel noticed Buckland held a blue bag in his hand.

"Certainly not as much as you," Buckland said with a pastoral tone. Both a clergyman and a geologist, he seemed to know what hat to wear in any circumstance.

"Are you well, Daniel? I heard you were hurt."

"I'm all right, sir."

Buckland put a hand on Daniel's arm. "Come , now, let's talk for a while."

Daniel walked with him to the vacant common room. Buckland set his bag on the floor with a clacking sound. The sound of bones.

"Will you attend the funeral this afternoon?" Daniel said.

"Certainly," Buckland said. "I feel obliged. After all, it was I who arranged for Mr. Bold's employment at the society, despite his father's objections. I convinced the earl that it would prove beneficial for his son to be around men of science."

Daniel bit his upper lip. "Did you want to tell me something, Reverend?"

"Oh, yes, certainly," Buckland said. "You must know that my *Bridgewater Treatise* will be published soon."

"Yes, sir, I'm anxious to read it."

"I know you are, my lad. That is why I wanted to warn you, and perhaps explain myself."

"Warn me?"

"Well, we have certainly discussed my views in the past about the relationship between geology and scripture."

Daniel nodded. "Yes, I studied your *Vindiciae* and your *Reliquiae Diluvianae*."

"Excellent, and what did I say in those books?"

"You wrote that geology was consistent with scripture and that it provided irrefutable evidence of God's creation and of the catastrophic nature of Noah's flood. Yet you argued that the evidence of the flood was only to be found in the upper formations of the earth, not in the sedimentary rock formations below."

"Exactly," Buckland said. "And that meant—"

"The earth was older than six thousand years."

"Yes, much older, because in the lower strata we find evidence of slow deposition of sediment followed by what seems to be rapid, catastrophic deposition."

Buckland bent towards Daniel. "And then we have the fossils, correct?"

Daniel nodded.

"Different strata, different fossils." Buckland put his hands in front of him, the right suspended over the left, then he moved the left above the right. "Ah! And the lower the strata, the more different the fossils are from today's living species."

"That's why you proposed the theory that those fossils represented several extinctions and recreations by God of new animals over long ages."

"You don't seem to agree with that theory," Buckland said, resting his hands on his tights.

"Why invoke these recreations? You should either interpret the Bible literally or—"

"Why literally?" Buckland fixed his eyes on Daniel.

Daniel shrugged. "Well—"

"Certainly, the Bible was intended only to be a guide to religious belief and moral conduct, not a science encyclopedia. While the biblical text, as any written record, is subject to human error, the geological evidence—the rocks—cannot be altered by man. We should listen to the rocks, Daniel, don't you agree?"

Daniel nodded, then looked away.

"Daniel," Buckland said, returning to his pastoral tone, "I know this may be difficult for you, but you're an intelligent open-minded man. Let go of your old beliefs, just as I have."

Daniel turned to face him, curious and suspicious at the same time. If Buckland only knew. Daniel no longer had the old beliefs.

"You see," Buckland said, "a large proportion of the fossils we find in the strata belong to extinct genera, and almost all of them to extinct species that lived and multiplied and died on or near the spots where they're now found. This shows that the strata in which they occur were deposited slowly and gradually, during long periods of time, and at widely distant intervals."

Daniel had read something similar before—in Lyell's *Principles of Geology.*

"In other words," Buckland continued, "I have left the catastrophist camp and moved over to the uniformitarian camp with Mr. Lyell. I'm now convinced that only present-day processes and rates should be used to interpret the past. In the *Treatise* I state my conviction that the Noachian flood was tranquil and not catastrophic—that it had no geological significance whatsoever."

Daniel blinked. Hearing those words from a member of the Anglican Church had an unexpected effect on him. They did not sound as shocking from Charles Lyell, a lawyer turned geologist—but from the Reverend William Buckland, they were. He couldn't even picture his father listening to those words, much less uttering them.

"Again," Buckland said, "I know how difficult this might be. If it serves your soul, read Reverend Chalmers' review of Cuvier's *Theory of the Earth*. Chalmers tries to reconcile geology with scripture by proposing many millions of years between the first two verses of Genesis. I'm not saying he's correct, but the interpretation has certain appeal for the untrained mind. His theory that in the second verse of Genesis the Deity is reconstructing a world that had perished in an ancient catastrophe appeased my mind a few years ago, though of course that view has no recourse in uniformitarian thought. Perhaps you can use that theory to bridge the gap until you are ready to let go of your old beliefs. What say you?"

Daniel forced a smile. Why was Buckland patronizing

him? He knew all about Chalmers's desperate compromise.

Buckland stood and extended his hand. "Well, I have some urgent business I must attend to. I'll see you at the funeral this afternoon."

Daniel rose fast, hitting his knee on the edge of the table.

"Yes, I'll see you then." Daniel rubbed his knee with one hand and shook Buckland's hand with the other. "I too have some inquiries pending regarding Alex's murder."

He bit his lip as soon as the words slipped out.

Buckland's pastoral smile vanished. "Bless you, my lad. You should leave that to the police. Pity this tragedy happened so close to the anniversary. For the good of the society, this matter must be treated with the utmost discretion."

His eyes fixed on Daniel, as if expecting his agreement. When Daniel said nothing in return, he raised his brows.

Was Buckland trying to silence him just like Lord Bold?

"Indeed it must," Daniel finally said.

"You're a good man, Daniel, and a good scientist. Please stay out of trouble."

11:52 A.M.

Scrope sat reading *The Times*, ignoring the 757 books shelved in his personal library.

An unwholesome odor tickled his nostrils. He lowered the newspaper.

"Ah, it's you," Scrope said.

He hadn't heard his henchman arrive. Lloyd stood in front of him, holding something in his hefty hands.

"Did you find what I'm looking for?" Scrope said.

"Yes." Lloyd offered him a set of papers.

Scrope took the two sheets—one a cheap-looking sheet with long scribbles, the other fine, with elegant calligraphy.

He read them both, then stood and handed the less elegant letter to Lloyd.

"Hmmm," Scrope muttered. He walked over to the fireplace and threw the second letter onto the flames. The paper shrunk inward as the fire consumed it and turned it to ashes. Scrope turned around and saw Lloyd reading the first sheet. He crumpled the letter in his fist and threw it in a wicker basket.

"Find him," Scrope said. "And get rid of him. Permanently."

3:00 P.M.

All around him, mourners in black sobbed as Daniel stared at Alex's empty coffin. Lord Bold had arranged an opulent funeral for his only son. Even the mutes, the professional mourners hired by the undertaker, were elegantly dressed, right down to black gloves and scarves.

At the rhythm of the death knell, a deep wound began to bleed again in Daniel. He thought about his brother and he thought about Alex and the mix of sadness and anger over them both churned in him.

James, Daniel's little brother—only eighteen months younger—had been his best friend up until his death at age six. They'd gone to the beach in Norwich to look for seashells and treasures in the shingle. James found the biggest whelk they'd ever seen.

"Look, Daniel, look what I've found!"

James ran down the beach with the shell against his ear, laughing with the breeze as he listened to the surf. He almost bumped into a tethered boat half hidden in the fog. Daniel caught up with him.

"Fish!" Daniel said.

A casting net inside the small boat trapped dozens of fish, a few still flapping.

"Grab some fish for mum," James said.

Daniel knew Father would beat them if he saw them stealing. James was already aboard, separating the net's lead weights.

"James, get out of there!"

James had a fish in each hand, still holding the shell between his right arm and his chest. Someone grabbed his left wrist.

"You little blighters!" It was the fisherman.

The fisherman grabbed Daniel with his free hand. Daniel bit the stinky hand around his wrist, and the man let him go with a push. Daniel's head went backwards against the sand.

Tears blurred his vision and a deep scream left his throat—not from hitting the ground but from the fear that overtook him. The fisherman was probably going to kill them. James for stealing his fish, him for biting his hand.

Still on his back, Daniel lifted his legs to kick the boat. His feet just stirred sand in the air. He scooted forward and tried again. Same result.

He opened his eyes and sat. The fisherman had pushed the boat into the ocean.

He ran toward the boat but reached only the waves. The wind blew with more strength as minutes passed. The fisherman made James stand with a net in his hands, as if he wanted James to fish for him. His brother looked terrified.

Daniel waved at him. "James! James!"

Then it happened. The wind rocked the boat and James fell into the sea.

Daniel shouted and waited to see his brother come out of the water. But he never did.

Daniel ran home crying and told his father everything. That night the current washed James's body, entwined in a

THE GENTLEMEN'S CONSPIRACY

net, onto the beach. They never found the fisherman, and Daniel's parents assumed he'd made the story up.

"The boy is always thinking up stories and daydreaming," his father said. "James's death was an accident. The good Lord took him so James could be in His presence."

Daniel followed Alex's empty coffin with his eyes until it touched the grave. Looking back up he saw Lord Bold, who nodded at him.

We will bury my son and tell everybody it was an unfortunate accident.

It was not an accident.

3:47 P.M.

Daniel could still hear loud sobs, even though the mutes were already gone. The sobs came from Alex's mother.

"My son, my so-o-on, my so-o-o-on…" Lady Bold wept louder and longer each time.

Lord Bold escaped to the company of calmer attendees. At this, Daniel saw his opportunity and approached Susan.

"Let's talk," he said, touching her elbow.

They walked away from the inconsolable mother and stood under a tree. Even in black she looked gorgeous.

"You are so beautiful."

Susan blushed and glanced around for her parents.

"Did you translate the letter?" Daniel said.

"Not yet. My mother wouldn't let me leave her side."

Daniel glanced at Lady Bold, who looked completely undone.

"My father says she needs fresh air. We're leaving for the country house tomorrow."

Daniel flinched.

"Father won't hold a funeral feast for a missing body,"

she said, "especially not with my mother's mental state. Meet me at the garden at nine."

He frowned and looked away. "I can't believe you're leaving—"

Susan touched his hand. "Meet me at nine, all right? We must speak about something important. The superintendent is suspicious."

He needed her, now more than ever. He kept his eyes on the thinning crowd. Ten feet away, Lord Bold exchanged handshakes and nods with the parting guests. That selfish man was sending Susan away. He'd like to slap some sense into him.

"Will you come?"

Daniel faced Susan, as if shaken from a dream. "Of course," he said after a few seconds. "After I meet with Greenough."

4:20 P.M.

Michael Oatts glanced at his police officer. "Don't be afraid, Willy, this is me territory."

William kept a watchful eye from side to side; his knuckles white around the baton tucked in his blue trousers.

"I've 'eard bad stories 'bout this place, sir. Lots of dangerous folk around 'ere. Even a bobby'd be lucky to get out with his frock coat on."

Oatts grinned. "That's true, very true. But you're with me today."

William opened his mouth but then as quickly shut it again. Swarms of ragged kids passed by to either side of the two men.

Oatts walked with the measured pace of someone who knows his destination but is in no rush to get there. This seemed to upset William, who would surely have preferred to hasten his steps.

Two filthy men jumped out of a makeshift hut and blocked their way.

"Ha-ha!" one of them said. He had a knife in his hand.

William pulled out his truncheon. His eyes moved between the two men and his boss. Oatts halted, cocked his head, and began twirling his mustache.

The men stared at Oatts, then nodded at him with fearful eyes and cleared the way. Oatts continued walking.

"Sorry 'bout that, Superintendent!" the man with the knife yelled from behind them.

William's jaw dropped. Oatts was now walking briskly.

"How did... What hap—"

"I told you, Willy. This is me territory. I ran these streets like every other poor Irish kid. But I'm not one of them any more—aye, Willy?"

"Aye, sir."

"They're like dogs. They can smell your fear. Be better if you got a hold of your emotions there, Willy."

"Aye, sir."

They stood in front of a building that seemed to have been washed in coal. William shook his head.

"I thought we were lookin' for the German gambler, sir. I don't think 'e would come to this godforsaken place."

"The man said 'e was 'ere, Willy. We're just goin' to confirm it."

Inside the building, heads turned from a long table where a dozen youngsters and an old toothless woman were gathered.

"G'day, lads, mum," Oatts said.

The filthy youngsters were of all ages. Oatts knew their type—wallet snatchers, under the command of the old lady. They muttered nervously among themselves, their eyes on

Oatts. Four of the older ones, teenagers, stood and strode to the exit. They looked back with contempt as they walked past William. The last one in line spat at William's shoes and ran out the door.

"We're lookin' for Jack," Oatts told the woman.

She sat straight and tightened her lips.

"We just want a little talk, mum. No more."

The woman hesitated for a few seconds, then nodded towards a large square hole to her left. On closer inspection, the hole turned out to be a stairway leading down to a lower level.

"Thank you," Oatts said and started for the stairs. William followed, ignoring the baleful stares of the kids.

The room below was dark except for a small candle in a far corner. Jack snored a rattling drunken breath. His eyes were covered by oily strands of hair, the lower part of his face by a forest of beard.

"Wake 'im up, Willy."

William shook the man like a bag. "Up, you filthy drunk!"

Jack sprung up in the middle of a snore, bumping his skull against William's nose.

"Aw, my nose!"

"Wha—, wha—, what?" Jack said.

Oatts refrained from laughing. William moved back from the bed, rubbing his nose.

"Here, Jack!" Oatts said.

Jack turned to him and belched.

"Who's there?" Jack said.

"Bring that candle over here, Willy."

William took the candle in one hand, the other one still on his nose. His eyes were watery.

Jack stared at Oatts under the light and grunted. "What do you want, Oat—"

The last syllable came out as a burp. Jack looked around

the room and blew through his lips when he saw William. Then he scowled.

"You'll need more than one bobby to take me out."

Oatts smiled. "Today's not your day, Jack. I just have a few questions for you."

Jack looked towards the stairs, then frowned at Oatts. "What is it?"

"Do you know a German called Honecker?"

"Depends."

"He may have killed a man. An important man."

"I'm not involved, Superintendent—"

"Then 'elp me see that."

Jack moved the hair away from his face and kept his gaze down on the floor.

"Honecker said he was with you Tuesday night, the night of the murder," Oatts said.

"That cheater beat me at a game of cards Tuesday. Got all I had. We came 'ere for the rest." He looked up at Oatts and cursed. "The German's a dirty cheater."

"Sure he is," Oatts said. "At what time were you here with 'im?"

Jack shrugged. "Some time after sunset."

Oatts nodded. "Who else was with you? I need to confirm your story."

"Julius was. Ask 'im."

"And where's Julius?"

"Probably at Pierre's. You know where—"

"Aye. Let's go, Willy."

A crowd of youngsters was gathered at the top of the stairs—more than were at the table when they had come in. They made way for Oatts, but William had to push his way through. Once outside, he let go a sigh of relief.

"They respect you, sir."

"Aye."

"But they could've hurt you if they wanted to, sir. They're so many!"

Oatts smiled. "That's why I brought you with me, Willy."

William nodded and filled his chest with air. Then he noted his truncheon was missing. "Bloody kids!"

6:59 P.M.

In the shadows of the cold evening, Daniel walked past the shops at Burlington Arcade and headed west. Large elegant houses rose on both sides of the street—this would be a fine place to live with Susan. As he walked, he daydreamed a future when she'd be his wife and he could hold her as long as he wished, look at her amazing eyes for hours, make her as happy as she could ever hope to be.

So easy to dream. He had no fortune to buy a mansion, and although Susan's inheritance would become his once they married, therein lay the problem. Lord Bold would never allow them to marry. Although educated at Oxford and a friend of his son, Daniel was still a middle-class country boy.

Daniel was thinking about what he might do to change Lord Bold's mind when the door to a mansion on his right opened. He flinched with a chill like the one at the library that morning, and with reason—the same man he'd seen at the library was now leaving the house. Lloyd. He could see his square face under the gas lamps at the entrance.

Daniel took cover behind a plane tree.

Lloyd crossed the path to the street and headed west, to Daniel's relief. In the last moment before disappearing at the corner, Lloyd shot a glance back his way. Then he was gone.

Had Lloyd spotted him? It was dark under the tree, but maybe he had. It seemed as if Lloyd had halted at the corner for a second. Daniel couldn't be sure.

The urge to run pounded in his chest. His eyes scanned the street number of the mansion. It was Greenough's place.

The urge grew stronger when he heard footsteps. What was Lloyd doing at Greenough's house? Now he heard sounds from both ends of the street. Lloyd? From where? The footsteps sounded closer.

Daniel ran. He realized too late he was banging against Greenough's door.

A startled butler pulled the door away from Daniel's knuckles.

"Mind you, lad—sir. What's the matter?"

Daniel stared at the ancient butler, breathing hard. The butler's face went from alarm to puzzlement.

What now? Daniel glanced over his shoulder towards the street. A couple walked by, muttering as they stared in his direction.

"Are you running away from someone, sir?" the butler said. His forehead wrinkles dipped between his eyes—probably a frown.

Daniel pulled himself up to his full height. "I need to see Mr. Greenough."

The old man examined him some time longer than a servant would normally—perhaps considering whether to kick him out—but in the end invited him in.

More than twenty minutes went by in the drawing room before Greenough showed up. Had Lloyd come back and was he now talking to Greenough?

"Mr. Young?"

Daniel startled. Greenough wore an impeccable suit, a gentleman in dress and bearing. Even Greenough's mention of Daniel's name carried a charm that bordered on seduction. Daniel stood.

"Yes, sir. Thank you for seeing me. I know my visit was unexpected."

Greenough's eyes emanated the sweet coldness of a man who thinks himself superior but maintains courtesy in the presence of his inferiors. This was not one to be trusted.

"Please sit down."

Greenough sat across from Daniel, legs crossed.

"How may I be of service, Mr. Young?"

Daniel's rehearsed speech was blocked by images of Lloyd in the library and leaving this house. Why was he afraid of Lloyd? He still didn't know that Lloyd had killed Alex.

"I recently joined the Geological Society and have been mentored by Reverend Buckland in the geological sciences. He thought—well, I thought—it would be very instructive to learn more about the society, and you being a founding member and the first pre—"

"For this you come to my residence at night?" Greenough said. "I thought you had more urgent matters to discuss."

Daniel went pale. He knew his speech wasn't very convincing, but he'd hoped—

"Well," Greenough said, "you're here now, I might as well answer some of your questions. But I don't have all night, Mr. Young. Tell me, what is it that you so urgently need to know?"

Daniel sighed. "Is it true that none of the founding members of the society was a practicing geologist?"

Greenough nodded. "We were all very interested in the new science of geology and some of us had a fair knowledge of the theories of the day. If by practicing geology you mean hammering rocks, no, we were not. Sir Humphry was, however, a practicing chemist."

"I've always wondered why William Smith was never part of the founding group."

Greenough shifted in his chair. "Smith was a very busy fellow, always traveling and working. He wasn't interested in joining us."

"Did he tell you that?"

"Well, no, he did not. But that's what I believe."

"Was he ever invited to the group?"

"Maybe. This was so long ago I don't remember. Perhaps he was. In any case, he probably couldn't afford the fees."

"What fees?"

"The group had dinner at five o'clock at the Freemasons Tavern and discussed geological issues. Each member had to pay fifteen shillings to attend the dinner or ten shillings and six pence if he couldn't attend."

The man could remember the exact membership fees of the society but not whether Smith was invited to the meetings. Could Greenough be hiding more than his class prejudices? This would all be much easier if he were a policeman and could ask questions directly. But what would he ask? He'd come with the idea of getting more information about Smith's letter, hoping to find a clue to Alex's murder. This was more complicated than he'd expected.

"Did you know Alexander Bold?" Daniel said. "He worked at the society's library."

"No, I believe not. It's curious you should ask that."

"Why?"

"I just had someone come not thirty minutes ago and ask me the whereabouts of the society's librarian."

8:06 P.M.

Daniel was too immersed in his thoughts to notice anything around him as he walked through the night. If Lloyd was looking for the librarian, maybe he hadn't obtained what he was looking for at the library. Old Shaw could be in danger. Worse yet, his Susan could be in danger if Lloyd found out she had the other letters. Perhaps he was looking for them?

But of course there was no way for him to know that Susan had the letters. In any case he had to warn her.

Daniel was headed down Piccadilly with Susan on his mind when he heard rushing steps behind him. He glanced over his shoulder, but shadows concealed the source of the noise. Not a soul was in sight. Daniel hurried his pace and veered towards Green Park—that way he could make sure whether he was being followed or not.

A few yards into the park, the black vegetation around him looked more threatening than any human being.

He had to keep his imagination at bay. The trees wouldn't harm him—what nonsense. In fact, they could help. He walked quickly towards a line of trees and squatted behind a trunk.

A cold wind blew against his face, and Daniel buried his chin in his coat. He peered around the trunk toward the street. Nobody. Not a sound. He hadn't heard the steps after he entered the park. It was as if whoever was behind him had vanished. Was that a good or a bad sign?

He leaned against the tree and the bark rubbed against his wound. He winced and reached for his head, lowering his chin to touch his chest—

Quick muffled steps on the grass, approaching from the front. A dark silhouette walked into view, a man, his features disguised in the moonless night. Daniel saw a hand pull a thin object from a side pocket. Cold sweat ran down his temples. It was a knife.

Something flashed from his brain down his spine. He wanted to scream for help, but all he managed was a guttural sound from the back of his throat. What mattered was that he sprang forward and charged like a horse.

Daniel's skull hit the man in his chest, and he fell flat on his back. Daniel stumbled on the man's large legs and landed upon him. The man screamed something unintelligible under Daniel's body, the warm breath seeping through his coat.

Two hands grabbed Daniel's shoulders from behind and pulled him up roughly.

"Don't play 'ero with us, mister!" the man behind him said. Irish?

Daniel winced at the foul breath in his face. He closed his eyes as all his strength left his limbs. But he was glad it wasn't Lloyd after all. Then a fist struck the pit of his stomach and he gasped for air.

The man Daniel had thrown to the ground was cursing when Daniel fell to his knees. A kick to his side spread him on the park lawn. He lay on old roots and dry winter grass, oblivious to the robbers' words. Why did everything become so foggy? He did not hear if they ordered him to hand over his watch chain or his money or his shoes, but he was later aware of their stripping him down to his skin, spitting on his face, and laughing a laugh of hunger and contempt.

The chilly silence after they left felt like a good omen. Curled like a shirtless fetus, he let a grin twist his mouth. It wasn't Lloyd. He was alive. He had his pants still. He was alive.

FIVE

MOTIERS, SWITZERLAND, 1765

Sultan's barks pulled Rousseau from his sleep. He shook his head and grumbled.

"*Qu'est qu'il—?*"

Shattering glass silenced both the dog and Rousseau, who stood from the bed at once, his hands trembling, his heart pounding. He inched forward, listening to the disturbance outside his bedroom. When he reached the foot of the bed, the room's door flew open, and a rock landed near his feet.

Rousseau screamed. He stared at the rock before him as if it were a rabid dog. After the furor of his book and the response of the church, people had thrown rocks at him in the market—but none had come close enough to hit him. This was the closest, and the first time anyone had dared attack his house.

He tiptoed his way to the door, staying away from direct view.

"Jean! Jean!"

Thérèse. He could not bear it if she were hurt.

Rousseau walked slowly, cautiously into the kitchen. Thérèse ran down the hallway and threw her arms around his neck.

"Thérèse, *ma chérie!*"

"It's the townspeople. They are mad, Jean, mad!"

"Rousseau *hérétique!*" a man bellowed from the back of the house.

Other voices joined, followed by a loud whoosh. Rousseau let his lover pull him against the wall as a volley of rocks turned what was left of the windows into a shower of glass. Thérèse began to cry. Tears brimmed his own eyes.

SIX

9:00 A.M.

Daniel's memory of his return home was hazy. He'd wandered for an hour before finding the way to his cousin's house. The servants warmed his feet with water heated to near scalding and the rest of his body with blankets, in which he fell asleep.

Last night was just a bad dream—although not as bad as the dream he had in his sleep, of Susan darting down a dark alley with robbers, killers, and even Alex's ghost chasing her. They were gnashing their teeth and yelling at her to give them the letters. Daniel had awakened sweaty and panting.

Now he was wide-awake and on the streets again. He wasn't sure of finding Susan home, not after missing their appointment last night. But he had to tell her why he hadn't met her, had to make sure she was safe.

The cab halted in front of the walking path to Lord Bold's centuries-old mansion. Daniel sprinted towards the deserted entrance. No carriages, no luggage. Too late.

He looked around, hands on his waist, and grimaced. He turned abruptly when the mansion's front door opened.

The housekeeper stuck her head out.

"Mr. Young," she whispered, and walked out. If the housekeeper was using the front door instead of the servants' entrance it was dead certain her masters weren't home.

She motioned for him to approach. "Mr. Young, please."

Daniel walked up to her.

She seemed afraid of someone seeing them. "I was waiting for you to come."

Daniel frowned. Her gaze shifted to an object in her hands.

"This is for you," she said. "A letter from Miss Bold."

She handed him the letter and went back inside the house. Daniel stared at the paper for a few moments, then glanced at the closed door. How strange but how wonderful to have an unexpected letter from Susan. Although it might only be the translation of Alex's letter.

Daniel felt the paper with his fingers, imagined he could feel the touch of Susan's white hands on it. He hid the letter under his coat. This was no place to read it. He retraced his steps to the street and went looking for a bench.

Pulling the letter back out, he sniffed the paper before opening it and the scent flooded his mind with the memory of Susan's eyes.

Dear Daniel,

I waited for you in the garden until the fear of being discovered drove me inside. Then I watched through my window for you until midnight. Where are you, my Daniel?

The grief over my brother's death is heavier on my heart with the knowledge that we will be apart for weeks. Yes, my father plans to leave my mother, my sister, and me at the country house for the rest of the winter while Parliament is in session. My mother's deep sorrow has affected me as well. Not only do I cry for my brother, it pains me to see Mother in such a state of grief. She won't touch any food and has made us all swear to wear nothing but black for a year. She says she will wear it the rest of her life. And Father does not even seem to care!

I was hoping to see you before we left, but my heart tells me that if you did not come it was because forces stronger than your will prevented you from coming, that what they say about you isn't true. I know you love me because your eyes cannot lie. I love you too.

Please forgive me for not translating the letter, but I dare not leave my mother's side for too long. I will take it with me to the country house and work on it as soon as I can. Then I shall send it to you through our housekeeper. Don't worry about her. She will keep the secret.

Take care of yourself, my dear Daniel, and think about me always.

Your love,
Susan

Daniel couldn't stop smiling as he folded the letter under the overcast sky. He opened the letter again and read the 'I love you too' a dozen times, until a shower of rain sent him running for cover under a tree.

The humid smell of leaves and the touch of wood under his fingers were oddly unpleasant—images from his assault flashed before his eyes. He felt sick. The delicious emotions inspired by the letter faded away. Still, the real meaning of the robbery was becoming clear. He was alive for a reason, right? He didn't die along with Alex, hadn't been spared so he could take life for granted. He felt he now had a chance to fulfill his calling, whatever it was.

Was he sounding like his father? Reverend Young would no doubt say something like that. Daniel could almost hear him: "God has great plans for you, son." But Daniel had lost interest in divine plans long ago. He'd be surprised if God hadn't given up on him. So what was he alive for? Why did Alex die?

"Why, God?" Daniel said to the gray sky. Thick drops slapped his face. If God didn't tell him, he'd find out anyway. He heard horses' hooves. Two men descended from a cab. Daniel leapt over the puddles and whistled to the cabby. He knew who would help him find the killer.

9:53 A.M.

Daniel paused before the façade. The infamous headquarters of the Metropolitan Police at 4 Whitehall Place. He entered the building and hesitated when a tall, burly bobby came up to him.

"I'm looking for Superintendent Oatts."

The bobby nodded and motioned for Daniel to follow him. He led Daniel to Oatts's unexpectedly small office—no more than eight or nine feet wide and some six feet long. The bare walls and scanty furniture helped; any added piece would crowd the only available walking space.

"Mr. Young, what a surprise," Oatts said, taking his feet off the desk.

Daniel's confidence in his decision faded now that Oatts was in front of him. When his brother died nobody made any effort to find the fisherman—not his father nor the authorities. True, the police force as such didn't exist until six years ago. The police from his childhood were an informal group of corrupt and inept guards. Had anything changed? Those same guards now had uniforms and a few rules. What difference would that make?

Oatts's stare pierced Daniel's intentions. He clutched his

THE GENTLEMEN'S CONSPIRACY

hands behind his back and moved from behind his desk. "Walk with me, Mr. Young." Oatts extended one arm toward the door.

Daniel nodded and walked out the door, then moved to one side to let Oatts lead the way. He wanted to say something—he was supposed to, because he was the one who came looking for Oatts—but he was mute. As they walked Daniel shot furtive looks at Oatts every now and then, but the superintendent kept looking forward.

They came to the back of the building and Oatts halted by a window.

"See the courtyard o'er there, Mr. Young? It once belonged to the Kings of Scotland. I've always thought that very interestin'. The Kings of Scotland!"

Oatts gave him a searching look.

"Remember this Honecker gambler I told you 'bout? Turns out his alibi's good."

Daniel looked away.

"Your friend was killed and you're the only witness. Could be you're involved."

Daniel blinked.

"But per'aps you're just afraid of pointing out the murderer," Oatts said. "You don't want to get killed yourself. Per'aps you simply don't trust me. Nobody likes the Metropolitan Police. The magistrates think we're taking over their power. The people think we're a threat. But that's changin'. Crime is down. People are seein' results. We're not that bad after all, are we, Mr. Young?"

Daniel looked down at the trim Irishman dressed in black. His father never trusted Irishmen. Why? Now that he thought about it, he didn't really know. He shouldn't have come.

"You're a man of few words," Oatts said.

Daniel inhaled, his lips quivered.

79

"You came." Oatts patted his arm. "That's what matters."

A man walked by and nodded at Oatts, who nodded back. Daniel pretended to examine the rug, which surely had seen better days.

"If I show I trust you," Oatts said, "would you trust me?"

Daniel tensed. "How?"

"I'll give you some information and then you decide whether you can help me or not."

He managed a nod.

"I found a rock at the place of the murder," Oatts said.

Rocks made Daniel tingle. "What kind of rock is it?"

"Just a rock. The size of a man's fist, covered in blood."

"Can you show it to me?" He was self-conscious of the eagerness in his voice.

Oatts cocked his head. "I've got you talkin' now, ain't I, Mr. Young?"

"I'd like to see it, Superintendent."

"Sure," Oatts said. "Why not?

They walked back to Oatts's office. The superintendent opened a desk drawer and took out a rugged mass. Daniel could see the dried blood around it; even a few hairs as he held the rock in his hands. The rock was black. He guessed what kind of rock it was but he had to be sure.

"We must make a geological assay of this," Daniel said. "Perhaps some chemical analyses."

Oatts frowned. "Make what?"

"Geological assay. To know what kind of rock it is."

"I don't know what you're talkin' 'bout, Mr. Young." Oatts reached for the rock. "But this is an important piece of evidence."

Daniel pulled his hand back. The superintendent frowned so fiercely that Daniel thought his eyebrows would touch his mustache.

"Would you trust me or not?" Daniel said.

Oatts threw his head back and laughed, catching Daniel by surprise.

"I got no other option. I said I would."

"Good," Daniel said. "I just happen to know the best place in London for this."

11:45 A.M.

Andrew Ure's laboratory was a marvel of boiling sounds and multicolored liquids flowing from column to flask that seemed to make the self-confident Oatts a little uneasy. Daniel, on the other hand, felt better than he had in many days as soon as they entered the lab.

"Good to see you, Daniel!" Ure's voice was deep but melodious.

"Dr. Ure," Daniel said, embracing him. "You're doing well."

Ure shrugged. "I won't complain. Work is good, and every now and then the Board of Customs asks for some analyses."

Daniel grinned and turned to Oatts, who stood with both hands in his pockets, eyeing Ure's tools and bottles.

"This is Superintendent Oatts, from the Metropolitan Police," Daniel said.

Ure extended his hand to Oatts and raised his brows to Daniel.

"Are you in some sort of trouble?"

"No, sir. Not at all."

"Good!" Ure said. "Take a seat then. If you can find a place."

Daniel and Oatts found seats but Ure remained standing.

"Still an aspiring geologist, Daniel?"

"I'm a member of the Geological Society now."

Ure rolled his eyes. "How do you like it?"

"Very much. I look up to the leadership. I'd expected to see you at some of the meetings."

Ure twisted his lips and waved a hand. "Ugh. I haven't been involved in the society since Sedgwick's attack on my book."

Daniel shook his head. He respected both men, but Ure was not a geologist *per se.*

"Anyway. Just be careful, Daniel, not to be led off the facts and into the play they're acting. Since Lyell became president the trend is so heavy toward old-earth geology and uniformitarianism that all catastrophist evidence is banned."

Daniel leaned forward in his chair. "Banned?"

"That's right. Last summer I visited Edinburgh and met with George Young, John Murray, and William Rhind. They told me the Geological Society had rejected their papers for the *Transactions,* and they suspected it was because they presented evidence for catastrophism."

Daniel frowned. "What evidence for catastrophism are they suggesting?"

Oatts spoke from a corner of the lab. "What's catastrophism and that other thing, 'uni' something, if you don't mind me askin'?"

Ure and Daniel turned toward him.

"Uniformitarianism," Daniel said. "It's a way of explaining geological phenomena like the mountains or the continents by causes that have always been the same and can be observed today. Lyell says rains, rivers, earthquakes, and volcanoes have always been at work in the world at the same quantity and intensity in the past as we see in the present, with no variation."

"Everything is an endless cycle for him," Ure said.

"Everything?" Oatts laughed. "That sounds plain silly to me!"

Daniel winced.

"Why so?" Ure said.

Oatts cocked his head and began fiddling with his mustache. "Well, I know nothin' 'bout rivers or earthquakes, but if I were to think like that in me job, I'd never catch up with the thieves of London. Criminals are always stealing new things in new ways."

Daniel said, "Yes, but geological events are not people."

"That's right," Ure said. "But the superintendent may have a point here. He could assume robbers will always use the same methods, if he wanted to, independent of what the robbers actually did. That would be his philosophical assumption. If he then found evidence of a new type of crime—very different from what he'd seen before—he could only hold to his philosophical assumption by denying the evidence or explaining it away. And that's what Lyell and his conclave are doing, shunning all evidence for catastrophism or reinterpreting it to fit their 'uniform causes' philosophy."

"Why would they do that?" Daniel said.

"I don't know why, I just know they are."

Daniel leaned back on his chair. He didn't like this conversation.

"What's that other word you were talking 'bout?" Oatts said.

Daniel ignored the question. His head was spinning. It was hard to fathom his heroes, the scientific stars of Britain, concealing evidence for the sake of a philosophy.

Ure looked at Daniel, then at Oatts. "Catastrophism simply recognizes that some geological events in the past—catastrophes, for example—shaped the earth in ways we don't observe today. There are many opinions on how many and how large these catastrophes have been, but I believe, along with George Young and other geologists, that the most significant was the flood of Noah."

Daniel regarded Oatts, who seemed interested. Ure continued. "The uniformitarians have denied all evidence for the flood. Take for example the finely preserved fossils of fish we've found. Uniformitarians say fossils form slowly, but that's not so. Let's see—"

Ure ran to his desk and snatched a paper out of a stack. "Here. This is an excerpt from George I've been planning to share with my students at the evening lectures." He began to read. "It is well known that scarcely any substance decomposes more speedily than fish; so that when we find fossil fish in a high state of preservation we may be sure that the strata containing them were deposited so rapidly as not to allow them time to become putrid, till they were safely encased in their present matrix. Now, fossils are often found in the finest condition, with no part of their structure injured; while we know that fish left dead on the beach, or on the banks of rivers, begin to decay in a few hours. The proper cause of their fine preservation was their being so suddenly entombed in the strata." Ure put the paper down.

"You see, geology doesn't prove our world is millions of years old. The rocks and fossils found by geologists provide rich evidence that a large amount of the geological record resulted from Noah's flood. Like George Young—and Daniel, you know how competent he is—I am convinced that God created the world about six thousand years ago."

Daniel's hands trembled with anger. He shouldn't be listening to this. Ure was a chemist, not a full-time geologist like Lyell.

"Let me tell you something else," Ure said. "Listen to this, Daniel."

Daniel gave him a cold look.

"When I visited with George later in the autumn, he took me to the Whitby Museum, where he has the fossil of this great crocodile. The bones of one leg were practically sunk into the bones of the other leg. The animal had been crushed by the strata above! You could see the pressure in its head and body. Only a catastrophe could explain that violent pressure. Don't you agree?"

"Sounds reasonable to me," Oatts said.

"How would you know?" Daniel said and stormed out the lab.

4:30 P.M.

Henry Cole stood at the doors of his chapel, watching the passersby. To those he knew he shouted a blessing; to the strangers he just smiled. But nobody crossed right now. The good Lord was sending his rain on and off.

From the street corner a middle-aged man came into view. He walked briskly, ducked under a newspaper he held above his head. He looked miserable and frowned as he glanced at the threatening sky.

A gust of wind rustled the trees, snatched the newspaper from the man's hands, and splattered it against the chapel's facade. Cole hurried down the stairs and around the rail. He picked the newspaper up and walked to the man, now squatting under the rain as if the sky were about to fall over him.

"Here's your paper, my friend," Cole said.

Just as the man reached for his makeshift, two words caught Cole's eyes: Geological Society. Cole pulled the newspaper close to his face to read the wet type. The man grunted an unintelligible protest.

The London Geological Society was celebrating its anniversary that evening. Cole skimmed the names of famous members who would attend and stopped over one: Adam Sedgwick.

The watered man grabbed the newspaper. "If you please," he said.

Cole took his hands off the paper and shook his head as if coming out of a trance.

"Go with God, sir."

The man and the newspaper parted, but the text he'd just read lingered in Cole's mind. Cole had wanted to send a personal message to Sedgwick, without success. Now he knew where Sedgwick was going to be—and among his peers. The event seemed like a perfect opportunity to contend for the faith.

7:00 P.M.

Dozens of gentlemen chatted in scattered groups as more arrived at the anniversary meeting. Hundreds of candles shone over the ivory mantles covering round tables. The mildew scent had been washed away and floral aromas flowed from every tabletop.

From his vantage point at one corner of the room Daniel could see Lyell busying himself at the fossil table and shaking hands with everyone who came through the door. Lyell forced a smile, but his sharp eyes seemed uneasy. It was obvious he'd rather work behind the scenes.

Daniel wasn't sure what to think about Lyell any more. Or Sedgwick. Or even his mentor, Buckland. Ure had sown a seed of doubt in him. The afternoon had been consumed in a storm of confusing thoughts. Uniformitarianism and catastrophism. He knew no greater scientific debate than that. And with Buckland's move to Lyell's side, catastrophism was surely dead. What was it Buckland said to him yesterday? That he was convinced the flood of Noah was tranquil and had no geological significance whatsoever. So Buckland still believed in the flood, he just didn't believe it was catastrophic. Lyell *did* render the flood as a myth.

And what about the evidence Ure spoke of? Daniel didn't want to return to what he once believed—that the Genesis record was literal history. That's what his father believed.

If what Ure said was true, Buckland's view of the flood would make little sense. The Bible's description of the flood was far from tranquil—it was like the worst catastrophe anyone could ever imagine. What was the point of believing in Noah's flood but not believing it occurred as the only account of the event said it did? Why didn't Buckland just say the flood was a myth and be done with it?

Daniel moved his eyes over the crowd, trying to spot Buckland. He was talking with Roderick Murchison, the retired army officer. Sedgwick joined them.

Why would Buckland compromise? Because he was a priest? He used to reconcile geology with scripture in all his writings, then gradually changed his mind. What would come next?

Sedgwick glanced at Daniel's corner, nodded a greeting, then walked to him. "Daniel!" Sedgwick said, offering his hand.

"Reverend Sedgwick." How ironic he was surrounded by priests.

Sedgwick put an arm around Daniel's shoulders. "How are you coping with your friend's death? Are you fully recovered from your head injury? I've been worried."

In a way, Sedgwick reminded Daniel of Lord Bold—they had the same coldness when speaking warm words, yet both were men of many friends and admirers.

Daniel forced a grin. "I'm well, though it's been—"

"Good, good. I'm glad to hear that. Look, we don't have much time to chat because Mr. Lyell will be addressing the society soon, but there's an urgent matter I must tell you about."

"What is it?"

"Two nights ago, a man attacked me on the street. Fortunately the police chased him away. It was dark and I couldn't see who it was." Sedgwick pursed his lips and passed a hand through his hair. "I'm afraid it may have been the same man who attacked you and your friend."

Daniel frowned. "But why?

"That's something the police will have to resolve, not us. All I know is that the society has many enemies. Especially those religious fanatics who want to impede the progress of science. If this man attacked me, he may try to attack you again. Perhaps you should travel away from London for a few weeks, go to Oxford, or visit your family in…"

"Norwich, sir."

"Right."

A shattering noise made them jerk. They faced the windows that looked over the street. Agitated voices and nervous movement followed a brief silence.

Daniel saw a stone lying on the floor among the broken glass. On the other side of the room, Buckland was apparently urging Lyell to take the lead and calm the attendees. Murchison trotted to the window, stepped on his toes and peered out to the street.

When Daniel turned back, he saw Sedgwick had gone to pick up the stone.

"Please be seated everyone," Lyell said from across the room. "This is merely an act of vandalism, no need to be alarmed. Let us not forget our purpose here tonight, to celebrate—"

Daniel let the words fall to the background. Sedgwick was looking intently at the stone in his hands. Daniel went towards him and peered over his shoulder.

The blackish stone—not very different from the one in Daniel's pocket—had some strange markings, like scratches. After a few seconds, Daniel could make out letters, then a sentence: YOU WILL ALL DIE.

7:30 P.M.

The rain had stopped but the fog was thick over the Strand.

"Cool night," Henry Cole muttered.

He rubbed his hands and hid them deep in his pockets. As his legs grew tired, Cole prayed the long walk was worth it. What was he going to accomplish? Only the Lord knew. As long as he was willing and obedient, God would use him.

The fog washed over the street on all sides. He couldn't tell how much longer he had to go. It was probably—

There. St. Marie-le Strand emerged from the fog to his left. He was making good time. Somerset House couldn't be too far now.

These were not streets he visited often, but he could certainly make his way to the Geological Society.

The stillness of the night surprised him. Perhaps the fog kept everybody away from the streets. Darkness was closing on him.

"Thy word is a lamp unto my feet, and a light unto my path," he muttered.

A faint brightness flickered in the night air. Cole shuddered. "Thank you, Lo—"

The sound of shattering glass pierced the fog. Cole's heart jumped inside his chest. Silence. Then, quick steps.

Panting. The sounds were closer.

Cole tried to focus his eyes on the flickering foggy light.

Panting. Running. A shadow covered the light—

And gave him a blow. Grunts. His back hit the ground.

A tall, heavy shadow towered over him. Cole opened his eyes and saw a face.

Pale eyes stared at him. Dead eyes. Then they were gone.

The man with dead eyes was running east down the Strand.

10:17 P.M.

Oatts glanced at his watch and sighed. Young probably wasn't coming home tonight. Two hours in the cold and the door to his house hadn't seen any movement.

Try coming back tomorrow? Fifteen more minutes, then he'd go home.

Two lamps glowed in the fog at each end of the street. Oatts hoped Young would walk below one of them soon enough—not because he felt tired (he never was) or because someone expected him at home (he lived alone), but because he was hungry. Good food was his weakness. And he now craved something like the meal he'd had with Ure that afternoon.

Ure was an interesting fellow, witty and honest. Oatts wondered how a man could be so passionate about such topics—topics Oatts himself had never taken seriously. He knew nothing about science and little about religion. Until he was six or seven his mother had dragged him to mass every Sunday. But once they moved to London, the only religion he knew was survival. That, he was good at.

In any case, this had to be more than warring doctrines. When the son of a Member of Parliament gets killed in such a brutal way, there's probably a political motive.

Oatts looked at his watch again. Five more minutes until his deadline. He grunted. Those five minutes could be put to better use.

He headed east toward one of the street lamps, hands deep in his pockets. A second later, Daniel emerged from the fog, eyes set on the ground. Oatts stopped while Daniel walked in his direction, apparently still unaware of his presence.

"Mr. Young," Oatts said, before Daniel would bump into him.

Daniel jerked as he looked up, eyes wide. He looked scared for a moment but then his face darkened with anger.

"May we talk?"

Daniel gave him a defiant look and said nothing.

Was it always so difficult to deal with this man?

"I don't know why you left so suddenly this mornin', but if somethin' I said offended you, 'ope you forgive me."

The defiant look vanished in a blink. "No harm done, Superintendent."

"Good. Now, we have pending bus—"

"It's quite late now, don't you think?"

Oatts sighed. This man was a mystery—an annoying one, at that. With a criminal, you could at least exercise some intimidation, create fear, play with his mind. But how could he deal with a man who wasn't afraid of him?

"I thought I gained your trust," Oatts said.

Daniel eyed him from head to feet with scornful eyes. Then he looked past his shoulders toward the house.

"This could wait until tomorrow. Now, if you'll excuse me."

Daniel began to walk away, but Oatts gave one sidestep to the left and blocked him. Daniel gasped.

"As you wish," Oatts said, extending one hand, palm up. "But first you must return what's mine. The rock."

After a few seconds, Daniel reached into a pocket and placed the rock in the superintendent's hand. Daniel's fingers were cold, and in the dim light Oatts could see his body trembling.

Daniel stepped past him and crossed the front yard to his house.

SEVEN

PARIS, 1766

The last few weeks had stirred a new optimism in Georges-Louis. He'd met with several promising candidates for the society and was close to completing and publishing the fourteenth volume of his *Natural History*. He was a rising figure in the French scientific community and wealthier than ever.

And now this. A letter from Rousseau, who was in England of all places. Last he'd heard the Swiss government had banned the Genevan from his own country. Georges-Louis sat by the window and glanced at the royal botanical garden. Snow surrounded every one of the king's trees and bushes like icy moss. He despised working for a monarch, but business was business—and the salary of 3,000 *livres* per year wasn't bad either.

The morning cold crept through the cracks in the floor, but the fireplace was at hand. He opened the letter.

> To G.L.
> From London, 12 January, 1766
>
> Sir, I regret that our correspondence had lapsed for many months, but you may already be aware of the circumstances surrounding my departure from my country and how, although I intended to go to Berlin, I ended up in London. This city, with its black fog everywhere, is taking a toll of my health.
>
> I am staying with the philosopher Hume, whom you may have met in France. He has a home in Buck-

ingham Street. I do not venture outside, not only for the aversion I feel to the streets of London but because I fear for my life. Terrible dreams of conspiracies against me assault my dreams every night. I lose sleep and wander tired around the house during the day.

A few days after my arrival in England, Hume introduced me to some of his friends, among whom I have detected brilliant minds. Be assured that I have not forsaken the duty you entrusted to me of recruiting worthy members for our society. With utmost discretion, I shared your vision and teachings with Hume and two of his friends, one Adam Smith, an economist, and one James Hutton, a naturalist like yourself. Mr. Hutton had read some of your *Histoire Naturelle*, and was greatly impressed. He particularly mentioned your essay on the "Theory of the Earth," and your rejection of miracles and catastrophes to explain the order of Nature. Mr. Hutton is most loyal to your view of a cyclical history of the earth. "There is no beginning and no end," he said to me many times that night, almost like the chant of a pious believer.

Georges-Louis grinned. The Genevan was at work. And this Hutton sounded intriguing—an adherent to the cyclical history of the earth. *What part of my essay did he enjoy more? Perhaps his personal favorite?*

He closed his eyes and recited from the depths of his mind. "It is the waters of the heavens which little by little destroy the work of the ocean, continually lower the height of the mountains, fill in the valleys, the mouths of the rivers and the gulfs, and bring everything to the same level, and which will one day return the earth to the ocean, which will then accept it, bearing new continents traversed by valleys and mountains, just like those we inhabit today."

He let the echo of his voice ring in his ears. *Merveilleux!* Few could write like him, few could think like him. If this Hutton was as shrewd as he seemed, he'd surely comprehend the meaning of the words: if one wants to understand the past or the future, one has only to look at the present.

Georges-Louis sighed and became aware again of his surroundings. He shook his head and stared at the papers in his hand for a few seconds. Then he skimmed the remaining seven pages of the letter. As customary, Rousseau lingered in picturesque descriptions of his surroundings and emotional state. The substance was already told. His next mind harvest would be in England.

Georges-Louis loosened his grip on the pages and let them slip. The paper crackled in the fire.

EIGHT

LONDON - SATURDAY, 20 FEBRUARY, 1836

3:19 A.M.

Daniel rolled over in bed. The night's events were still roiling in his mind, pushing all sleep away. He wished he could speak to Susan. He needed an ally in her absence. Someone. In the last few days, only one person seemed to really care and sympathize with him: Reverend Sedgwick.

Sedgwick had been attacked. He saw the black rock with the scratched message YOU WILL ALL DIE. He would surely be interested in knowing what Daniel knew about the other black rock that Oatts found and about Lloyd's sneaking into the library. Sedgwick was a clever scientist. Who better than him? Oatts? No. The policeman would never think scientifically. Only scientists could solve this mystery.

Didn't scientists like Lyell, Buckland, and Sedgwick solve the riddle of the ages and the history of the earth by studying nature? Just by looking at rock formations and fossils, scientists like Sedgwick can tell what happened in the distant past. If Sedgwick can do that, certainly he can deduce who killed Alex.

But what if Sedgwick wants to let the police take over? No, the police are not trustworthy. He would make Sedgwick see that. He'd tell Sedgwick how the police let his brother's killer get away, tell him how Superintendent Oatts so easily believed Ure's conspiracy theory. Yes. He would see Sedgwick in the morning. It would all work out well.

9:56 A.M.

Daniel had already knocked at Sedgwick's door when a cab halted in front of the house. He tried to see who would descend, but whoever it was they weren't in a hurry. Then the door of the house opened before him.

A butler not too different from Mr. Welsh at his cousin's house stood there.

"Sir."

He looked so much like Mr. Welsh that Daniel felt the urge to ask whether they were brothers.

"Do you..." Better not to make a fool of himself. Daniel smiled. "Is Reverend Sedgwick at home?"

"Indeed," the butler said. "Are you expected?"

"No, I'm not."

The butler twisted his lips. "I will announce you. Please come in."

A large but overly furnished foyer greeted Daniel. A faint musty smell came from the wooden furnishings.

The butler extended an arm. "The drawing room is this way, Mr... your name, ple—"

A woman burst into the entry from a door at their left, panting. "Please come righ—"

"What is it, Margaret?" the butler said.

"An accident in the kitchen. "One of the cooks, Bessie, she cut her finger."

The butler rolled his eyes and excused himself. He followed the woman, who avoided looking in Daniel's direction. What odd behavior.

Alone with the musty odor, Daniel felt sick to his stomach. He turned right in search of the drawing room. The modest room had only a blackened fireplace and three chairs covered with mantles. With nowhere to sit, Daniel crossed his arms and walked towards the window that looked over the front of the house. The cab that had come while he was at the door was now gone, but he could not see anybody in the street—nor hear anybody at the door. Then a carriage pulled by fine horses stopped where the cab had been. Some wealthy visitor had arrived.

Daniel stepped to the window to see who the visitor was. A chill ran down his spine when he saw the two men who came out of the carriage. Scrope and Lloyd!

They walked the short distance to the house in quick steps. Lloyd's square face seemed made of stone—a stone that would smash Daniel at the first opportunity. Daniel couldn't shake the idea that they'd come looking for him. Absurd. How would they know he was here? His pulse quickened. His head ached.

A knock on the front door. What was he going to do? Steps out in the musty room—the butler. He'd probably send them to the drawing room.

Daniel's body trembled as he looked around the room for a place to hide. He had snuck away from Lloyd twice before but this time had nowhere to go. He could hear the door opening.

He cringed at the sound of voices and dived below a chair. Stretched over the floor, the chair's mantle covered him down to his knees, leaving his feet to stick out toward the back of the room. If his heart weren't pounding so loud in his chest he'd be able to hear something.

The butler's voice reached him. "The Reverend is expecting you. Right this way."

Expecting them? Daniel jerked and hit his head against a leg of the chair. His days-old wound received the impact. The world turned fuzzy. Nothing made sense now. Why was Sedgwick involved with Scrope? Scrope was a member of the Geological Society, but so were hundreds of others. What could their dealings be? He had to find out.

Daniel held his position for a whole minute but not a sound could be heard. They weren't coming to the drawing room.

Ready to leave, he scooted back an inch, when the butler's voice froze him under the chair. "Sir?"

What would he say if the butler walked in so far he noticed Daniel's feet sticking out from the mantle? That he was looking for a missing coin?

The butler seemed to walk away, the steps vanishing into the musty area. Daniel waited a few seconds before sneaking out of the drawing room. Sweat damped his hands. The cautious voice in his head screamed to get out of the house, but his legs kept moving him away from the front door.

Beyond the musty room he followed a narrow hallway with two closed doors on each side. The hallway ended with another door, not completely closed. Daniel walked toward it and peered through the opening into what seemed to be a large study. He could see Scrope's profile and the arm and leg of someone sitting beside him—probably Sedgwick. He couldn't see Lloyd.

Scrope chuckled. "I'm certainly satisfied, Adam. Those bigwigs in Parliament had no choice but to swallow my words when they realized the implications of Lyell's work. You shall see their embarrassment when we oblige them to deny the effects of the deluge. What would have been heresy a few years ago will be accepted like physics when not only the Geological Society but the Royal Society are attached to the liberal side."

"We have a new victory," Sedgwick said. "Buckland is now completely on our side. And who better than Buckland to help us assimilate all catastrophist evidence?"

"Buckland?" Scrope said. "The Mosaic geologist par excellence? Tell me, Adam, how did you accomplish that feat?"

"You may give Lyell some credit for that. Lyell lured him

out of his devotion to biblical dogma while I showed him the political advantages of uniformitarianism."

"Marvelous!" Scrope said. "At this pace, it will only be a few decades before our scientific and political leaders embrace atheism."

Daniel gasped. Scrope turned his face toward the door and Daniel yanked his head out of view. Had they seen him?

Conversation in the room ceased. Daniel heard heavy steps moving in his direction. He would bet his life the steps were Lloyd's. In three strides Daniel reached one of the closed doors in the hallway and turned the knob. It was unlocked. He snuck into a dark room and closed the door as quietly as possible. Right before it closed, he saw a figure emerging from the musty-room side of the hallway. The butler? What if he'd seen Daniel come into the room? What if both Lloyd and the butler saw him?

The room was so dark Daniel couldn't see a thing. He shuddered. The small room felt like a prison cell. How had he gotten into all this trouble?

With his palms against the wall he felt his way toward the back of the room, but three feet later, he hit a barrier—a large wooden cabinet that felt like a wardrobe. Now what?

His heart jumped when he heard sharp words outside the room. It sounded as if Lloyd and the butler were arguing about something. Daniel crouched, then lay on his stomach. With his palms on the floor, he slowly moved his head to peer through the bottom of the door. Two opposing pairs of shoes. Words like *door, spying,* and *open* reached his ears— no more. Then two more voices with their respective footwear joined the quarrel.

Daniel's head wound tingled and the pain returned. They were going to open the door and discover him. He closed his eyes. A flood of implications swept through his mind. Sedgwick was in some sort of plot with Scrope, and

Ure was telling the truth about the society suppressing evidence. For what purpose? He still didn't know. But it didn't matter. Lloyd was going to kill him just as he'd killed Alex. The quarrel stopped. Daniel opened his eyes and saw that only one pair of shoes remained outside the door—Lloyd's.

10:32 A.M.

Oatts scooted one step back and waited for the door to open. What he would do once it did, he didn't know. Whose house was this, anyway? A few minutes ago, his ear against the door, he'd heard a commotion inside. Surely Daniel was causing trouble—or was in trouble. Whatever was happening, he felt an urge to participate.

The door flew open to the view of an agitated butler. He wiped the sweat on his brow and struggled to regain his posture.

"Sir?"

Oatts glanced over the butler's shoulder and saw two men standing a few feet away from the door. He'd seen one of them enter the house with a third man, whom he couldn't see now. Where was Daniel?

"I'm Superintendent Michael Oatts from the Metropolitan Police. I'd like to speak with..."

Oatts reached for the notebook in his pocket and shuffled the pages, hoping the butler would finish the phrase.

"Let him in, Mr. Welsh."

Oatts glanced up toward the two men behind the butler, who now moved out of the way. The short man Oatts had seen enter turned around and walked to the back of the house, the other man came toward him.

"I'm Reverend Sedgwick. Please come in, Superintendent."

Reverend? What was Daniel doing in the house of a reverend?

"Thank you."

Oatts stepped in and glanced around. No sign of Daniel. At the end of a hallway two men were entering a room. The door closed behind them. Oatts tensed.

"What can I do for you?" Sedgwick said.

Oatts kept staring at the door at the end of the hallway.

"Who's the gentleman that was 'ere with you? I think I've seen him before."

"Perhaps. He's a Member of Parliament. George Scrope."

"I see." The name wasn't familiar.

Oatts turned to Sedgwick, who raised his brows just a little. The reverend's face seemed polite enough, but Oatts noted Sedgwick's left boot moving up and down while his fingers rubbed the corners of his coat.

"Do you have any more visitors today, Reverend?"

"No, I don't. Now, may I inquire about the purpose of your visit?"

"Just those two gentlemen back there? No one else?"

Sedgwick rolled his eyes. "Yes, just the two of them."

Oatts walked about the room, fiddling with his mustache. A musty smell filled the air. His uneasiness grew. For some reason, the reverend was concealing Daniel's presence in the house.

Sedgwick cleared his throat, probably irritated by Oatts's wandering, but he needed time. Time to figure out where Daniel was, figure out what to do next.

As Oatts passed by a small table, his coat brushed against it, toppling a stack of letters to the floor. Sedgwick grunted and Oatts bent down to pick up the mess. He took his time, placing one over the other, seeing how much he could read without opening them. The last two were sealed with a design he'd seen before—two letters, G and S. He held the seal up to his face and searched his memory until it came to him. He smiled and put the letters back on the table.

"When did you join the Geological Society, Reverend?"

"Well, um, that was many years ago. Why?"

"I see." Oatts cocked his head, trying to conceal his satisfaction. Now he had an excuse to be there. "You must know everyone there very well."

"I wouldn't say it that way, but—"

"Including Alexander Bold, aye?"

For a second, a shadow crossed Sedgwick's face, as if pricked by fear. But he blinked, looked away from Oatts, and the shadow vanished.

"Yes, I knew Alexander," Sedgwick said, shaking his head. "Good lad. Pity what happened to him."

The man didn't mean what he said—it was obvious from his voice. Hiding something for sure.

"Who killed him?"

Sedgwick frowned. "What?"

Those reactions were what Oatts loved the most about his job.

"Any idea who the killer is?"

"If I had such information I would have certainly informed the police already. What about you, Superintendent, any ideas from your investigations?"

"No suspects yet." Oatts resumed his pacing.

"Oh, pity!"

Sedgwick was not trustworthy. If finding Daniel weren't his first priority, Oatts would enjoy setting a trap for the reverend.

He knew more than one way to get the information he sought. But Daniel wasn't around. And he didn't feel right about the two men at the end of the hallway, either.

"I'm dreadfully thirsty," Oatts said. "I would like a drink, if you don't mind me askin'?"

"A drink. Of course." Sedgwick walked past him toward the way the butler had taken. "Mr. Welsh?"

He waited for a response, hands on his waist.

"Mr. Welsh, where are you?" Sedgwick turned to Oatts. "Please excuse me." Then he disappeared through a door.

Oatts glanced down the hallway. This was his chance.

10:53 A.M.

The coldness of the dark room crept into Daniel's body. Although Lloyd's feet were gone, he feared the knob he couldn't see would turn at any moment.

He pressed his back against the wall. Muffled voices caught his ears between breaths—otherwise he could only hear his irregular breathing. This was ridiculous. He should just go out and face them.

But that was madness. He could get himself killed.

Could he really believe that? Sedgwick wouldn't allow a murder in his house. He was a reverend, for God's sake.

Daniel bent over to peer out through the slit, not expecting to see anything but the old red carpet that lined the hallway. Black boots.

He'd seen those same boots before.

Daniel sprang to his feet and pulled the door open. Oatts stared at him with owl eyes, apparently as surprised as he was. Daniel's hands tingled. It occurred to him that someone could be watching. But he was still inside the room. Nobody else could see him.

"Mr. Youn—"

Daniel reached for Oatts's arm, pulled him inside the dark room, and shut the door. Oatts's black silhouette moved awkwardly as if spinning around itself. Soon Daniel felt an unimaginable force lifting him from his shirt. His feet left the ground and his back smashed the wall. Where did the little Irishman get so much strength?

"What's your game, Young?" Oatts spat the words out. "You've no idea who you're messing with! You—"

"I mean no harm, please!" Oatts's knuckles dug in his chest. The chill was gone from Daniel's body. A sweat crown formed on his forehead. "Please."

The grasp on his shirt yielded. Oatts grunted. "Speak."

Relief washed over Daniel. "Did you see the men out there?"

"Aye."

"I'm hiding from them. They don't know I'm in the house."

"Why are you hidin'?"

The story would take too long to tell. Noise stirred in the hallway again.

"I'll explain later," Daniel muttered. "Get us out of here."

"I'll do that very thing." His tone was rather jovial. Interesting how Oatts's emotions could swing so briskly—just like the door, which opened and closed in two seconds as Oatts emerged into the hallway.

Daniel swallowed and bent down on his knees to follow Oatts's shoes below the door.

"Sorry, reverend. I guess this ain't the water closet." The superintendent sounded so casual he didn't seem to be pretending.

10:57 A.M.

The reverend's expression wrinkled like a wet sponge. Oatts offered back a blank look.

"The water closet is this way, Superintendent," Sedgwick said.

Oatts nodded and walked to the small door by the kitchen, just as the butler came out with what seemed to be his drink. He closed the door behind him. He counted to fifty, grinning at the plan developing in his mind.

Oatts came out and found the butler standing by himself in the living room. He took the glass from the butler's tray and peered at its contents. Wine. Excellent. He shook the glass a little bit and the wine rose up to the edge of the glass.

Sedgwick reappeared from the room at the end of the hallway, where his visitors probably waited for the reverend to get rid of Oatts. He would gladly leave, of course. But first things first.

"Well, reverend, if you're sure there's nothin' you can tell me about the murder, I'll let you go back to your visitors."

"I'm sorry I can't be of more help, Superintendent."

Oatts's eyes focused on Sedgwick's feet. He needed him a little closer.

Sedgwick stopped three feet away from him. That would have to do. Without looking at the glass, he tipped it over and poured the wine in his mouth. The liquid stopped at the back of his throat, filling his mouth and then coming back out again. The ejected wine traveled three feet and splashed on Sedgwick's coat.

"Oh, my," Oatts said. "I forgot I can't drink wine! Doctor's orders."

Sedgwick's face turned red. He glared at Oatts. "Look what you've done!" His breathing became agitated. But just when Oatts expected him to say things no man of the cloth should utter, he muttered something unintelligible and walked toward the stairs across the living room. Oatts turned to the troubled butler.

"You should help your master, don't you think? And do pass on my apologies to him."

The wide-eyed butler followed Sedgwick and Oatts followed them with his eyes until they disappeared in the second floor. It was time for Young to come out of his hiding place.

11:42 A.M.

Daniel sighed with relief as soon as they entered the gentlemen's club on Waterloo Place and Pall Mall. This was his retreat—the bachelor's haven in London. Oatts hadn't said much on their way there, just eyed him suspiciously from time to time. The superintendent was obviously not comfortable around him and Daniel didn't blame him—his behavior in the last few days didn't exactly give Oatts any reason to deem him trustworthy. But how could he trust a policeman?

Oatts seemed to shrink under the looks of the club members. He didn't belong here. But he'd come to the club at Daniel's request. He'd snuck Daniel out of Sedgwick's house. He'd trusted him with the rock. If there was anyone trustworthy it was Oatts.

Oatts halted and glanced around. Daniel pointed to a table and they sat.

"I owe you an apology," Daniel said. "I haven't been straightforward with you."

Oatts smirked.

This could be hard. He had to get through to the superintendent. It was his only chance to get some help.

"Look, I have my...reasons to be wary of the police."

The superintendent frowned as he fiddled with his mustache.

Daniel sighed. "But now I know none of those reasons apply to you. You've shown me your trustworthiness, and I—well, I'm grateful for that."

"No problem, Mr. Young. But I can't keep 'elping you if you don't start tellin' what you know, aye?"

"Of course."

Daniel told him everything from the morning he saw the letters until their encounter at Sedgwick's house. Oatts seemed intrigued by the second rock that had broken the glass at Somerset House. His face grew serious. He shook his head and stared into the distance.

"So Lloyd has to be the killer, don't you agree?" Daniel said, trying to bring him back. "I witnessed the murder, now he wants to kill me."

The superintendent blinked and turned a silent stare to Daniel.

Daniel leaned forward. "Lloyd shows up everywhere I go. He must be following me."

"Per'aps. But I wonder what kept him from attacking you so far. Lloyd got a very good chance, didn't 'e, Mr. Young?"

"What do you mean?"

"I'm just sayin', maybe you're imagining things."

"How can you say that? I saw him at the library, I didn't imagine that."

" I believe you, Mr. Young. But me job is to put the facts together, not the fears. You said the librarian wasn't there that day?"

"We were supposed to meet, but he was sick."

"Was he really?"

"That's what they told me."

Oatts rubbed his chin. "Per'aps they sent him home so this Lloyd could search the library."

"I don't think they would—"

"There's no need to defend the reverends, Mr. Young, we're just doing some guessin' here."

Daniel leaned back on his chair and dropped both hands to his sides. Was he still blindly defending the society's leadership? After listening to Sedgwick and Scrope that morning, how could he do that? There was something rotten with the reverends, as Oatts called them. Of course, Lyell wasn't a clergyman, but a—

"There's only one way to prove my guessin'," Oatts said.

"What's that?"

"Ask the librarian."

NINE

MONTBARD, FRANCE, 1772

Georges-Louis regarded his reddened fingers one more time before glancing at the oven. The tin sphere that served as control in his experiment began to melt. He reached for the other spheres and placed them on a table in the cellar.

"Pierre? Be sure to write down the time elapsed when I tell you."

The young Pierre-Simon Laplace frowned at the sight of the thirty spheres on the table—all one inch in diameter but each of a different metal or mineral.

With a rapid movement, Georges-Louis touched the two hot spheres he'd just drawn from the fire.

"*Sacrebleu*, still hot!" he said, blowing air at his burned fingers.

After a minute, he touched the spheres again. He lifted one of them in his hand and put it back on the table very rapidly.

"The iron sphere is cooling down. I can hold it in my hand for a half-second. Write down in your chart the number of minutes that elapsed for the iron sphere."

"*Voilà*," Laplace said.

Georges-Louis did the same with the sandstone sphere. "Now," he said. "This one takes longer."

Laplace looked at his watch and recorded the minutes on the chart.

Georges-Louis walked toward Laplace, shaking his right hand in front of him.

"Potot de Montbeillard suggested these experiments a

few years ago, when I told him my theory for the cooling of the earth."

"*Oui*," Laplace said. "You mentioned the theory before. I find it rather odd."

Georges-Louis chuckled. Laplace had a brilliant mind but was still very young.

"Perhaps because you do not fully understand it. It's rather simple when you see the progression of my thought." He began pacing. "Long ago, a comet hit the sun obliquely, tearing off about 1/650 of its liquid matter. This matter divided into rotating spheres, which are, of course, the planets. Hence, the primitive earth was a sphere of molten matter rotating on its axis. The centrifugal force of this rotation removed the least dense matter, thus forming the moon. Very slowly, the earth cooled down and became a solid mass."

He strode to the table and picked up a cool sphere. He held it before his eyes for a few seconds, then brought it closer to Laplace's eyes.

"Do you see this metal sphere? It has holes, wrinkles, and waves as a result of the cooling process. The same happened with the earth, the wrinkles being the primitive mountains of the globe."

Laplace nodded, his eyes fixed on the sphere. He took it from Georges-Louis' hands, turned the sphere in his palms. Then he looked up to the chart he had been working on.

"So with these times, you plan to calculate the age of the earth."

Georges-Louis grinned. "I already did."

"And? What is it?"

Georges-Louis considered his new pupil for a moment, the bright mathematician interested in astronomy. Was he ready to hear *his* truth or was he still a slave of old dogmas? The night before, Laplace had mentioned how his father intended him to become a Roman Catholic priest, but he'd had other plans for himself. Georges-Louis narrowed his eyes. There was only one way to know. He would tell him and observe his reaction.

"From my experiments with the spheres, I estimate around 75,000 years for the earth to reach its current temperature. That is the number I will publish in my book."

"But the earth isn't just a sphere cooling in the air—"

"You're right. The earth cooled off in the vacuum while still being heated by the sun. And considering that life, the first sea mollusks, could have only appeared 36,000 years after the formation of the planet—it was too hot before then—there may not be enough time to account for the production of all the calcareous matter of the globe's surface. Many hidden causes were in operation during the cooling of the earth."

"Then what do you believe is the age of the earth?"

Georges-Louis hesitated. "At least ten million years, probably more. Many times more."

Laplace nodded. "That sounds reasonable. Why are you publishing the 75,000 years number then? Do you fear the church's theologians?"

Georges-Louis snorted. "Not for a moment! For those theologians, 75,000 is as outrageous as ten million. The real reason is to avoid obscurity and confusion over an already difficult matter. The human mind, accustomed to short periods of time, considers a hundred years a long time. It cannot imagine a thousand years, let alone millions of years. I don't want to plunge my readers into the dark abyss of time. What's important here is that I have demonstrated with physical evidence that the biblical chronology is wrong."

"I can see many holes in your theory, M. de Buffon," Laplace said. "Just like the holes in this sphere. It's promising, but it needs refinement."

The young mathematician was right where Georges-Louis wanted him to be.

"That is why I'm sharing these with you. D'Alembert, your mentor, has spoken highly of your genius. I'm convinced that you could refine my promising theory and cover all those holes you now see in it." He grabbed the paper with the chart and threw it in the fire. "You will do better than that."

TEN

8:05 A.M.

The chimes of church bells echoed through the empty streets of the Old City of London.

Oatts's eyes lingered on a poster touting the grand concert by singer Liza Vestris. He should find the time to attend that concert. *The Last Days of Pompeii* was still running every evening—as were dozens of other plays, whose posters covered the bricks of every public wall.

Acting was the life he would have pursued if he hadn't been pushed into this one first. But then again, trapping murderers seemed to be a more righteous cause than entertaining the nobility. And here he was, trying to trap the murderer of a nobleman.

He looked down the row of rat-infested apartments. Four buildings down the street, a faded green facade bore the number on the note in his pocket. The green building was the best kept of all the structures in the neighborhood.

If the librarian, a Mr. Victor Shaw, were a religious man he would probably be at church. But the man was sick, aye?

Oatts knocked on the door and it just squeaked open. He stepped inside and noted the peeling paint of the interior walls, hanging like dead petals. At least it was tidy. He was looking up the stairs to the second and third floor when the door to his back opened.

"May I 'elp you, sir?" a woman's voice said.

Oatts spun on his feet. A bush of disheveled hair topped a plain face with red chubby cheeks.

"Aye. I'm Superintendent Oatts from the Metropolitan Police. I'm looking for Mr. Shaw."

The woman gasped. "Oh, heavens, the police. Mr. Shaw? Has he done anything wrong? Poor Mr. Shaw, what has he done? He's such a good man, very quiet—he does enjoy the drink, I'll say that, but he always pays the rent on time, very polite man. No trouble, mister, no trouble never."

"He's done nothing wrong, mum. I just want to talk to him." Oatts eyed her from head to toe, judging how much to say in order to gain her cooperation. She seemed harmless in the yellow dress and the stained white apron that she probably wore day and night. "And check that he's all right."

"Oh, poor Mr. Shaw's not all right at all, so sick he went away to his sister's that she'd take care of him, you know? The other night he was coughing blood, I think, and looked so very tired, the poor old man."

"To his sister's, you say?"

"Oh, yes, that's what his letter said, you know? A few days ago I come out early mornin' and find this letter and the next month's rent in my box, and that's where he says he's away to his sister's, poor man, I sure 'ope he's all right."

"Did he say where his sister lives, mum?"

"No, no, he didn't say. He left the message he was going away and no more, you know? That and the next month's rent."

The woman wiped her hands on her apron as if talking had made them dirty. The hand flapping was temporarily replaced by repetitive nodding. Oatts debated between leaving with the little information he now had and subjecting himself to her babbling for the sake of new information that might or might not come.

The landlady stopped wiping her hands and stared at

him. Then she shrugged. "That's what I told the other man."

"What other man?"

"The man who come on Thursday asking for Mr. Shaw. A very tall handsome fellow with a straight face, said he was a relative—I saw no resemblance, you know—and he wanted to find him soon. I could tell him no more than I'd told you, but this man kept asking and turned all upset at me for not telling him more. But what could I do? I kept telling him the same until the man left—that angry he was, you know?"

"A well-dressed blond fellow?"

"Aye, yellow loops, like those Germans," she said. "Do you know 'im? Is he really a relative of Mr. Shaw?"

"Lloyd," Oatts muttered under his breath. Daniel's hunch was right. The librarian was in danger if this Lloyd was after him. He had to either find the librarian first or keep Lloyd away. Oatts stared at the old floorboards and considered his options. How strong was his case against Lloyd? Not strong enough to throw him in jail. And if the man worked for a Member of Parliament, all the harder to convince the chief to incarcerate him without proper evidence. No, he needed more proof, not just to catch the bandit but also the masterminds of whatever Scrope and the Reverend Sedgwick were planning. This murder investigation was turning into something unexpected. A bolt of excitement ran over his skin.

Oatts came out of his thoughts to see the landlady wiping her hands again on her apron. He glanced up the stairs. From Daniel's story, it seemed that Lloyd—or his boss—was after a bunch of old letters. Did they think the librarian had the letters?

"Have you been to his flat since he left, mum?" Oatts said.

She shook her head. "He paid his rent and the place is still *his*, so why would I do that? No, no, no, no."

Oatts scowled at her. She probably had been there, more than once. She looked the nosy type.

"Maybe we should take a look," he said. "And see if we can find the address of his sister. You don't know how important it is that I find him."

The woman raised her brows. "I don't think we can do that, sir. What would all the other tenants say if they see I let a stranger into a renter's flat while he's away? No, no, no, we ain't doing that, sir, no."

Oatts stepped forward toward her. "May I remind you I'm from the Metropolitan Police?"

She shrugged. "What difference does that make? The other tenants don't know that. And who's ever heard about the police entering a good man's house without reason?"

"I see now." He tilted his head and reached to his mustache with two fingers. "Per'aps you've heard about the police jailin' uncooperative folks 'til they open their mouths and tell what they must."

The woman looked down at the floor and twisted the apron in her hands. "I...I might of heard something like that, I'm not sure, sir. A person never knows what to believe about all the things they say in the streets." She glanced back at him. "Is that true, sir?"

"Do you really want to find out, mum?"

She shook her head.

"Which one's his flat, then?"

The landlady pointed up the stairs. "First door on the second story."

8:54 A.M.

Shaw's place was as plain as a jail cell. Hard to believe this was a librarian's apartment. Oatts couldn't see a single book in the flat, nothing that would reveal what Shaw did for a living. In fact it felt like the place of a man who merely goes by each day. Only the basic survival items lay atop a worn-out table from another era. It was either very neat or scattered—Oatts couldn't make up his mind about it. It was as if the washbasin, the towels, and the brushes were perfectly arranged within themselves but didn't follow any particular pattern on the table. As he looked closer he knew why. The items were new, never used. Why did he leave without his new effects?

"How long has Mr. Shaw lived 'ere?" Oatts asked the landlady, who stood by the door, her face a mask of disapproval.

"As far back as I can remember," she muttered. "He was already 'ere when I came twenty years ago."

Interesting. He looked at the nearly bare walls—only a framed newspaper clipping hung above the lonely, unmade bed. The clipping was a piece from an 1816 account of the Geological Society's new apartments at 20 Bredford Street, Covent Garden. That was probably the place the society rented before moving to Somerset House. A few paragraphs down, the piece mentioned the library and the librarian by name.

Oatts smirked. For a man who must have a great respect for the printed word, he found it ironic that Shaw's name was the only print to be found. Oatts moved away from the wall and scanned the room for the letters.

The landlady's silence was suspicious. Just a few minutes ago in the hallway she could hardly shut her mouth, now she was mute. Perhaps his jail threat put—

The door frame was empty.

Oatts frowned and strode to the door. He stuck his head out of the flat and looked both directions—down the stairs and down the hallway. No sign of her. All the better, he could search the place in peace.

He was turning around when the landlady's voice broke the stillness.

"Superintendent!"

Oatts bent over the rail to see the woman shouting up at him.

"You won't believe who's here! That *relative* of Mr. Shaw's I was telling you 'bout!"

From his position over the rail, Oatts could only see the legs and feet of a man standing by the landlady—the hallway that led to the stairs to the third floor covered the rest. The feet turned and disappeared.

Oatts ran down the staircase in three steps and sprinted after the man, past the frantic landlady and out to the street. He saw nothing in front of the building but heard galloping to his right. A carriage to the north quickly disappeared from his sight. A familiar carriage he had seen just the day before.

ELEVEN

PARIS, 1779

Georges-Louis enjoyed the enthusiasm of his latest apprentice as much as the scenery at his familiar royal botanical garden.

"*C'est fantastique*, M. De Buffon," Lamarck said. "I'm now an official member of the French Academy of Sciences. How may I repay your help?"

"It's my pleasure, Jean-Baptiste. Believe me, this is only a milestone in your successful career. I have many plans for you—if you're at all interested in what I have to say."

"But of course, *monsieur*. Without you, my book wouldn't have seen the light of day. I look up to you. Please tell me."

Georges-Louis grinned. "*Voila*. For now you may work here at the botanical garden as an assistant botanist. I have also arranged for you to do some research at the *Jardin des Plantes*."

"Botanical research?"

"*Mais oui*," Buffon said, rolling his eyes. "You may study more flowers there, but you will also find that animals can be a more interesting path of research."

Lamarck's eyebrows drew together. "Animals? But I have no experience, no knowledge of—"

"Never be afraid to learn, Jean-Baptiste. There is so much to discover!"

His pupil offered back a timid nod. Perhaps he was not convinced. But time was on their side. Just like Rousseau and Laplace, Lamarck had the one quality he thought most important in his protegés: materialism. In a few years, Georges-Louis's dangerous ideas (that's how he liked to think of them) would be published, debated, and no doubt accepted—and none would carry his name. Just the way he wanted it. Destroying dogmas involved more than one man, more than one lifetime.

"Come here," Georges-Louis said, walking to a pond in one corner of the garden. "I want to show you something." They stepped near the pond and Georges-Louis pointed to the water. "Imagine that these fish lived in a dark cave underwater. Their eyes would have no use—they would become useless organs. Do you know what would happen to the descendants of those fish in a few generations? They would be born blind! If you study animals, Jean-Baptiste, you will find that as animals adapt to their environment, they develop gradual changes in their morphology. Do you see this?"

"No, M. de Buffon, why would they lose their eyesight?"

"Because of disuse, Jean-Baptiste, because of disuse." He put a hand on Lamarck's shoulder and they resumed their walk around the pond. "This may seem somewhat arcane now, but you will comprehend the law of disuse eventually. For now, you must understand the law of adaptation and changes. Think for instance about a giraffe trying to reach for the leaves on the high branches of that tree you see there. As the animal stretches its neck higher and higher, its neck becomes longer. Then, I believe, it will pass this trait to its descendants—and that is how giraffes came to have long necks. Do you grasp this concept?"

Lamarck stared at the trees with a frown, seemingly mulling over the words and the images Georges-Louis had described.

"I believe so," he said. "Would this happen to humans as well?"

Georges-Louis laughed. "You'll find that humans and animals are not so different from each other."

TWELVE

11:05 A.M.

Daniel waited at the back entrance for the Bolds' housekeeper to emerge. What could be taking her so long?

He glanced at his pocket watch. Perhaps the other servants were keeping her busy. There could be a lot of activity at this time around the house, especially if Lord Bold was due to arrive soon. Daniel had tried to come by earlier but he couldn't avoid taking care of his cousin's businesses any longer. So he'd visited the shoe and the soap factories, collected the earnings from the accountants, and deposited the money in the bank. Now he'd come here to collect the translated letter.

The housekeeper opened the back door and stuck her head out.

"Mr. Young," she said and stepped out. "I apologize for my delay, sir. One of the maids informed me about a terrible incident." She half-closed her eyes and shook her head. "Someone broke into the house last night. We're—"

"Is anyone hurt? Was anything stolen?"

"Everyone is all right, sir. We haven't found anything missing yet. But one window was broken and Mr. Alexander's room was torn apart."

So Lloyd had come looking for the letters. The superintendent should know.

"Here," the housekeeper said. "Miss Susan sent you this."

123

He plucked the letter from her hands.

"I must go now, sir. Please excuse me."

He should probably go somewhere safe to read the letter, but his hands couldn't wait. What if there was something else from Susan this time—a love letter, perhaps?

He unfolded the letter and skimmed the first few paragraphs. It was Susan's handwriting, but the letter wasn't directed to him.

14 January, 1796

Dear Jacques-Louis, Comte de Bournon

May the spirit of freedom and fraternity find you well. I'm writing to you in French so as to not forget the language. I pray in advance you forgive my errors. Only you are kind enough to understand my love for France and the revolution. May one day England embrace the spirit of the revolution.

Now, let me recount the happenings in London. Pepys keeps rambling about the suggestion from La-Place and Lamarck that we should gather around Hutton in Edinburgh. He doesn't agree with them that England may be more easily taken if we begin in Scotland. Pepys and Babington think that a better strategy is to establish the society's presence in London and to make it public (including its long-kept secret name). "What better facade than to hide in plain sight?" is what Pepys says. They are planning to meet at William Allen's place next winter. For my part, I believe that as long as the society's ulterior motives remain veiled, it's fine. The Askesian Society may be known as a philosophical club and no one will ever suspect of our gatherings. Of course, they ask not for my opinion, because I know nothing about science or philosophy (although I'm learning as much as I can; you would be proud of me).

I know they keep me around because they see me as your protégé and, because of my history, they expect me to do the dirty work. It seems that my debts with the law in England were forgotten after so many years in France. For that reason, I hope no more butchery will be required of me (but rest assured I will do whatever necessary for the good of the cause).

Is it true that you will come to London this autumn? I wish to see you soon, my friend.

Liberté, egalité, fraternité!

A.S.

Dear Daniel,

At last, I can send you the translated letter. I have looked at my brother's notes and he did not seem to know the identity of the author, A.S. What is the Askesian Society? This is all so mysterious! I want to hear what you think about all this. Write to me, please. I miss you so very much.

Your love,

Susan

A million thoughts flooded Daniel's brain. The Askesian Society? The name sounded familiar but he couldn't remember what it was. Pepys? All Daniel knew was that William Pepys was one of the thirteen founders of the Geological Society. Laplace and Lamarck in a secret society? Who was

A.S? Adam Sedgwick? No, impossible. Sedgwick was merely a child in 1796.

Askesian Society. A.S. The Geological Society. Comte de Bournon. William Pepys. It was time to connect all these elements.

2:15 P.M.

"The Askesian Society?" Ure raised one brow.

Daniel nodded. He felt awkward returning to Ure's laboratory after his behavior the week before, but Oatts wasn't at his office, and he couldn't think where else to go. Ure would surely know something. Fortunately, he didn't seem to resent Daniel's outburst.

"I haven't heard about the Askesian Society in thirty years," Ure said. "I believe it was in 1796 that William Allen and other young scientists—young then, not now—started meeting twice a month at his laboratory to conduct experiments and present papers on any topic they were inclined to. The name came from the Greek *askesis*, which means 'training,' if memory serves. It was a promising club, but after a few years they disbanded."

"What happened?"

"Some of the members went to the Royal Society or the Linnaean Society. In fact, some of the disbanded members, including William Allen, got together again to form the Geological Society in 1807. Soon afterwards I was invited to join as an Honorary Fellow."

"Were Laplace and Lamarck also members of the Askesian Society?"

Ure frowned. "The French scientists?"

Daniel nodded.

"I don't think so, no," Ure said. "The only Frenchman

directly involved with the Askesians was Comte Jacques-Louis de Bournon."

Daniel's eyes widened. "Comte de Bournon?"

"Yes, another of the founders of the Geological Society. He fled France after the revolution. Why do you ask about Laplace and Lamarck? These are all strange questions, Daniel."

Should he tell him about the letter? Daniel stared at Ure for a while, whose face darkened.

"Are you all right, Daniel?"

"I wish Oatts were here to think of something," Daniel said.

"What?"

"Superintendent Oatts, you know—"

"Yes, I know who he is. But I'm worried about you. The other day you storm out of here in anger and today you're asking peculiar questions. What's the ma—"

A knock on the door. They both turned to look when the door pushed opened.

"You got my message!"

Oatts walked in and took off his hat.

"Aye," Oatts said. "And I brought the rock."

Daniel grinned, happy to see the superintendent. "I'm confident I know already what kind of rock it is. A volcanic rock. It came to me when I saw the other rock that broke the window at the anniversary."

"Is this the rock that was used to kill your friend?" Ure said.

"Yes."

Ure nodded. "But not everybody carries a volcanic rock around. These aren't found on the streets of London."

"Right!" Daniel said.

Oatts walked closer to them. "I see now. You're saying then that the killer didn't pick the rock from the terrace but brought it with him?"

"Perhaps the killer stole it from someone's rock collection," Ure said.

"Perhaps," Daniel said. "But perhaps he had no need to. I'm sure Scrope has a rock collection, and Lloyd has access to it."

Oatts fingered one tip of his mustache. "I don't know, Mr. Young. Why take a rock—and then drop it—that can be easily associated with his boss? Not only that, but there's the rock that broke the window. What's the meaning of that? This Lloyd mate don't seem the sloppy type that would use such a conspicuous weapon, do you think?"

Daniel could not believe his ears. Oatts was actually defending Lloyd.

"But then again, it might be possible," Oatts said. "He's gone searching at least twice for the librarian. That fellow is dirty, all right."

Daniel stood. "So he really is after Mr. Shaw? You saw him?"

"Aye. The man ran away as soon as soon he found I was there. But I couldn't get hold of the librarian. Seems he's away at his sister's."

This was serious. Lloyd was after the letters. He hoped Susan was all right.

11:53 P.M.

Susan dropped her pen at the sound of crackling branches outside. She gazed out the window into the dark woods but saw nothing. She could hear the dialogue between leaves and wind and pictured the green vibrating and breaking free from the twigs. But this was not what had startled her. It sounded more like someone had stepped on fallen branches.

She crossed the room to check that the windows were

locked. Mother and Emily were sleeping; Mr. Hunter, the keeper, could be awake but he wouldn't be walking around the house. He knew better than to spy on them.

Five minutes went by with no further sounds. Now she was imagining things. Alex's death and all this trouble with the letters had her mind playing tricks. Father said they'd be safe at the country house. She shouldn't be afraid, all would be well.

She blew the candle out. Her eyes adjusted to the darkness, but sleep eluded her. In its place a deep cold embraced her, leaving her even wider awake. It felt almost like a presence—a physical aura looming in the room. What if there really was someone out there?

She inched toward the window. Nothing seemed to move. The night would have been perfectly black but for a few stars that pierced the sky. So peaceful. The country house had always been a place of peace. This was where her best childhood memories resided—riding horses, spying on the adult guests, setting up practical jokes on Mr. Hunter. And this was the place where she'd met Daniel. During his first year at Oxford, Alex brought Daniel here for the hunting season. After that they came back as often as they could. A few hunting visits later Susan had fallen in love with Daniel's face, with the way he moved, with the cadence of his voice.

"Daniel," she whispered to the shadows. If she were in London, they'd go for a walk at Hyde Park and—

The door clicked.

Susan whirled around.

The door opened, slowly. Her feet and hands lost all warmth.

A tall figure stepped inside. She wanted to scream but she was too frightened.

Two short steps, then whoever it was halted as if aware of her stare.

Susan gasped for air but barely anything came in—fear choked her. She knew what would happen next: she would die and meet Alex in heaven, or whatever awaited their souls on the other side of life.

The intruder seemed to hesitate for a second, then moved toward her.

Thirteen

London · Tuesday, 23 February, 1836

2:10 p.m.

"I came as fast as I could," Daniel said, panting in the foyer of the Bold's mansion. "Is she all right?"

"Yes, sir," the housekeeper said. "Right this way."

She led him up the stairs to the second floor. Sweat ran down his temples but his fingers were cold as the day outside. He tried to bring saliva to his dry mouth but all he accomplished was to bring up the sour taste of the acids churning in his stomach. Even his week-old head wound hurt.

"He's after all of us," Daniel murmured to the air. The journey here from home was hell—poring over the brief letter from the Bolds that urged him to come and see Susan, who had been robbed at the country house. The lack of details was maddening, excruciating.

"Are you sure she's all right?"

They were at the left end of the hallway already. The housekeeper shifted to one side and faced him with a smile.

"See for yourself, sir."

Daniel hurried into Susan's bedroom. Lord Bold and Dr. Gray were chatting on one side of the room. Susan sat on her bed, eyes closed, her back against the headboard.

"Daniel," Lord Bold said. "So nice of you to come." His stern expression made Daniel feel as if his shirt's collar had suddenly shrunk around his neck.

"I came as soon as I knew, sir, my lord." Daniel glanced

at Susan, who opened her eyes at the sound of his voice.

Lord Bold stood near him. "They brought her early this morning. After what happened last night, nobody felt safe at the country house any more."

"Excuse me, sir." Daniel pushed past Lord Bold and sat on the bed beside Susan. She reached a hand to him. All pain and fear left him at her touch.

He wet his lips, now that he could.

"I... I was so afraid that—oh, Susan!"

She giggled.

"Why do you laugh?" Daniel cried.

She put a hand to her mouth. "I can't help it. Just last week you were in bed hurt and I was suffering over you. But don't fear, I'm well. Not even a scratch. I fainted when I saw the stranger in my room, that's all."

"But who—"

"I didn't see him. He walked in the shadows. He may be a phantom for all I know."

Daniel managed a weak smile. "Are you serious?"

"About him being a phantom? Oh, I don't know. Unless phantoms like to read."

His smile turned into a frown.

Susan glanced over Daniel's shoulder and then leaned forward so that her face came just inches away from Daniel's face.

"He took the letters. All of them."

"What?" he said, louder than he wished.

"Yes," she whispered. "I had them on my desk. He took nothing else from the house, just the letters."

Daniel put his hands over his eyes for a moment.

"This is a terrible blow, Susan. We needed the information in those letters!"

Daniel sensed a presence behind him.

"What letters?" Lord Bold said.

PART II

"For in six days the LORD made the heavens and the earth, the sea, and all that is in them, but he rested on the seventh day. Therefore the LORD blessed the Sabbath day and made it holy."

Exodus 20:11 NIV

"Let's be honest—if one just reads God's Word, without any outside influences whatsoever, one would never get the idea anywhere of millions of years. This idea, which contradicts Scripture, comes from outside of it."

Ken Ham

ƑOURTEEN

LONDON - FRIDAY, 26 FEBRUARY, 1836

5:57 P.M.

George Scrope rubbed the back of his neck. He scanned each piece of furniture in his office to check that everything remained in perfect order.

"I'll send you a message regarding the generalities of the meeting tonight," he told Sedgwick, who was heading out the door. "The particulars we can talk about in person tomorrow."

"Are you sure this isn't about his son's death?" Sedgwick said.

"He assured me the purpose of the meeting is political."

Sedgwick nodded, but Scrope could see the worry in his face.

"Be of good cheer, my friend." Scrope patted Sedgwick's back. "I can handle this."

"I know." Sedgwick glanced at his watch. "I must make haste. Lord Bold will be here soon. Farewell, George."

"Farewell." Scrope closed the door and paced the office until he heard the anticipated knock. Exactly at six o'clock, right on time. What else could be expected from Lord Bold?

"Come in," Scrope called.

He could do this. He'd never been nervous before Parliament when it came to squashing his enemies, so why did he feel this dryness in his mouth, this numbness in his fingers? Lord Bold was just another quaint Tory who would eventually be removed when the republic was established.

The door swung, Lloyd pushing it open, and right behind him came Lord Bold, almost as tall as the towering Lloyd, but slimmer. Scrope wiped a drop of sweat from his forehead. What if the king had sent Lord Bold to spy on him? No, that was nonsense. And even if it was true, it would all work in his favor. He could use any scare tactic the king attempted to denounce the abuses of the monarchy. Yes, he could easily outsmart any Tory, any time. He wouldn't be intimidated by this man.

"Milord, please come in."

"Thank you." Lord Bold acknowledged him with a light movement of his chin, not quite a nod.

They sat across each other. Scrope noticed Lord Bold's eyes inspecting every corner of the office coldly. Scrope hated the intrinsic pride of men like Lord Bold. They sought perfection in their surroundings and looked down on those who didn't meet their high standards. The sooner he finished this meeting, the better.

"What may I do for you, milord?" Scrope said.

Lord Bold clicked his tongue and his lips twisted a little to the right. His whole body seemed to lose its stiffness. He glanced back to the door as if to make sure it was closed.

"George, I'm through with the king," he said.

"Pardon me?"

"I have to confess that my sentiments are not new. I've been harboring my differences with his majesty for many years but have held fast to my traditions as a Tory. I cannot hold my peace any longer."

Scrope forced his eyelids to blink. No, this wasn't a dream. Lord Bold, one of the king's most loyal subjects, had just confessed his disloyalty. "I beg your pardon, my lord," Scrope said, "but it's hard to believe those words coming from your mouth. If they're true, why are you telling me this?"

Lord Bold bent forward, glanced at the floor, then up at Scrope again.

"Only you would listen to my concerns, and we both know why. Telling this to my colleagues in the House of Lords would only cause havoc, and I would be politically isolated. But you—we all know your sentiments against the king and your ideas of establishing a republic in England. I believe you have found some support in the House of Commons."

"Scant support, I might add."

"Of course, of course. The bloody revolution in France is still fresh in our minds. Parliament is terrified that something similar might happen in our country, so any talk about political reform—and especially something as radical as a republic—will be immediately rejected."

"I'm aware of that." Scrope was starting to feel annoyed. "It hasn't stopped me, however, from bringing the issue before Parliament. I will keep advocating for a republic in Britain until I see its fulfillment."

"I admire you for that."

Scrope doubted that Lord Bold had expressed his admiration for anyone in the last twenty years. Should he feel flattered or insulted? He didn't know.

This conversation smelled treacherous. It was not what he had imagined—on the contrary, he'd expected to disagree, even to argue strongly with one of his political enemies. He was even prepared for any accusation that could come regarding Alexander Bold's death.

But this? No, never.

"I want to learn more about your ideas," Lord Bold said. "And perhaps advance some of them in the House of Lords, albeit gradually and with extreme prudence."

"Are you mocking me?"

Lord Bold stiffened. "Far from it!"

Scrope wanted to believe him. Having an ally in the

House of Lords would be their greatest victory since the re-form of 1832. But could he trust this Tory?

"If these sentiments you have talked about aren't new but have been there for several years," Scrope said, "why speak only now? You have served the king faithfully until today. Your votes in Parliament, not unlike the Duke of Welling-ton's, have always gone hand-in-hand with the king's wishes. So what has changed now?"

"Fair questions that deserve fair answers. For one part, I no longer have an heir to take my place in Parliament, and this has led me to ponder my political legacy. I've realized I ought to be true to my beliefs, not the capricious desires of a selfish king."

Scrope regarded the man across from him. What would the others at the society think about all this? He'd no doubt have a difficult time convincing them that Lord Bold want-ed to advance the republic. Sedgwick would laugh at the very idea!

"Have you heard about Comte de Buffon?" Lord Bold said.

Lord Bold was talking about Buffon! He smiled and said, "Buffon worked at the Royal Botanical Garden for the king of France for most of his life. Yet it's known that Buf-fon was not a monarchist, and many of his ideas inspired those involved in the revolution. Why do you think that is?"

Scrope could not find words to answer.

Lord Bold leaned forward in his chair. "I will tell you why. Buffon was a clever and practical man. He loved mon-ey—which his work for the king provided—and he had a vision. He knew that more could be achieved when his op-position did not see him as a rival but believed him to be an ally. Think of me as following Buffon's footsteps."

Scrope leaned forward and a smile spread over his face.

"There are no better footsteps to follow!"

9:00 P.M.

The wood crackled in the fireplace of the Bolds' drawing room as Lord Bold related his meeting with Scrope. Daniel whistled, amazed at the man's acting ability. Apparently, Scrope had bought Lord Bold's charade. Their scheme was proceeding as planned.

Susan and Oatts seemed as mesmerized as Daniel. During the past few days Daniel had seen a facet of Lord Bold he'd never known before. After Lord Bold overheard Daniel and Susan discussing the letters, no earthly force could have kept him from finding the truth—though in fact, his commanding presence alone was enough to make Daniel spill the story.

Lord Bold had dismissed the doctor and listened to the whole tale with an expressionless face. Daniel expected some kind of reprimand for having hidden the letters, but Lord Bold simply walked to the other side of the room and stood by the window, his gaze intent on the garden below. Daniel looked at Susan, who merely shrugged.

Finally Lord Bold spoke. "Alexander was smart enough to realize he had stumbled onto something important but foolish enough to steal the letters and tell no one who could do something about it—like his father. Now he is dead, and I regret deeply that I never won his confidence."

"Well, sir, if it's of any consolation," Daniel said, "Alex didn't tell me, either."

"Never?"

"Well, he did mention the letters the day he was—"

"It doesn't matter, Daniel. I am aware of my failings as a father. It is obvious I was doomed to repeat my father's mistakes, though thankfully not all of them." He closed his eyes briefly. "In any case, it seems as though a French secret society made its way to England, and Alexander had the bad fortune to be caught in the middle. Now we all are caught."

Daniel didn't miss the implicit suggestion that they might end up murdered.

"Do you recall all the names in Alexander's diagram?" Lord Bold said.

Daniel felt one of his pockets. "In fact, that diagram wasn't stolen. I carry it with me." He extracted the piece of paper with the names of the Askesians and handed it to Lord Bold.

"May I keep this?"

"Of course. I know all the names by heart now."

Lord Bold read the paper. "I will find as much as I can about these people. I want you to come back in two days with Superintendent Oatts to discuss this further. I may have to request an audience with the king and explain our findings."

But two days later, Oatts convinced Lord Bold to gather some solid evidence before going to the king. And it seemed their plan was working.

"So what happened?" Susan said.

Lord Bold turned to her, then looked back at Oatts and Daniel.

"Scrope invited me to meet with him and other sympathizers of the republic. He never mentioned the word 'society,' however. We must see what comes out of this tomorrow."

FIFTEEN

LONDON · SATURDAY, 27 FEBRUARY, 1836

11:00 A.M.

A breeze from the Thames blew through the desolate courtyard at Somerset House, and Lord Bold fought the wind
for the rights to his hat. He stayed close to the wall of the
north wing until he reached the apartments of the Geological Society.

Once inside, he sensed an unnatural silence. Had he mistaken the agreed-upon hour? There were no carriages outside on The Strand other than his. Perhaps he should go back
and check with François, but the possibility remained that
Scrope was waiting for him somewhere. He hated to be late.

Lord Bold cleared his throat and climbed the stairs to
the second floor. Also empty—empty and eerie. How disap-
pointing. He was actually looking forward to this game of
deception. When had he last taken a risk? Thirty years ago
perhaps, early in his career when he'd been less favorable to
the king's wishes for Parliament. After that they forced him
to fit in, to live up to his father's reputation and the honor due
English tradition. This precarious position he'd put himself
into now had nothing to do with that honor. He was meeting with a Whig and his accomplices to speak against the
king. If the Whig and his republicans showed up.

Every door down the hallway was closed except for the
one to the society's museum. Elaborate cabinets filled with
rocks lined the walls. He stared through the glass of one.

They all were just rocks to his eyes, looking much the same. He'd heard rocks were supposed to tell stories about the places around them. Wasn't that what geologists claimed? That when they found a rock they could tell you the history of the terrain in which the rock was found? He could only wonder whether those stories really came from the rocks or from the geologists' imaginations.

His cheeks burned. A rock had taken the life of his only son. Geology was nothing more than—

"Lord Bold."

He startled at the sound of Scrope's voice close behind him.

Lord Bold turned, his heart still agitated (oh, how he hated to be spoken to from behind), and saw Scrope's malignant smile. This meeting promised to be as tense as a political debate.

"Right this way, please," Scrope said, leading the way to an office ten feet from the rock cabinet.

Walking behind him, Lord Bold had a clear view of the shorter man's bald spot. Scrope was an ugly little fellow, but powerful. Lord Bold raised his chin.

Three heads rose as the two men entered the office. Lord Bold knew them: Lyell's clueless face behind an old desk, Sedgwick bored and slouched in a chair, Buckland walking toward him with open arms.

"Milord," Buckland said.

"My dear William," Lord Bold said, returning his brief embrace.

Odd. He had expected to see more people—at least a few other members of Parliament. It seemed this society was very ill-equipped. How on earth did they plan to establish a republic in England with a lawyer and two reverends?

Lord Bold looked around. "Is this our quorum, George?"

Scrope seemed taken aback. "Well, yes."

Perfect. Now he needed to make them lose confidence in themselves and place it in him. Scrope would be easy, and Buckland was a docile sheep. The other two were unknowns.

Lord Bold took a deep breath, then plunged. "I assume you have wider support for your cause than just the number of people in this room. Certainly the demise of a centuries-old institution like monarchy requires more than four men in morning coats."

Both Scrope and Lyell lowered their eyes to their coats and back up. Buckland seemed to swallow his thoughts as he walked backward to a seat besides Sedgwick, who narrowed his eyes.

Lyell seemed as pathetic as Scrope. But this Sedgwick—

"Do not underestimate what one man can do," Sedgwick said, "much less four. Many others work for our cause, though they know nothing about it." He grinned. "And yes, there are many more members in this…" He glanced at Scrope. "This society."

Scrope nodded but said nothing.

"Society?" Lord Bold said. "Do you mean the Geological Society?"

"Yes—"

"No."

The *yes* had come from Lyell,the *no* from Sedgwick.

Buckland shrugged. "*Yes* and *no* are correct answers."

Lord Bold gave them a cold look. He knew where they were going but couldn't risk showing them how much he already knew.

"We're getting ahead of ourselves, Adam," Scrope told Sedgwick. "Please, let's sit and talk a little about politics."

Lord Bold frowned. Not a good turn. They could talk politics for hours without getting back to the topic of the society. He fixed his stare on Buckland.

"What do you mean that both *yes* and *no* are correct answers?"

Buckland shifted in his chair, his eyes avoiding the others. "Well, certainly, the Geological Society has no political mission per se. But there is a society within the Geological Society, so to speak, which seeks political reform."

"By political reform you mean the republic?"

Buckland shrugged and nodded. "Ultimately yes, but—"

"But we are patient," Sedgwick said. "And any political reform that takes powers away from the king and gives it to the people is good enough for us."

Sedgwick's voice bordered on hostility, but he'd given Lord Bold the most useful information so far.

If he could just link the letters to them—unequivocably—then Oatts could make a case against these men.

"Tell me more about this society within the society," Lord Bold said. "Does it have a name of its own?"

"Indeed," Buckland said.

"But only its members know its name," Sedgwick said.

Lord Bold twisted his mouth. "I see. And I am not a member."

Sedgwick shook his head in agreement.

What a nuisance.

"Why then did you invite me here?"

"I didn't," Sedgwick muttered.

"Adam!" Buckland and Scrope said in chorus. Lyell had buried his nose in a book on his desk.

"I apologize, my lord," Scrope said. "Adam is a little upset because of some personal businesses—and because— well, because you are a Tory, and it feels odd to have such an important Tory among us discussing such contentious matters. My friends here did not know about your visit until this morning."

"Of course, I understand," Lord Bold said. "You said it would be beneficial to meet with your like-minded friends here today. Naturally, I expected an open discussion of ideas."

Sedgwick's face softened a little. But even if it softened further, the damage was done—Lord Bold would not trust Sedgwick. What if his hostility came from a guilty conscience? What if Sedgwick was an accomplice in Alexander's death?

Scrope cleared his throat. "Our open discussion of ideas might offend you, Lord Bold, since our political convictions are so far apart."

"I thought we had established already that our convictions are not that far apart after all."

"So it seems," Scrope said, "to the surprise of us all."

"Speak up, then, if you may," Lord Bold said.

Scrope nodded. "We have two main purposes: abolish monarchy—"

"And abolish religious dogma," Lyell said.

They all turned to Lyell.

Scrope laughed. "Charles is especially adamant about the issue of religious dogma. I think they are intertwined. Monarchy and religion sustain each other throughout Europe. As long as theological dogma persists, it's almost impossible to destroy monarchy. We must begin by abolishing the tenets of superstitious faith."

Lord Bold glanced at the reverends Sedgwick and Buckland. Neither seemed uncomfortable with this talk about abolishing religious dogma.

He himself wasn't a truly religious man, conforming to the formalities of the Anglican church, no more. If he were religious he probably wouldn't lie to these men about his political convictions.

He would one day enjoy seeing the king crush them. For now he had to keep them talking.

"And how do you intend to do that?" Lord Bold said.

"We are already doing it," Sedgwick said, "through the Geological Society."

11:05 A.M.

Daniel glanced at his watch and tapped on the table with his fingers.

"They must be meeting now. I can't wait for your father to come back and tell us everything."

Susan paced around the drawing room. "I'm worried about him, Daniel. What if they try to hurt him?"

"I don't think Scrope will do your father any harm. It would be too risky. But just in case, the superintendent is keeping a close watch to make sure your father is safe."

"Waiting here like this is so unnerving!"

"I know what you mean." Daniel had hardly slept the night before—morning found him staring at the ceiling of his usual guest room in the Bold's mansion. He still couldn't believe Lord Bold was involved in the investigation. And in a sense, there was no one better than Lord Bold—neither he nor Oatts could infiltrate the circles in which Scrope moved.

"What else can we do?" Susan said.

He considered her question and remembered his thoughts during the sleepless night. He needed to know who this "A.S." was. Comte de Bournon, the recipient of the letter, had died a few years ago. But William Haseldine Pepys still lived.

"I'm going to visit Pepys today," Daniel said, "see if I can unravel something new."

"Excellent. I'll go with you."

"Now, wait a minute—this is no business for a woman."

"Don't treat me like a child, Daniel. Of course this is my business. Alex is my brother, remember?"

"I know, but—"

"Do you think that because I'm a woman I can't be of any help? I can think too, and better than most men."

"Susan, I've never said that—"

"Do you think more of yourself now because you wander

146

around with a policeman? Let me remind you who found the letters first and translated them. I did!"

"I know that, dear, but going with me would only complicate things more. How would I explain your presence at his house? I at least have the excuse of being a member of—"

"What are you hiding?"

Daniel's jaw dropped. "What are you talking about?"

"The superintendent said you were hiding something. You're a suspect in my brother's death."

"A suspect? You've gone insane. What's wrong with you?"

Susan slapped him. Stupefied, he only felt the pain after she'd walked out of the room.

11:30 A.M.

Lord Bold stared at Sedgwick. Had he heard him correctly?

"I would not have guessed that the Geological Society was interested in religious matters," Lord Bold said.

"Not officially, no," Lyell said. "But our scientific inquiries have significant effects on religion."

"Indeed," Buckland said. "Most of my views on religion have been shaped, in one way or another, by geology."

Lord Bold frowned. "What does geology have to do with religion? And what does this have to do with a republic?"

"More than you think," Lyell said. "If we can convince the world that the science of geology disproves the Bible, then we can remove the king's claim to divine authority."

The king's spokesman had a saying, if Lord Bold remembered correctly, that monarchy was the most natural form of government because nature was ruled by God, the absolute monarch.

"Can geology do that?"

Lyell grinned. "We're working on it. It's just a matter of

showing that nature is ruled by geological forces and not divinity. I use, for instance, the force of erosion—"

"Please, Charles," Scrope said. "Let's not bother Lord Bold with technical details. Let it suffice to know the society plays an important role in the establishment of a republic. What we need to discuss is not the society's role, but Lord Bold's."

They all looked at him. His mind went blank. He had been so focused in making sense of their religious talk that he'd become passive in the conversation. He'd lost control again. This was completely unacceptable. He pursed his lips and returned all their stares.

"You must not be seriously considering that I talk about geology in the House of Lords. That would be ludicrous! I have no interest in the subject. Never had, never will. Everybody would see right through me if I did—my lack of expertise in the subject would be palpable. The fact is, you will need more than geology to get your republic. Obviously you are not men of arms, hence a military route is not an option—a good thing, as I see it. You are men of ideas, and this subtle attack on religion may pay off eventually, or it may not. In any case you will be required to explain how your republic will work, what institutions and what leaders will replace the monarchy. Or do you seriously expect the forces of nature to rule the people of England?"

The four pairs of eyes locked on him in what looked to Lord Bold like disbelief and confusion. Now seemed the perfect time to leave. They would have no other choice but to seek him again—and then he would have the upper hand.

Scrope cleared his throat. "You must know, my lord, that our society draws the expertise of more than geologists. Others like the Swiss Rousseau have already written about the inner workings of the republic. What we need—"

"Gentlemen, I must take my leave now." Lord Bold stood up. "I have other commitments I must attend to. Mr. Scrope, you may tell me about your ideas on how to run a republic in the near future. Please excuse me."

He walked briskly out the door.

12:02 P.M.

Oatts saw the carriage move away from Somerset House, whistled loudly, and ran to meet it. The horses halted.

François nodded as Oatts climbed inside. Lord Bold looked tired and haggard. If Oatts didn't know better he would have said the man was drowsing. But he hadn't had time to fall asleep, aye?

"Superintendent," Lord Bold said.

Oatts removed his hat and gave a slight nod. "I kept an eye on Lloyd, sir, but he didn't do much besides walking to the terrace for a while and then back to his hidin' place behind a column in the courtyard. Any luck with your meetin', sir?"

"Not as much as I expected." Lord Bold's voice sounded tired. "They are definitely part of this Askesian Society, although they were secretive in that regard. Nonetheless, their confessed motives include the establishment of a republic and other anti-religion nonsense. They behave more like idealist fools than cruel murderers. Politically they do not worry me in the least."

"I see now."

Oatts looked through the window, mulling Lord Bold's words. It seemed like another dead end for the investigation.

"It didn't cross my mind then," Lord Bold said, "but now I wonder, did any one of them kill Alexander?"

He remained silent for a few seconds before answering his own question. "I doubt it, Superintendent. Before today I would have voted against Scrope—he knows how to play the rough politician in Parliament. But now I have seen him for who he really is: a self-deceived son of this generation."

"Aye, that may be true. But the question isn't if they killed your son but if they conspired to have him killed."

Lord Bold sighed. "That I don't know, Superintendent. I do not know."

1:12 P.M.

Daniel strode down Earl's Court Road searching for Pepys's place. The simple three-story house sat in a pleasant spot with farmland in sight.

He kicked the courtyard door open. The door turned on its axis and hit a rock with a cracking sound.

He grumbled. If Susan wanted to behave like a child and make a scene, fine. She was impulsive—he knew that—but such a strong hand came as a surprise. Was this the real Susan, or was it just an unbearably strained Susan? The last week hadn't been easy for her. It hadn't been easy for him, either. He rubbed his left cheek. Did she slap him on the left or the right cheek? He couldn't even tell.

A dark cat ran out of the house, its fur shaved off from the base of its tail halfway through its torso. The cat shrieked and darted through Daniel's legs. A man emerged from the house, apparently in pursuit of the cat. The man's eyeballs, buried deep in his face, seemed to protrude at the sight of Daniel. He shifted his eyes down the cat's escape route and twisted his lips in disappointment.

"Excuse me, sir," Daniel said. "Are you Mr. Pepys?"

The man rested his hands on his waist, and Daniel noticed a razor with dark hairs in the man's right hand. He observed Daniel for perhaps half a minute, as if trying to determine if he was an acquaintance or a stranger.

"Depends on who's asking."

Daniel sighed. "I'm Daniel Young, sir, from the Geological Society, and I—"

"Never heard of you."

The man turned and walked into the house. What a strange man. Was it Pepys or not?

The door remained open and Daniel hurried inside. He didn't want to lose sight of him. "Mr. Pepys?"

"Yes, yes, just leave the door open in case the cat wants to come back, which I very much doubt. Now I'll have to hunt another one."

Pepys moved deeper into the house and Daniel trotted behind, until they reached a large room that resembled a small factory, with metallic tools, white and green casts, a large fire oven, and a strong odor Daniel couldn't quite identify. Pepys dropped the razor on a table and dipped his hands in a water basin. Daniel examined the tools on the table, which looked like none he'd seen before. Pet torturing devices? Pepys must be a lunatic.

"What is it the Geological Society wants with me?" Pepys said, still washing his hands. "I renounced my fellowship years ago and am not interested in coming back."

He spun around.

"Well," said Daniel, who was starting to feel intimidated, "my visit isn't actually official society business."

"What is it, then?"

"I have some personal questions I'd like to ask you."

Pepys's frown made Daniel uncomfortable, but he decided it would be better to be forward and see what happened.

"Look, Mr. Pepys, my best friend was killed a week ago. He worked at the Geological Society. It seems he feared for his life, and we know this because of some letters he had at the time of his death."

"What kind of letters?" Pepys said, walking toward him, something like intrigue flickering in his eyes. "Threat letters?"

"Well, they were certainly a threat—"

Pepys grabbed the razor from the table and raised it in front of his face. He glanced back and forth from the blade to Daniel's eyes.

"This is a surgical razor I'm working on." Pepys's eyes searched Daniel's face. "Now, what is it you want to ask me?"

Daniel glanced at the razor, thinking about the cat.

"There are some initials in one of the letters we think stand for the name of one of the early members of the Askesian Society. But we don't know who."

"Initials? What initials?"

"A.S."

Pepys' face tightened as if an arctic wind had frozen his features.

"Who sent you? Is this a practical joke? Or are you trying to scare me?"

"Do you know what the initials stand for? You must know."

Of course he knew. A.S mentioned him by name in his letter.

But Daniel didn't dare say it. There was no telling what Pepys would do if upset. At the moment, he looked depressed.

"I told them I wanted nothing more to do with them. I'm a true Quaker, don't you see? I was young then, foolish. He—he said the violence was over with, then the new ones came and took over."

"Who? Who said the violence was over with? A.S.?"

Pepys's voice trembled as he spoke. "Yes. How come you don't know him? What is it you really want? Why are you here?"

"I've told you, sir. My friend was killed—"

"I want nothing more to do with them, do you hear me?" Pepys cried, lifting the razor over his head. "Get out of my house! Get out!"

THE GENTLEMEN'S CONSPIRACY

2:15 P.M.

Daniel wandered around Kensington trying to shake off his frustration. It really had gone badly with Pepys. The image of the half-shaved cat and the razor needled him.

Passersby scowled at him. He stopped at the intersection of two streets—one went down to his cousin's house, the other to Susan's. Where should he go now? He wanted to drop out of the world. Well, not really. He wanted to be at peace with Susan again. He wanted to tell her about the razor—that would make her understand why it was better for her not to have gone. He wanted to tell her A.S. was alive and Pepys was surprised that Daniel didn't know him. He wanted Susan to help him make sense of that. And of course there was Lord Bold's story about the meeting with Scrope.

Could he really miss that? No, he couldn't. And so he walked away from the street that led to his house and went down the road to the Bolds' mansion.

3:30 P.M.

What could be taking them so long? Susan peered down the hallway from her room and saw the study's doors still closed. Father and Daniel had been there for more than thirty minutes. She wanted to know what went on at the meeting with Scrope, but Daniel arrived before she had a chance to ask. And of course she wouldn't go into the study, just to remind him of his bad behavior.

Susan sighed. Never before had she hit him—or anyone else. What had gotten into her? Why would Daniel want to hurt her brother? But there was no reason to keep her away if he weren't hiding something.

Perhaps he was just treating her like a child, as her father did. She'd thought Daniel was different. Father never let mother or her, much less Emily, participate in anything exciting. A woman's life should consist of more than tea parties and the pianoforte. She longed to be bold—she smiled at the irony—like Alexander.

The hallway seemed gloomy. Cold air had crept into the house and not even the servants would venture outside the heated rooms unless necessary. She was free to spy. Susan wrapped a shawl around her shoulders and inched forward.

Father's deep voice was but a murmur behind the closed doors at the end of the hallway. She could imagine Daniel smiling and nodding politely. Daniel never cared much about social conventions, unless it served to please Lord Bold. Maybe that was why Daniel hadn't let her go with him to see Pepys: he wanted to impress her father. Just like that time at the country house when Daniel readily took the glass father offered him after dinner, though he said he never touched whisky.

"I only wanted to gain your father's favor," he'd said. "I didn't drink the stuff." Susan was far from impressed. In any case, he would have to redeem himself.

She glanced down the stairs as she passed them. Empty. She stood a few feet away from the study. Her father had developed an interest in the room over the past week—all since knowing the letters had been hidden there. Did he believe there were more secrets to be found? Alex probably never had the chance to conceal more enigmas.

Susan considered the doors. That's where she showed Daniel the letters for the first time. Their love ought not to be so complicated. She let out a soft low sigh. He kept sneaking into her mind. All she wanted to do was find out what happened at the meeting. No more. The doors of the study swung open and light flooded into the hallway. Susan gasped and froze. Daniel stood at the door.

"Thank you again, sir." Daniel turned, pulling the doors closed behind him. "Susan!"

With the study doors closed, the hallway went gray again. Light came through here and there from the west-side rooms. Daniel's face, a few inches from Susan's, was but a shadow. She tried to imagine the face she knew, but the image that popped to her mind had red marks on one cheek.

"Susan? What is—"

Susan couldn't contain the burst of laughter.

"Sorry," she said, covering her mouth. But the memory of Daniel's frown only made her laugh harder. What would he think of her?

"What's going on, Susan?" Daniel said.

Why couldn't she stop laughing? Light washed over her.

"Good heavens, Susan, what's the meaning of this?"

Father. The laughter halted instantly in her thorax. It felt tight. She brought her hands to her throat as she gasped for air, but somehow the oxygen was stuck. Daniel reached for her arms.

Breathe. She needed room to breathe.

She moved one foot backward and tripped on the hem of her dress. As she fell, Daniel caught her shawl—it slipped from his fingers and she fell flat on her back.

3:47 P.M.

Back at the study, Daniel waited for Susan to drink her water and catch her breath. Lord Bold had stayed for two minutes, then left. Ever since meeting him, Daniel had the impression Lord Bold couldn't spend much time in the same room with women, even his own family.

"I'm all right, Mary," Susan told the housekeeper.

Color had returned to her face. Good sign. Had reason

returned to her mind? He would not try to understand her, though in truth there was nothing he wanted more.

Daniel walked to the window and pulled the curtain aside, but all his senses were directed behind him. He could hear every movement of the housekeeper, the chair creaking when Susan shifted, the setting of the cup on a tray, the water Susan was gulping.

"You should try the cannabis for your poorly times, miss," Mary said.

"Thanks, Mary, but the cramps aren't really that bad."

Cramps? All the more reason for not taking her with him to see Pepys. She should be resting instead of walking around the house. His mind wandered to Pepy's workshop. Dreadful thoughts.

After a minute or so, Daniel no longer heard the housekeeper. He turned and saw Susan closing the brown doors.

They stood alone, facing each other in awkward silence. He knew one of them had to break the silence with an apology, but she had to ask forgiveness for two offenses—the slap and the mockery—while he didn't really have to apologize. He hadn't done anything wrong.

Susan alternated her gaze between his face and the furnishings around the study, seemingly gathering courage to speak. "I didn't intend to laugh like that," she said. "I don't know what came over me."

Daniel nodded. That was a good start.

"Well?" she said. "How did it go?"

"My visit to Pepys? It was…"

"I mean Father's meeting."

Unbelievable.

"It went well," he said, as drily as he could. He didn't want to talk about that. He wanted to talk about Pepys, the cat, the razor. Though this new attitude in Susan didn't particularly incline him to talk at all.

Susan raised her brows. "Just well?"

"That's what your father says. Didn't you ask him?"

Her face reddened. "I'm asking you. Why would I ask you if I'd already asked father?"

Daniel could tell from her tone she was irritated. He wished he were somewhere else.

"All right, there's no need to get mad."

She inhaled deeply and closed her eyes. Her hands clasped the edges of her dress. If she tried to slap him again, he'd run.

"I don't want to fight," she said.

He felt lighter immediately. "Neither do I."

Susan opened her eyes and crossed the room to sit on a chair, pressing a hand to her stomach. Daniel sighed. At least she wasn't walking out on him again.

"Now, please tell me about the meeting," Susan said. Her tone was still far from the sweet voice he was used to. He missed it.

He glanced at the door, hoping someone would interrupt them.

"What's the matter?" Susan said.

"Nothing." He noticed that her face seemed to be turning pale. She crossed her arms around her stomach and bent forward. "Are you feeling sick?"

Susan winced. "It's nothing to worry about. Tell me what happened with Scrope."

Should he tell her or fetch some help? She looked miserable.

"You don't look well, Susan."

"Just tell me about the meeting."

Daniel lifted his hands. "All right, as you wish—"

The doors flew open and Mary burst in.

"Miss Susan, it's your mother. One of the maids found her on the floor in Mr. Alexander's room."

4:45 P.M.

Susan sat on Alex's bed watching her mother tremble.

"You must eat something, mother. Enough is enough. Just look at you, so weak."

"Drink this tea, mum, please," Mary said.

Seeing her mother in such state, Susan felt a fool for having argued with Daniel. She looked around, but he'd left. She'd been unfair, too hard on him. Daniel had never seen her in this mood. Part of her still wanted to chastise him, but another part wanted to make peace. "Oh, my God," she muttered. Now it dawned on her. Here lay mother, ill from the loss of her spoiled child. She lived and breathed only for Alex, her daughters mere accessories in her daily routine. And Father, well, he only lived and cared for himself. But Daniel was unique in her life. Only Daniel shared her secrets and loved her sincerely. She just couldn't drive him away.

Lady Bold sipped the tea and mumbled something unintelligible. She seemed better now. But Susan didn't feel right. Not without Daniel. Was he gone? A panic overtook her as she pictured her life *sans* Daniel.

She stood and left the room. In the hallway, she began to run.

"Daniel? Daniel?" She almost stumbled down the stairs. Her heart pounded in her chest. "Daniel!" No answer. She felt tears brim in her eyes.

SIXTEEN

PARIS, 1795

Jean-Baptiste Lamarck tried to ignore his hunger, directing his thoughts instead to the specimens at the *Muséum d'histoire naturelle* he still had to classify. He'd come up with a new term to describe the organisms with a backbone like that of man: vertebrates. His belly rumbled. A day and a half had passed since his last meal—at least Charlotte and the children ate more often than him. He sighed. Work could occupy his mind in such a way that his stomach became irrelevant, but there was no work before him, just the asphyxiating tobacco smell of Laplace's house.

Laplace, sitting across from Jean-Baptiste, laughed heartily—probably at one of Hutton's jokes. But Jean-Baptiste hadn't heard. His head swirled, dizzy from wine on an empty belly. He stared at them, feeling like a stranger who had no business with their merry mingling.

Laplace and Hutton liked each other. Of the society, Jean-Baptiste liked only Buffon. But the master was gone. He missed Buffon's cordial speech and delicate manners. It would soon be seven years since his death. He would have to take some flowers to Buffon's grave.

"*Allez*, Lamarck!" Laplace said. "It's not every day that James comes down to visit. That's why I called you, to offer the welcome he deserves."

Jean-Baptiste forced a smile. "*J'en suis désolé*, my mind just drifted for a moment."

"Well, then," Laplace said, "stop your drifting and pay attention. James is publishing an expanded version of his

Theory of the Earth. I've asked him, now that he's in Paris, to speak about his geology to the members of the philosophical club." Laplace turned to Hutton. "Oh, and I forgot to mention that many of the attendees at the club are members of the society as well."

"Is that so?" Hutton said, never looking at Jean-Baptiste, who simply rolled his eyes. He didn't care much about Hutton anyway.

Laplace grinned. "*Oui, oui.* The club was an idea of Lamarck's to attract new minds and recruit members for the society."

Hutton raised his brows. "So Lamarck finally came up with a good idea?"

Jean-Baptiste watched them laugh. He didn't have the energy to loathe Hutton, so he just closed his eyes and imagined the wing patterns of the insects preserved at the *Muséum.*

"Wake up, Lamarck!"

He didn't hate Laplace, either. Buffon had warned him about Laplace's insufferable pride. Jean-Baptiste opened his eyes. "*Oui?*"

Laplace blinked as if something unexpected had happened. Hutton patted Laplace's arm. "So, what about your theory?" he said.

Laplace shook his head and turned to Hutton. "Oh, it's almost ready. Of course I'm following what Buffon insisted on, an evolution from chaos to explain the origin of the solar system."

Jean-Baptiste had never expressed much interest in Laplace's mathematical formulas, but his astronomical speculations were fascinating. Buffon would be proud.

"It's like this," Laplace said, standing up and walking to the middle of the room. "In the distant past, the sun was a giant rotating cloud of gas. I call it a nebula. Due to cooling and gravity, the gas contracted and flattened into a disk as it began to rotate faster—then BOOM!" He opened his arms. "Rims of gas came off the contracting disk. These gases then condensed and formed the planets, and the remaining gas ball in the center is the sun. This theory explains why the planets revolve around the sun!"

Hutton straightened up. "And am I right to suppose that you have worked out all the details to make your theory credible?"

Laplace smiled. "Of course, *mon ami*. My theory will convince the world that there is no need for a god to account for the origin of the solar system, or the universe."

Hutton nodded and stood to pace the room while rubbing his chin. His monstrous nose made a large shadow on the wall every time he walked past the fireplace.

"Buffon's triangle is almost complete, then. My geological evolution and your cosmological evolution form two of the sides. Now we need only explain the evolution of life."

"That's Lamarck's task," Laplace said.

Their eyes turned on him, and Jean-Baptiste felt smaller than ever. Why now? His stomach emitted an embarrassing growl.

"Well?" Hutton said. "What's your theory, Lamarck?"

Jean-Baptiste hands began to sweat. "I haven't worked out the details as yet. I know I will use chemistry to advocate for the spontaneous generation of life, and I've given some thought to the similarities between organisms to argue for a common descent from simpler forms to more complex organisms." His voice came out weak, but he couldn't help it.

"You must publish something, then," Hutton said.

Jean-Baptiste looked down and said, "I'm not ready yet."

The light dinner at the tavern poured some strength into Jean-Baptiste but still he felt miserable. Hutton despised him

and was now turning Laplace against him. He closed his eyes
and rubbed his temples. He had to think about something
else. To hell with Hutton!

He shot a glance at Laplace, who stood in front of the
ten attendees at the philosophical club and signaled for silence. Jean-Baptiste went to the back of the room—that way
he could be as far as possible from Hutton when he rose to
speak—and sat on a stool by the door.

Laplace began to talk. "*Bienvenue, mes amis....*".

Jean-Baptiste lost track of Laplace's words when the door
creaked softly and inched open. Jean-Baptiste saw a hand
push the door open wide enough for a man to walk in.

"*Excusez mois,*" the man said.

Jean-Baptiste knew him: The aristocrat Jacques-Louis,
Comte de Bournon. The name was so reminiscent of George-
Louis, Comte de Buffon, that Jean-Baptiste had taken a curious interest in the fellow since the moment he heard the
name. A stranger walked in behind de Bournon.

The stranger caught up with de Bournon, not caring that
the door remained open. Jean-Baptiste frowned and closed
the door himself. When he returned to his stool, Hutton
was already beside Laplace with a pathetic smile below that
beak-nose of his.

Jean-Baptiste glanced at the heads in the room. Where
had de Bournon and the stranger gone? Then he saw them.
They sat by the lively English pair of Pepys and Babington. Everybody knew them—riotous and eccentric. Anyone in the street could tell they were not French, even from
a great distance. Their gait and laughter gave them away.
They seemed to be hushing and nodding to the stranger.
Perhaps de Bournon was introducing the stranger to them.
Curious. Maybe the stranger was also a Briton. They suddenly stopped their hushing and turned to face Hutton.
Jean-Baptiste copied them.

"The past history of our globe must be explained by what can be seen happening now," Hutton said. "No powers are to be employed that are not natural to the globe, no action to be admitted except those of which we know the principle. With that philosophy in mind, I set out to form my theory of the earth, which I will now expound to you."

Jean-Baptiste groaned. How could they expect him to write a theory of life in such a short time? He needed more research. He needed to refine his ideas.

Hutton's voice grew stronger. "The solid parts of the present land appear in general to have been composed of the marine sediments and other materials similar to those now found upon sea shores. Hence the land on which we rest is not simple and original, but a composite formed by the operation of second causes."

None of this was new to Jean-Baptiste. Buffon had taught them that.

"The rocks we see today are made up of materials derived from the ruins of former continents. But the reverse occurs as well when these rocks erode and decay. This destruction and renewal, this great geological cycle, has occurred so many times that we find no vestige of a beginning, no prospect of an end."

Jean-Baptiste's head felt light. He realized that Hutton had fulfilled his promise to Buffon—he'd developed a believable materialistic theory that contradicted the biblical chronology. And with such audacity! Just by saying there is no beginning and no end, Hutton gave nature the most intriguing quality of the Christian God: eternity.

And what about him? Jean-Baptiste's task was to come up with something as daring and contentious as Hutton's theory. But he had to go beyond the origin of rocks and continents. Yes, he had to aim higher in the chain of nature. And he'd do it. He'd aim for man.

SEVENTEEN

London - Sunday, 28 February, 1836

10:26 A.M.

Sweat covered Henry Cole's round face. A few drops actually reached the pulpit as he shook his hands in the air. His voice came out loud and strong, keeping the fourteen parishioners at the chapel that morning awake and—from the look of some—scared. And they should be scared, because he was not preaching on a light matter.

"We have already inconvertibly established it," Cole bellowed, "from the lips of eternal veracity, that neither the earth, nor the material of which it was formed, nor any creature that is found therein, existed before the first day of revealed creation. Whatsoever phenomena, therefore, of order or confusion, of combination or disorganization, of quiescence or convulsion, the researches of the geologist may discover, all must inevitably be the production of the beauteous creation and destroying flood recorded in the annals of everlasting truth. But I am fully aware that such meditations as these are not receivable amid the loud and flattering plaudits of a talent-admiring and science-idolizing multitude. I undeservedly count, therefore, the costs of all the vituperation and contempt that will be poured upon me. They will call me a scientific ignoramus and my work religious cant, but I am quite prepared to meet that--and ten times more. But let admired philosophers and scientists know that vituperation is not the refutation of eternal truth!"

Cole paused only long enough to swipe some sweat with his hand.

"Citing the researches of geology, some claim that the first chapter of Genesis is merely poetic legend. If these divine-authority-denying and inspiration-denying principles of geological skepticism were not read in public print, who could possibly bring himself to believe that they existed in a Christian land, and in the hearts of revelation-blessed mortals? And further, who would ever venture to suppose that such principles were openly avowed in the public worship of God, in both universities of Britain, by ordained ministers of the word of God and of the gospel of Christ? What the consequences of such things must be to a revelation-possessing land, time will rapidly and awfully unfold in its opening pages of national skepticism, infidelity, and apostasy, and of God's righteous vengeance on the same!"

Cole cut short his gasp for breath when he saw someone moving in the unlit section of the chapel. This someone emerged from the shadows into the morning light that washed through the windows and sat in the back pew. Cole narrowed his eyes and saw the man's face—the same face he'd seen at The Strand, the face with the dead eyes!

All thoughts of his sermon were gone. He just couldn't keep his eyes away from the man in the back pew. The fourteen parishioners turned to see what had caught the preacher's attention. The man widened his dead eyes and twitched his lips.

Cole pointed at him and spoke with a trembling voice to the phantom of his recent nightmares.

"You, sir!"

The man stood and stumbled away from the pew, then fled to the street.

"Wait!" Cole raised his habit and descended the pulpit as fast as he could. His heart ached for that tormented soul—

yes, because that's what he was, a poor tormented soul. *I must reach him.*

The parishioners stood and gasped as he crossed through their midst. Cole ignored the murmurs and ran toward the door, but a woman in the middle section grabbed his robe.

"Pastor, you need to visit my man," the woman said. "He's terrible sick."

"I will, child, I will." Cole loosened her grasp. "I must leave now."

He rushed the few feet left to the street. What would he tell the man when he found him? He didn't know—but the Lord would put the words in his mouth. "Let me reach him, dear God."

Only a few passersby walked outside the church, and Cole saw the man hurrying away to the east.

"Please, sir, wait!" Cole cried. But the man would not halt.

Cole caught up with him after three blocks. Panting and desperate, Cole reached for the man's arm. The man grunted and shook off Cole's hand.

"Let go of me!"

Too breathless to speak, Cole bent over with his hands on his knees and watched the man cross the street and enter Grey's Inn.

"I will pray for you."

2:00 P.M.

Susan looked one more time at the garden before opening the back door of her house. She smiled and walked inside. What a good day: the cramps were gone and mother had begun eating again.

She saw her reflection as she walked past a mirror. How she wished she didn't have to wear black—and how she wished she could see Daniel. But she just couldn't go visit him by herself. Would he come by today?

She heard noises in the drawing room and walked closer to inspect.

She was about to open the door when she heard footsteps behind her. Turning, she saw her father, almost trudging, staring at the floor in deep thought. She slipped into the water closet next to the drawing room. Father didn't see her, she was sure of that, otherwise he would have sent her away. She really wanted to know who waited in the drawing room. It could be Daniel.

Susan locked the door to the hallway and walked to the other door on her left—the one that opened into the drawing room. She could hear her father entering now. She pushed the door open a mere two inches and peered in. Two men waited inside. One short and bald; the other tall and evil-looking.

"Milord," the short man said.

The tall man stood two steps behind the short one with a flinty expression and his hands clasped behind his back.

"Mr. Scrope," Lord Bold said. "I did not expect to see you again so soon."

Susan gasped.

"You departed so abruptly from our meeting, my lord, that I felt obliged to pay you a visit. We have some serious unfinished business to discuss."

Susan felt a knot forming in her stomach. Scrope sounded so intimidating. But her father didn't even flinch.

"Please, take a seat."

"Thank you," Scrope said.

She didn't like his smile. Who knew what intentions it masked?

"Now, then," Scrope said. "I believe you're aware that the things we discussed are to remain confidential. You must not speak of them with anyone else."

Susan tried to see her father's response, but he'd taken a seat out of her view. And she didn't dare open the door further.

"What are you afraid of, Mr. Scrope? Do you think I might tell the king? Remember, it was you who invited me to your gathering. Perhaps you regret that decision. Or perhaps you regret having said some things you said. Is that so?"

Scrope cleared his throat and looked away for a few seconds.

"Well, now, my colleagues insist that you're not trustworthy, my lord. We have given you our—"

"And what do you think, George? Am I trustworthy?"

"I don't know." Scrope paused for a few seconds. "I came here today to make sure."

"Do you know what I think?"

Scrope shook his head.

"I think you risked your career and your position with your colleagues by trusting in me. Why? Because you think I can be an advantage in attaining your objectives. Your friends do not see it that way, but you do. You are a Member of Parliament. You know you need support in the House of Lords to further your agenda—if you are to promote the republic. I could be playing with you, that's true. Maybe I don't want to advance your cause. Maybe I do. But you have made a mistake coming into my home intending to silence me."

Susan felt a chill at hearing her father be so daring. Scrope's face looked tight, closed.

"If anything," Lord Bold continued, "our meeting merely displayed your unique approach to politics—mixing science and religion. Honestly I see no future in that, but I am open to hearing your political ideas. If you came to discuss how to run a republic, you are welcome to speak and I will listen. But if your idea is to force me into a stupid conspiracy, you may as well leave my house now."

Scrope jumped to his feet, making Susan jolt. The bald man's face radiated hatred.

"You don't know who you're dealing with!" Scrope brandished his right index finger. "You cannot even fathom what we're capable of. So don't even dare stand in our way!"

"What kind of ridiculous talk is that, George? We are nobles. We do not use violence!"

Susan couldn't tell if her father was frightened, but she surely had started to panic. Her hands trembled and her breathing had become spasmodic.

"Oh, no, Lord Bold, I never commit violence. My hands were not made for that. Stephen here, however—he's hard to control."

The tall man behind Scrope unclasped his hands and moved them to his chest in two fists.

Susan put a hand over her mouth. Her whole body trembled now. She didn't hear her father say anything. What could he be thinking? What if they harmed him? *Would they?*

Scrope crossed his arms over his chest. "Just remember, Lord Bold, that these are dangerous times. You recently lost a son. It would be a shame if something were to happen to one of your daughters."

Susan stepped back and stumbled against the wall. *Oh, God. I made too much noise...*

She pressed her palms against her chest. She couldn't faint, she just couldn't.

She regained her balance and pushed open the door to the hallway, not caring about the noise. She ran past the stairs that led to the upper stories, through the foyer, the dining room, and into the kitchen. The cooks stared as she darted down the stairs to the servants' level, panting.

Susan felt as if her heart might explode from the fear. And all she could think about was Daniel.

He would protect her.

"François! Where's François?" she asked the maids gathered in the laundry room.

"He's out with the horses, miss," one of the maids said.

Susan looked around. Where should she go? She hadn't been down here since she was eleven.

"That way, miss," the maid said, pointing to Susan's right.

Susan rushed through a narrow hallway that led to the east of the house. After a dark passage, the hallway opened into the far corner of the garden. A stone path marked the way to the stables. Susan yelled as loud as she could, frantic.

"François!"

The coachman emerged from a smelly hut, eyes wide. "Miss Susan?"

Susan tried to catch her breath before speaking. "François, you must take me to Daniel's house, you know where he lives."

"But, miss, I can't. Your father wouldn't allow—"

"Today he will," she said. "Now let's go."

François shrugged and walked to the stable to prepare the carriage.

2:12 P.M.

Cole sat on his cot, still thinking about the man with the dead eyes. Why had he gone to his chapel? It had to be more than coincidence. The Lord was surely at work in this.

He closed his eyes. "Speak to your servant, Lord. What should I do about this creature?"

In the silence he waited quietly for a thought or a feeling to guide him, but his mind kept drifting to the unopened letters on his desk. He pushed the thought aside and concentrated again in his spiritual listening. "Here I am, Lord," he whispered.

Two minutes passed. Nothing. Cole opened his eyes and saw the letters on the desk. He might as well read them now, then go visit the sick man the woman at the church had told him about.

Cole took the letter on top, broke the seal, and unfolded it. A letter from his old parish in Norwich. How good to have news from them—

"Oh, my Lord!"

3:10 P.M.

"Here we are, miss," François said from the front of the carriage.

Susan peered through the window at the house in front of her. Her heart was still racing. She glanced at her trembling hands. Was this a good idea? What if she got into trouble? She sighed. What could possibly be worse than the wreck they were in right now? Scrope sounded like a dangerous, wicked man.

Against any conventions her mother would have insisted on, Susan descended from the carriage and walked up to Daniel's house. She knocked twice.

Twenty seconds passed. Maybe he's not home. What now?

The door opened and a short, chubby butler stood under the doorframe. He peered around her as if looking for someone else.

"Mum."

Susan smiled, trying to control her shaking, gulped, finally spoke.

"Please, I must speak with Daniel." The butler stared. "Urgently," she said.

"Yes, mum, please come in." For a second she thought the butler had rolled his eyes, but his voice sounded cordial.

As soon as she stepped in she saw a man hurrying down the stairs. He looked like Daniel but had darker hair and a neatly trimmed mustache. His trot turned into a relaxed gait once he saw her standing by the door.

"Oh, we have a visitor," he said. "A beautiful visitor."

He walked to her and bowed slightly. "Richard Lewis, madam. It's a pleasure to make your acquaintance."

"Susan Bold," she said.

Now that the man was in front of her Susan noticed he was almost her height, unlike Daniel, who was five inches taller. But it was difficult to say who was more handsome.

"Welcome, Susan Bold," he said with a warmth that made her lose her train of thought. "May I inquire about the motive of your visit? I don't think we've met before."

"I…"

"Susan?"

Now Daniel hurried down the stairs. She felt a mix of relief and anxiety. Relief at seeing him here. Anxiety because she wanted to run into his arms but for obvious reasons could not. And there was a third feeling she couldn't quite pin down, a feeling that had something to do with this Richard.

"Daniel," she said in the sweetest voice she could manage.

His face brightened at once, and she felt as if her soul had been freed from a dark prison.

"Susan, what—?"

"Oh, my Daniel."

He drew closer and she hugged his neck, then stepped back, embarrassed.

"I'm sorry, Daniel."

"Well, well, well, cousin," Richard said. "I see you have beaten me to the heart of this pretty lady."

Daniel rolled his eyes. "And I see you have met my cousin. I apologize, Susan. He sometimes can be too forward."

Richard shrugged and smiled. "I'm afraid that's me!"

Susan glanced at him. What an unusual man.

Daniel scowled at Richard and shook his head.

"If you'll excuse me," Richard said, "I'll let you two discuss your business." And he walked off with the butler behind him.

Susan followed them with her eyes until they were out of sight.

"Susan?" Daniel said.

She turned and faced him, suddenly remembering the reason for her visit. But she had to make sure he wasn't angry at her.

"Daniel, I'm sorry for—"

"Yesterday is behind us, Susan, don't worry. Are you alone?"

She nodded.

"Why? What happened? Is your mother well?"

"She is, and I'm well too—now, at least. It's just…something terrible—oh, Daniel, I'm frightened."

"What? What is it?"

"Scrope came to speak to father today and *threatened* him."

"What? How dare he!"

She leaned her head on his shoulder. "I was so afraid, Daniel, I didn't know where else to go."

Daniel gently slid her head to his chest and she heard the galloping rhythm of his heart.

He spoke to her ear. "It's all right, dearest. I'm here."

She let him caress her hair. His breath on the top of her head felt warm and soothing.

"You must tell me everything," he whispered. "But not here. My cousin may overhear us and I'd prefer he not get involved."

She raised her face and her gaze lingered a while. He

smiled and raised his brows. "François is outside," she said. "He can take us somewhere else."

"Perfect!"

3:42 P.M.

Bile in his throat. Sharp pressure in his forehead. Daniel felt like jumping off the carriage and going after Scrope. But the real danger was Lloyd. Now who could deny that Lloyd was the killer? Lord Bold and Susan had seen his wicked intentions. Scrope himself had incriminated his henchman.

Susan's face reflected nothing but anguish.

"What are we going to do, Daniel? My father is fearless sometimes. He's capable of standing up to them. But these people are bandits, barbarians."

"We must tell the superintendent," Daniel said. "He'll know what to do. Your father should speak with him."

Daniel dug in his pocket for the small notebook he used for geology lessons and tore off a page. He scribbled a note.

"I'll send word to the superintendent to meet us at your house and we'll all speak with your father. I believe that's better. What do you think?"

"I don't want to go home right now. Would you take me somewhere nice?"

"Everything will be fine," he said. "You'll see."

The carriage slowed down and Daniel looked outside. They were in front of the Grand Entrance to Hyde Park. He grinned. These were not the best circumstances for romance, but Hyde Park brought pleasant memories of afternoons with Susan. Daniel called François to halt, put the notebook back in his coat's right pocket, and opened the door. He stepped down first and helped Susan out of the carriage.

"François," Daniel said. "I need a favor. Please take this

note to Superintendent Oatts at the Metropolitan Police and then come back for us. That's no place for Susan, we'll wait here."

François looked distressed. "Mr. Young, I could lose my job for this. Lord Bold doesn't know where I am, and I've taken his daughter—"

"This is very important—it's for the safety of your employer. You may lose your job anyway if something happens to Lord Bold."

François frowned.

"It's true," Daniel said. "Remember Alex."

The coachman's face suddenly turned grim. "D'accord. I'll go."

"Thank you, François."

As the carriage departed toward Knightsbridge, Susan took Daniel's arm and gently led him to one of the park's foot entrances. Daniel's hands tingled. This was the way he liked to be with Susan, close enough to breathe her peach-like scent.

He searched her eyes—she looked so worried it hurt his soul. If Daniel had been afraid just imagining Lloyd was chasing him, how must Susan feel after hearing Scrope imply that Lloyd would harm her? Yes, she had reason to be terrified. He had to take the fear from her mind, at least for a while.

"Let's walk to Kensington Gardens," he said as they stepped inside the park.

She nodded. They took the footpath parallel to the king's private road.

"I love it here," Daniel said.

"I love the park too." Susan's voice sounded timid, and she tightened her grip on his arm.

"Oh, I wasn't talking about the park, although I share your fondness for it."

She stopped and looked at him in the eyes. "Then what?"

"Here. With you. That's what I love—being at your side."
Susan smiled and blushed. Daniel smiled back. It felt so good to make her smile; to make her feel loved. They resumed their walk and talked of inconsequential things for a few minutes.

"You know," Daniel said, "my cousin just returned from Switzerland, says he fell in love with the Swiss Alps. He's even talking about moving there permanently."

"Really?" She stared at the vegetation.

"Do you want to know what else he said?"

"Uh-uh."

"He said that since he has no heir, he'll leave me his house in London and part of his business when he moves."

Susan turned to him. "How generous!"

A chill ran through Daniel's body. Perhaps this was the perfect moment to tell her what grew in his heart the moment his cousin offered him the inheritance Daniel's father could not provide.

"Yes, Richard is very generous. But what would I do with a house so large?"

"Oh, I don't know."

Daniel took a deep breath. "It would be better to share it with you—as my wife."

Susan stopped and dropped his arm, her mouth opening a little.

"Oh, my Daniel, how can we speak about marriage under these circumstances? Look at me. I'm still wearing black for my brother. And my father—"

"I'll talk to him."

She lowered her gaze for a moment.

Daniel felt as if someone had punched him in the stomach. His face must have shown it, because Susan touched his cheek tenderly and shook her head.

"Please, Daniel, it is not that I don't love you—I do. And

I do want to marry you someday. But this isn't the best moment—"

"I know," he said, forcing a smile. He knew she was right, but it hurt that she didn't show more excitement. She had released his arm but was now holding his hand.

They followed the path as it turned right and joined the crowd crossing the bridge over Serpentine River.

Daniel thought it strange to see so many people at the promenade, but then again, it was Sunday and the weather was the best in more than a week. They had to slow down behind other pedestrians.

"Tell me more about your cousin," Susan said.

Her tone had turned jovial but Daniel suspected it wasn't natural. Perhaps she wanted to make up for turning him down.

"Richard is a clever little charmer—but you know about that by now. He's only ten years older than me, and already a widower."

"Really? What happened?" Susan said.

"His wife committed suicide. I think she had a mental illness."

"Bless his heart. That's so sad."

Daniel glanced at the water below and thought about the day Richard found his wife hanging by the neck.

"Yes, she—"

Someone bumped against Daniel's back—much too hard.

The shove made him lose his grip on Susan's hand. He almost fell on his face but managed to put a foot forward near the edge of the bridge. Then he felt a blow on his right side and a sharp prick on the skin above his waist.

Only a second later, he felt someone pulling up the back of his coat and shoving him forward again.

Too late he realized he was falling headfirst into the Serpentine.

4:57 P.M.

Susan stared up in confusion at the dozen people surrounding her. What happened? Where did Daniel go?

One man bent over and offered his hand. "Are you hurt, mum? Let me help you up."

She took the man's hand and stood. Her right shoulder hurt, as well as her left elbow. Someone had hit her shoulder and she fell on her elbow—that was it.

"Daniel?" Susan said.

"There, mum," a boy said, pointing down at the river. "The man that was with you. He fell in the water."

Susan gasped and put her hands over her mouth. She hurried to the edge of the bridge and peered down to the water. Almost dusk, yet she could see the swans and the surface of the Serpentine quite well. But no sign of Daniel. No! He had to be—

"I saw him, mum," the boy said.

"Where?" she said, staring at the river.

"He ran away, mum."

"What? You said he fell in the water!"

"No, not him! The man that pushed your friend. He ran away over there." The boy pointed to the far end of the bridge to their left.

"I don't care where he went!" Susan yelled. "Where is my Daniel?" She covered her eyes as if she could contain the tears now wetting her face. "Daniel—"

"Look!" a voice cried.

"I see 'im!" Another voice.

Susan looked back at the river. Daniel swam with difficulty toward the shore.

"Oh, thank God!" Susan cried.

But from the bridge, Daniel seemed to struggle to stay above water. Susan pushed her way through the curious who had gathered around her and were blocking the way—doing nothing as a man drowned in the river.

She reached the end of the bridge and turned right, away from the foot path and toward the riverbank. Dozens of trees and tall grass stood in her way. Maybe she could go back to the path and walk around the area of trees—no, that would take too long. There was no time to lose.

She sprinted down the green maze of trees and called for Daniel again and again. Moving blindly through the tall grass, she kept putting her feet in the wrong places, until she stumbled to the ground. She landed on her hands, but the grass covered her face and hair. Pain stabbed her ankle. But Daniel was still in the water—she had to reach him. Her black dress took on a mix of earthy tones that matched the scenery in the park. A gap between two trees allowed her to see the water. She headed in that direction.

Sweat ran down her temples. She had never run as much as today and she feared her airways would narrow and she'd start wheezing. But the image of Daniel drowning kept her moving forward. Alex had died in the river. Daniel's fate ought to be different.

Reaching the riverbank, she looked west. Daniel scrambled to the shore ten feet away from her.

"Daniel!" Susan lifted the hem of her dress and limped toward him over the shallow water.

Daniel collapsed face down on the ground.

"Oh, my Daniel," Susan cried and knelt to his side. "Daniel, please, talk to me."

Daniel grunted and pulled himself over to rest on his left side. The haft of a knife protruded from the right side above his waist.

"Dan—there—there's a knife—"

"Let me…catch my breath," Daniel said.

Susan felt as though she could barely breathe herself.

"You need a doctor. You must be bleeding—"

"What? I'm all right," Daniel said, looking at her with damp eyes. "I just swallowed some water, that's all."

"No, Daniel, he stabbed you. See—"

Daniel tried to sit. "Aw. My side does hurt, but—"

His eyes fixed on the knife. He passed his left hand beneath his coat, right where the knife had entered. Susan couldn't believe it. It was as if he did not feel any pain.

"Did it cut you too deep?" Susan said.

Daniel sat straight and took his coat off. The knife came off along with the coat. Susan felt her mouth drop. Daniel panted. He spread the coat over his legs, then pressed with one hand over the fabric around the knife and pulled the blade out with the other hand.

Susan shook her head. "I don't—"

"My notebook," Daniel said, as he pulled out a notebook from his coat pocket. It had a deep slash in the middle. "It saved my life."

5:32 P.M.

François found them walking in the dark toward Hyde Park Corner. Susan complained about her ankle, which was probably swelling, but Daniel just nodded. His mind reeled. This was the third time in less than two weeks he'd escaped death. Good luck or divine protection? Either way, he didn't want to test his luck or tempt God again. From now on he had to be more careful.

He glanced backwards. Nobody seemed to be following them.

"At least we know they're serious about their death threats," he said.

Susan winced. "Please don't say that. This is very serious!"

She seemed to have entered a bad mood again. Perhaps because of the pain in her ankle. Strangely, he felt good, despite the cold creeping into his bones and his wet clothes. They boarded the carriage and remained silent all the way to Daniel's house.

"Oatts must be waiting for us at your house," Daniel said, descending from the carriage. "Perhaps I should put on some dry clothes and go with you."

Susan shrugged.

Daniel sighed. "How is your ankle?"

"Not good."

"I'm sor—"

"Just go change and come back quickly! The sooner I'm home the better. We shouldn't have come here in the first place—"

Daniel walked away, shaking his head. He just couldn't understand her mood swings. "François, please wait for me. I won't take long." If it weren't important he speak to Oatts he'd have told François to leave without him.

The coachman nodded. "*D'accord.*"

Daniel shivered. He'd better hurry. He knocked at the door, which swung open.

"Daniel!" Richard said.

Daniel had expected Mr. Welsh to greet him.

"I was waiting for you, cousin. Come in, quick!"

"What is it?"

"Look," Richard said, placing something in his hands. "A letter from Norwich. I also received one, but this one is yours. Terrible news, Daniel, terrible news."

Daniel felt a lump forming in his throat.

"I say, you're all wet," Richard said. Daniel ignored his cousin and looked with dread at the letter. Terrible news from home? How ironic it would be for one of his parents to die while he was escaping death.

He turned the sealed letter in his hands. Didn't he have enough problems already? He sighed and loosened the seal. He recognized his mother's handwriting.

Dear Daniel,

I pray this letter finds you well. Your father and I always remember you in our prayers and ask God that you will keep a good conscience and a pure heart.

Now I must ask you to come home. Your father is very ill. I sense he will soon die and part to be with Christ. He tells me so every day. The only thing that holds him back from surrendering himself to death is his desire to see you one last time. 'Tell Daniel to come,' is what he says. Your father has not lost his mind or alertness, although he is weaker every day. It grieves me seeing him like this.

Please come and do not tarry. Grant your father his last wish. I know you need to make peace with him too. Even though you never told me, I could feel your resentment against him. Perhaps it is time to forgive. Remember that we love you with all our hearts.

Mama

The world seemed to stop around Daniel. Dad was dying. The strong massive man whose presence commanded as much authority as his exhaustive sermons—dying?

Daniel felt as if darkness were surrounding him. He should be sad, he knew that, but all he felt was a cold emptiness as if all feeling for his father had been locked away deep in his soul. His body trembled and he realized that Richard was shaking him.

"Daniel, you must be strong. How do you feel?"

Daniel stared at his cousin. Richard seemed truly concerned. Why wasn't he?

"I—I don't know how I feel," Daniel muttered. "This is so…" What was the word? "Unexpected."

The butler stood between Daniel and Richard and cleared his throat. "Sir, there is a carriage waiting outside."

"Are they waiting for you, Daniel?" Richard said.

Daniel nodded.

"Mr. Welsh," Richard told the butler. "Go tell them that my cousin will not be coming out again." Richard turned to Daniel. "You're in shock. That's normal. But you must leave as soon as day breaks. You can take my town coach. Do you hear me?"

He nodded.

5:45 P.M.

Oatts fiddled with his mustache while Lord Bold drank his whiskey. Lord Bold's face remained impassive, but his fingers tapped the glass nervously. Oatts looked around. The drawing room had become an everyday stop for him this past week.

"How unfortunate," Lord Bold said. "It seems Susan overheard my conversation with Scrope. Otherwise how would Daniel have known?"

"Aye," Oatts said. "It's true then, sir?"

Lord Bold rested the glass on the bar table and nodded once.

"I am undecided, Superintendent, what to make of Scrope's words. The man is a pathetic charlatan who bought himself a seat in Parliament. He has no class, no taste, no nobility. But he thinks he does. And that makes him dangerous."

"You shouldn't underestimate 'im, sir. Not after your son's death."

Lord Bold paced around the room but didn't once look Oatts in the eyes, which made the superintendent uneasy. He never cared about the snobbishness of the higher classes, but Lord Bold's indifference frustrated him. He worked for the man, for heaven's sake. At least he could pretend to be interested.

"Scrope came with this other man—what is his name? The one Daniel thinks is the murderer."

"Lloyd," Oatts said.

"Yes, Lloyd. He seems to do the dirty work for Scrope's conclave."

"Aye. I'll keep an eye on 'im. Lloyd will fall sooner or later. I'll send one of me bobbies to watch this house and escort you wherever you go."

"Thank you, superintendent. I would not want to impose a heavy burden on the police. Vigilance over my house is warranted for the safety of my daughters. No need to worry about me. François is as good a guardian as any of your men."

Oatts nodded, although he doubted that François could take on Lloyd by himself.

"What will you do, sir?"

"Scrope expects me to keep silent about their doings, but it is too late for that now. You and others already know of it. He may also wish that I join his political cause, but all this was a hoax from the beginning. I have no intention of joining their ridiculous conspiracy. I trust you will find the necessary evidence to bring these men to justice before another tragedy occurs. So do it quickly, superintendent."

Oatts felt blood rushing to his head and bit his lips.

"Aye, sir."

EIGHTEEN

LONDON, 1802

"Lamarck?" Pepys said, peering from above his lens. "What's he saying *now*?"

Jacques-Louis de Bournon smiled. Pepys had inherited Hutton's attitude towards Lamarck.

"He's finally published the theory we were waiting for. Some are calling it the transformation of species, others call it biological evolution because Lamarck says that all living species come from simpler organisms."

Pepys stopped reading the newspaper and turned to face him.

"Listen to this," Jacques-Louis said, turning to the page he had marked. "It appears that time and favorable conditions are the true principal means which nature has employed in giving existence to all her productions. We know that for her time has no limit, and that consequently she has it always at her disposal." Jacques-Louis glanced at Pepys, buried in the red chair of his drawing room. "He then goes on to explain the circumstances that nature uses to produce new organisms."

Pepys grumbled and Jacques-Louis handed the book to him.

"Read for yourself," Jacques-Louis said. "We should present these ideas to the society members tonight."

"Not tonight."

"Why not?"

"We have other matters to discuss," Pepys said, narrowing his eyes as he examined the cover of the book. "Luke

Howard is presenting a paper. Let me read this first and then, perhaps, I will consider presenting a report to the society."

Jacques-Louis shrugged. "As you wish."

"Lamarck may be going too far this time," Pepys muttered.

"Too far? What do you mean?"

Pepys looked at him but said nothing.

"Tell me!" Jacques-Louis said.

"Is he also saying that humans are a random product of nature?" Pepys said.

Jacques-Louis grimaced. "What's the problem now? That's what we have always aimed for—explaining everything without God. Everything. You know that."

"Yes, but it's one thing to be a materialist in regards to rocks and even the planets—but to ourselves? It's just—"

"*Fermez-la!*" Jacques-Louis snapped. He couldn't believe they were having this conversation. "You knew what you bargained for when you joined Askesis. You swore to abandon your religious nonsense and embrace materialism. It's too late to back up."

He snatched Lamarck's book from Pepys's hands.

"You will not mention your doubts again. If you do I'll let Ananias teach you a lesson."

Pepys's face wrinkled with terror.

ℕ𝕀ℕ𝔼𝕋𝔼𝔼ℕ

LONDON - MONDAY, 29 FEBRUARY, 1836

6:00 A.M.

The sun rose with a pale light. Daniel rubbed his palms while Thomas put his luggage on the coach. So cold. Still he waited until Thomas took the reins of the horses before stepping in himself. He knew the trip would be lengthy and wasn't eager to sit in the coach longer than necessary.

He thought of the morning many years ago when he'd left Norwich to study Natural Philosophy at Oxford. His father said he was proud Daniel had earned a scholarship, but Daniel knew the truth. He was disappointed his son would not become a clergyman.

"Don't worry, Dad," Daniel said. "I'll use my knowledge of science to bring glory to God."

"I pray you will, son. It's the least you can do for your Savior and for your family."

Daniel saw in his father's eyes a fear that was almost a prophecy—he feared and he knew Daniel would fail him. He'd never believed in him.

"You can still study for the ministry at Oxford. The Church of England might pay you well."

Daniel grimaced and let the comment go. They had discussed the topic *ad nauseaum*. "Never let earthly knowledge deceive your mind or drag you away from God," his father said—a phrase Daniel had heard countless times in the previous weeks. But when it came to his life's work, he wanted to try something different, do something different than his father.

And so he did.

What would they say to each other? Knowing his father, he'd probably avoid talking about his illness or imminent death and would instead ask a hundred questions about Daniel's life. How is life in London? Are you planning on getting married? Have you been attending church? Oh, yes, that last question would be asked for sure. And what would he say? "No, father, I quit attending church the day I left yours. At first I was too busy with my studies, then I realized I couldn't trust the church." That would be a deadly blow for Reverend Young, no doubt.

The ride turned bumpy once they left London. Thomas seemed to be taking to heart Richard's admonition to get to Norwich as soon as possible. The horses galloped steadily while Daniel's body shook all over.

"Thomas!" Daniel yelled out the window. "The idea is for me to be alive to see my father!" The coachman didn't seem to hear him.

The wheels bumped over a rock and Daniel hit his head against the coach's hard top. The pain made him wince. He passed a hand over his hair and felt the scab on the back of his head. He thought about Alex, about his own brushes with death—and realized something was wrong with him. Seriously wrong. His useless yell to Thomas and the thoughts he'd just had about his father were desperately cynical, even cruel. A wave of regret washed over him.

He closed his eyes and grasped the seat to remain steady. When did he become so different from his father? When did he turn into a skeptic? It didn't happen overnight, but he could easily pinpoint the day he crossed the line: a partly sunny morning in the spring of 1830.

Daniel's head was spinning as he left the classroom that

THE GENTLEMEN'S CONSPIRACY

day, the words of his professor reeling in his mind: "We have many reasons to believe now that the earth is millions of years old. We have only to study the fossils to notice that strata with marine shells alternate with strata with land and fresh-water shells. Further, we notice that both fossils of ter-restrial and marine animals are found in the strata close to the surface. Ah! And what about fossil human bones? We have only found these in the most recent strata. This is not the result of a global flood but of a slow succession of events!"

How would he bring glory to God through science if ev-erything he learned contradicted his beliefs? He gasped as he came out of the building and slumped under a nearby tree. He wanted to hear the authoritative voice of his father, but that voice had become weak. Daniel let his eyes wander to the spire of Christ Church Cathedral in the distance. Per-haps his father was not here, but he could seek an audience with the bishop.

He found the bishop walking the grounds outside the cathedral. They had spoken once before but Daniel doubted the bishop would remember him.

"Bishop Bagot," Daniel said.

The bishop turned to him and narrowed his eyes, as if trying to recognize Daniel's face. "Yes, son?"

"May I have a word with you?"

The bishop nodded. "If you don't mind walking with me, yes. I enjoy the morning sun."

Daniel walked alongside the bishop, trying to organize his thoughts. Why did he walk so fast?

"My soul is troubled," Daniel said. "And I need some counsel."

The bishop nodded, looking ahead.

"My father always taught me to believe scripture as the true word of God, starting with the book of Genesis." He paused and considered his next words carefully. "Now, my

191

geology professor and some others on campus say the book of Genesis is not literal history but a—"

"Do they really say that?"

Daniel blinked. He couldn't say those were their exact words.

"Well, that's what they mean, don't they? They say that facts and observations indicate the earth is older than six thousand years and the Noachian flood was only responsible for the formation of recent valleys. That's not what my father taught me. That's not what the Bible says!"

The bishop smiled, still looking ahead. "You don't have to worry, son. You may still believe what your professors say without departing from the faith. You're not the first concerned student to come to me with such troubles. You see, the age of the earth is not important for the Christian. I must say it's not even clear from the text when the world was created. Pious preachers have come up with reconciliatory interpretations. Some say the geological events described by today's scientist easily fit between the first two verses of Genesis. Yet others say the six days of creation represent long ages of time."

"Are these preachers competent geologists?" Daniel said, shaking his head. "Do they know what they're talking about when they reinterpret the Bible or are they simply salvaging their beliefs?"

The bishop looked at him for the first time. "What do you mean?"

Daniel felt angry now. "What if along comes a new theory of the earth? Would they reinterpret the Bible again to fit the new theory?"

"That I don't know, my son."

"Isn't the Bible the truth? Does the truth change?"

"God is the truth, son. The Bible is just the Bible, a moral code."

Daniel stopped but the Bishop kept walking, not even turning back to him.

Either the bishop was wrong or his father was wrong. He couldn't decide.

Oddly, however, he wished his father were wrong. Hadn't his father been wrong about James? Reverend Young believed only what he wanted to believe. If his father didn't believe him, why should he believe his father?

The bishop turned at the far corner of the building and then was out of sight. Daniel sighed. The old bishop lacked any conviction about what he preached. The only reasonable and consistent person Daniel had heard so far was a geology professor.

9:10 A.M.

Oatts stepped out from behind the plane tree as soon as he saw Lloyd leaving Scrope's house. He cursed. Lloyd boarded a coach that pulled out from the back of the house. Oatts couldn't let the scoundrel get away.

He looked around and jumped on the first cab coming his way. The cabby recoiled. "Wha—"

"Hullo, chap," Oatts said. "Just follow the coach o'er there. And don't miss it, aye?"

The cabby frowned.

"Here's the chink," Oatts said, handing him a coin.

At this, the cabby parted his lips in a toothless smile and whipped his horse.

"Won't miss it, mister, if you 'ave more."

"Aye, aye." Oatts looked at Lloyd's coach getting away. "But go faster. They have two beasts and you have just one."

"Hey! This ain't any regular 'orse. 'E runs like the wind!"

The old horse seemed to be in the last run of its life, trotting painfully behind Lloyd's carriage—which, to Oatts's relief, wasn't going very fast.

Turning on St. Thomas, Oatts lost sight of the coach. He cursed. "Where is it?"

"Ain't nothin' to worry 'bout, mister, they stopped just ahead. See?"

"Stop 'ere, cabby!"

He saw Lloyd talking to another man at the entrance of a shop. The man's face looked familiar but Oatts couldn't think of his name, distracted by the cabby, who kept asking for his pay. The man handed a note to Lloyd, who glanced at it and put it in his coat pocket.

Oatts grumbled. Should he get off now? What if Lloyd got back into the coach?

The cab stood in the middle of the street, and Lloyd would only have to look their way to see him—and he probably knew already who Oatts was. Better not risk it. He jumped off the cab and dug into his pockets for money. Then he looked down to count the coins on his hand.

"Here you g—" Oatts noticed movement out of the corner of his eye. Lloyd had returned to his ride. Its horses whined and moved forward.

Oatts grabbed the handle of the cab and pulled himself up.

"My ride's not o'er yet, cabby. After them!"

9:12 A.M.

Daniel watched the rough terrain beyond the road. He saw a mudslide caused by recent rain. Water was a powerful force. In retrospect, there were too many things his geology professor at Oxford didn't tell him. Like the evidence for the flood that Ure pointed out. Or the fossil trees that spanned

THE GENTLEMEN'S CONSPIRACY

several strata—when the layers covering the trees suppos-
edly formed over long ages.

He felt so angry. Angry with his professor, angry with
Buckland and Sedgwick, angry with the Geological Society.
Angry with himself. He could have kept believing like his
father or even the bishop. Instead he chose to believe what
he thought were facts.

For so long he'd resented his father for not telling him
what waited outside home. They all betrayed him, keeping
the truth from him.

But did his father really know? Was he even wrong? Perhaps not. Daniel hadn't decided. Sedgwick and the others
knew well they were manipulating truth for their advantage.
Not only that, they were trying to kill him. Susan and her
father were also in danger. As long as Lloyd remained free,
he could harm any of them. Daniel hoped Oatts would be
able to stop him soon.

10:15 A.M.

"They came this way before, mister," the cabby said. "Per'aps
they're lost."

Oatts shook his head. They didn't seem lost to him. Probably they were going around in circles to see if they were being followed. Well, he couldn't back up now. He'd just have
to keep playing the chasing game and see where it led him.

"Slow down, cabby."

They were entering Islington. What was Lloyd doing in
this place? He jumped off the moving coach onto the street
and ran inside a shop.

"Stop there, cabby!" Oatts said.

"Aye, mist—mister, my pay!"

Oatts ran across the street, pulling his hat down so it

195

wouldn't fall. He hoped the cabby would see the shillings on the seat soon and stop his yelling.

Two drunkards tried to get into the shop before Oatts, who rolled his eyes. He noted the sign on the window—a gin shop. He pushed his way through the drunkards and stepped inside. A woman in ragged, dirty clothes sat in a corner giving gin to her infant. Two older children fought over a sip while the lone host served gin to the other customers. No sign of Lloyd.

Oatts walked to the back, making his way through boxes and bottles, full and empty. He could see a vertical line of flickering white light at the end of a narrow hallway. The back door. He covered the distance in three steps and pushed the door open. He found himself in a deserted alley. Two rats scurried away through the trash on the ground. To his left was a brick wall, but to his right, the alley led to a side street.

Damnation! Lloyd had outwitted him and escaped. At least they were far away from Lord Bold's place, so there was no immediate danger of an attack. He combed his mustache with his fingers and headed for the street.

It seemed obvious now that Lloyd knew he was being followed. Oatts's eagerness to keep him in sight and the recklessness of the cabby gave them away. In the future he had to be more—

He noticed an open door on the wall to his left. A sudden movement from the door, and a man came fast at him. Oatts had time only to raise his forearms before his face. The blow against his skin and bones hurt like the devil. He heard the wood slat hit the ground, then he was out of air. His abdomen burned and his torso bent forward.

Lloyd said, "You tried my patience enough, peeler!"

As Oatts gasped, Lloyd grabbed him and shoved him face first against the wall. Pain crushed against his left cheek and down his chest. His mind traveled back to a day a boot pressed his head against the dust and his body shook, kicked by a bunch of Irish-hating scum. Oatts clenched his teeth, put his palms against the wall and shoved himself backward with all his might. His upper back hit Lloyd's stomach, whose body seemed to envelop Oatts's smaller one. Lloyd slumped to the ground, Oatts landing on top of him.

As Oatts tried to stand, the bigger man wrapped his arms around him and pressed hard. Oatts felt as if his ribs were being broken, but his arms were free of the asphyxiating embrace. He formed two fists and swung his arms above his head. Then he struck both of Lloyd's ears at the same time.

Lloyd's body trembled and his extremities gave away. Oatts rolled on his side and jumped to his feet. Lloyd's face contorted in a painful grimace, but Oatts knew the shock from the blow to his ears would soon pass. He bent down on one knee, clenched his right fist, and struck Lloyd's temple so hard he knew his hand was injured.

He didn't care. Lloyd lay unconscious in the middle of the alley.

2:05 P.M.

It had taken two bobbies to put the mighty Lloyd in the dark, damp cell at the Islington police station. Oatts walked back to the cell and looked at him through the bars.

"'Aving a good time, aye? Per'aps you feel like talkin' now. What were you up to in Islington?"

Lloyd ignored him. If he didn't confess any crime, it would be hard to keep him locked up—especially if his boss, the Member of Parliament, had any influence on the commissioner. Couldn't trust the justice system when everyone had a price.

Oatts put a hand in his pocket and felt the folded paper

he'd taken from Lloyd while he was unconscious. At least he had that.

"Do you know the punishment for attackin' a policeman?" Oatts said.

Lloyd just kept staring at the floor. Oatts studied the man for a few seconds. The set jaw and shortly trimmed hair made his face look boxy, and his skin had a yellowish cast.

"The magistrate will surely send you to the 'ulks. Nasty prison boats if you ask me. Worse than the little cell you're in 'ere."

The corners of Lloyd's mouth lifted up slightly.

"You think it's amusin'?" Oatts said.

"Tomorrow I'll be free and you'll be demoted," Lloyd said.

Oatts cocked his head. "Is that so?"

The prisoner grunted.

"So you're expectin' your powerful boss to rescue you, aye? But what if he never knows you've been arrested? No way to 'elp you, aye?"

Oatts noticed the change in Lloyd's smug expression.

"You could be labourin' in the 'ulks long before your boss finds out what 'appened to you." He turned to the guard standing by the hallway that connected the offices to the cells. "Hey, guard, what do you do with the prisoners in 'ere?"

The guard walked closer. "Excuse me, sir?"

"The prisoners—where do you send them?"

"Ah, all 'round, sir," the guard said. "Depends on the crime. Debtors go to the Marshalsea. Thieves and pickpockets they send to Newgate. But the most wicked ones end up in one of the 'ulks on the Thames."

Oatts could see Lloyd's uneasiness. "This is a wicked one," Oatts said. "A murderer."

The guard eyed Lloyd with contempt.

"I want no murderers in 'ere," the guard said. "I know a soldier, sir, that takes these fellows to the 'ulks and sends 'em to America or Australia. You want me to call for 'im, sir?"

Oatts kept his gaze on Lloyd but spoke to the guard. "Would the soldier come tonight?"

"Aye, sir!"

Lloyd stood abruptly from his bunk and shoved his arms through the bars, trying to grab Oatts's neck. Oatts jumped back after seizing one of Lloyd's thumbs—then twisted Lloyd's finger until the bone cracked. Lloyd let out a cry and snatched back his hands, backing into a corner of the cell.

"Well deserved!" the guard yelled.

Oatts grimaced. This Lloyd was pulling out old habits in him. He couldn't get carried away. Better do things by the book.

"Go fetch a doctor for 'im," Oatts whispered to the guard. "And keep 'im secured. I need to speak to the chief super-intendent, but I'll be back tonight."

8:11 P.M.

If Daniel felt exhausted, he could hardly imagine how the horses might feel. They had stopped briefly only twice along the way to Norwich.

He stuck his head out to speak to Thomas. "Turn right and follow that path over the bridge. That will take us di-rectly home."

Home. What an odd, bittersweet word.

His hands were clammy and he wiped them on his trou-sers. The pain in his mouth made him realize he was biting his lips too hard. Out the window, his parents' house came into view. A strange excitement overtook him.

"That's it, Thomas. Right here!"

He stepped out quickly and ran across the front yard like a child, although now he covered the same distance in just a few steps. He halted. What was he doing? He just couldn't go in like that. He turned to Thomas and watched him unload the luggage.

Now what? Daniel closed his eyes and took a deep breath, hoping that courage would come to him. Then he turned back. He could see candlelight flickering beyond the window glass.

How would his mother welcome him? Would she reproach him for sending only a handful of superficial letters in the last six years and never coming to visit? But she'd asked him to come now.

He took two steps forward, and knocked. His mother opened the door. Her skin had lost the smoothness he remembered, and her hair had turned the color of winter.

"Daniel!" She threw her arms around his neck and kissed his cheek several times. "The prodigal son returns home."

The first reproach. He didn't feel like a prodigal son at all. But that was just the way his mother was. He hugged her and felt awkward.

"Hello, Mama."

"Let me look at you!" She stepped back and inspected his face and body as one inspects a vegetable at the market. "You're a grown man now. Come, come inside. I'll make sure the coachman brings everything inside and give him directions to the inn."

The house was exactly as Daniel remembered it. Time had stood still in his absence. The creaking chairs, the cramped theological library, the basket with his mother's embroideries near the fireplace, the portrait of little James hanging on the far wall. The aroma of tea.

"You must greet your father," his mother said from behind.

Daniel glanced at the door to his father's room and his heart skipped a beat. Someone was walking out that door.

He thought his father would be bed-bound. How was he walking? Had they tricked him into coming?

"Do you remember Mr. Cole, Daniel?" his mother said.

So it wasn't his father after all. Daniel narrowed his eyes to see the man's face in the dim light: an unaffected smile under small eyes.

"You might not remember me, lad," Cole said. "You were but a little boy when I served at the parish with your father."

"I do remember you—a little. I used to be afraid of you."

Cole smiled wider and moved to one side, clearing the way for Daniel. Ready or not, this was the time to face his father again. He took a deep breath and walked right through the door. The room felt hot—it seemed at least ten degrees hotter than the room he'd just left. Daniel loosened his shirt's collar.

"Your father can't stand the cold," his mother said, "so I keep the fire burning in here."

There on the bed lay his father. His breathing was ragged, his chest moved up and down irregularly. He must be half the weight he'd been when Daniel last saw him. Daniel felt an urge to run. The vault in his chest where all feelings were stored threatened to explode like dynamite.

Daniel took a step back and bumped against his mother.

"Go on, son," she said. "Talk to him."

"Let us pray he wakes in a lucid period," Cole said.

Daniel turned to his mother, confused.

"Sometimes he's just delirious and makes no sense at all," she said.

"But your letter said —"

She shrugged. "It's a recent thing."

Daniel inched forward and sat on a chair beside the bed, letting the seconds slip by.

His mother drew closer and motioned with her head for him to stop lingering and just speak out. Daniel could tell she was getting impatient and he nodded like a child.

"Dad?" His voice left his throat as a faint whisper.

His mother frowned. "You have to speak louder than he snores."

This proved harder than he'd expected.

"Dad!" Daniel's voice came out so loud that even his mother jolted.

The man on the bed jerked and began coughing.

"Daniel's here, Jonathan," his mother said.

The sick man's eyes opened a little, seeking for something until they lingered on Daniel's face.

His father smiled. A dam of emotions burst inside. Daniel felt a lump in his throat suffocating him, pushing its way up, and finally tearing in his eyes.

"My... son," his father muttered with difficulty.

Daniel felt his father's hand reaching for his and took it. It felt cold and bony.

"Hello, dad." He wiped his tears with his free hand.

"I—missed you."

Daniel smiled, thinking of something to say while his heart melted.

"I... lo— love you. Do you know that, son?"

Daniel nodded. Now he did feel like the prodigal son, receiving his father's undeserved love. The ungrateful, rancorous son returned with mere guilt in his hands. Only one thing felt right.

"Forgive me, dad. I—" Tears slipped down his cheeks.

His father took a deep breath and closed his eyes.

"No, son, I need your forgiveness." The words came loud and clear, followed by a violent coughing spell. Once the coughing stopped, he sank in the bed, looking exhausted.

Daniel's body trembled. Why did his father need his forgiveness? His mother gave Daniel a glass of water and helped his father drink from another.

"I was... wrong," his father said.

"I'll tell him, dear, don't wear yourself." She put the water on a side table and looked at Daniel. "We loved your brother very much."

Daniel's heart raced.

"And naturally his death caused a lot of pain in your father. That's why he said some things he shouldn't have said. He said he didn't believe your story about the fisherman."

"I should... have," his father said. "I do now."

Daniel felt weak as he stared at his father's eyes.

"I...I'm sorry, son. I'm sorry I didn't believe you."

Overcome, Daniel bent forward and kissed his father's forehead.

"Yes," he said. His mind felt drained.

8:13 P.M.

"Escaped?" Oatts snapped. He felt like strangling the guard. "The cell's still locked!"

"I—I closed it," the guard said. "'E was with the doctor and I was in the w.c. when it 'appened."

Oatts cursed. The chief expected him to take Lloyd to headquarters tonight.

"What about the doctor?"

"Well...'e left." The guard's hands trembled.

"What's the doctor's name?"

The guard wiped the sweat on his forehead. "Uh—why?"

"What's 'is name?"

"'Is name is Dr.— Smith?"

Oatts curled his lips. He didn't believe a word of it. He looked at the guard with contempt, then noted something sticking out of one of his pockets. He grabbed the guard by his coat and pushed him against a wall.

"How much did he bribe you with?"

"No…no, sir, I never—"

Oatts smashed the guard's round sweaty figure and pulled the bill sticking out of the pocket.

"This is more than you get paid in a month!"

The guard mumbled something unintelligible. Oatts released him and threw the money to the ground. He shouldn't have left Lloyd with this piece of trash. With Lloyd free, nobody was safe. He had to catch him again.

"Now speak!" Oatts said showing the guard his fist. "Is 'e still near?

The guard shook his head. "It 'appened after you left."

Oatts snatched the keys from the guard and opened the cell.

"Did the doctor ever come by?"

The guard looked to the floor. "No, sir."

In two sudden moves, Oatts shoved the guard into the cell and locked the door. Then he picked up the bill.

"Newgate or the 'ulks for you?"

8:17 P.M.

George Scrope flared with anger at the sight of Lloyd's swollen head. As far as he knew, nobody had defeated Lloyd before. Then he looked at the broken thumb. The superintendent was a beast.

Lloyd sank in a chair, probably mulling his hatred. Scrope had to think, but emotions clouded his mind. He needed Sedgwick, where was—

"Sir?" The butler. "Reverend Sedgwick is here to see you."

"Excellent," Scrope said as Sedgwick came into the study, hat in hand.

"What's so urgent, George, that it couldn't—"

Sedgwick's mouth dropped at the sight of Lloyd.

"The Irish beast," Scrope said.

"What?"

"Your friend the superintendent. The one who doesn't drink wine, remember?"

"He did that to Stephen?"

Scrope told Sedgwick everything that had happened to Lloyd that day.

"It seems Lord Bold told the authorities about my visit," Scrope said.

Sedgwick gave Scrope a cold stare. "This is all your fault, George. Why did you have to bring him to us?"

Scrope nodded. He felt bad already. "I know. The question is what do we do now?"

"We have to silence Lord Bold. There's too much at stake. And the same goes for the superintendent."

"So what do you propose?"

"Be creative, George, you know better than I when it comes to that."

Scrope glanced at Lloyd, who had left his chair and now stood by the fire. What could he be thinking about? Usually expressionless, his face seemed to steam with ire.

"Oh, and one more thing," Sedgwick said, and nodded in Lloyd's direction. "He shouldn't stay here. The superintendent might come looking for him."

10:04 P.M.

Eating his mother's mutton again felt like the perfect closure for Daniel's night. She spoke about the years lost with Daniel's absence while he and Cole devoured the food and his father snored in his room.

His mother picked up the dishes.

"What happened with Mrs. Lubbock?" Daniel said.

"The servants left us," his mother said. "But without children in the house, what need do we have of servants? We get along well enough by ourselves." She took the dishes to the kitchen.

Daniel sensed Cole's eyes fixed on him and turned.

"What is it?" Daniel said.

"You look different," Cole said.

"I'm a grown man, of course I'm different."

"Different from when you first came in. There's peace in your eyes now. Incredible what forgiveness can do to a man's semblance."

Daniel nodded politely but wondered if Cole was some kind of religious lunatic. He certainly didn't want to discuss his feelings with him.

"So what are you up to these days, Mr. Cole?" Daniel said.

"Aside from my duties as the shepherd of my congregation, I consider it my call to contend for the faith. That is why I'm writing a book on geology."

Daniel's eyes widened. "Geology?"

"Yes, geology, it—"

"I didn't know you were a geologist!"

"Oh, no, my lad. I'm not a geologist but a student of the word of God, and as such, I feel it my duty to condemn every impious doctrine, such as the ones taught by so-called men of God like the Reverend Adam Sedgwick."

Daniel shook his head. Unbelievable. He tried to figure out what Cole could possibly say about Sedgwick's work.

"Have you actually read Sedgwick?" Daniel said.

"Of course," Cole said. "How else would I refute him?"

"And just what is it you want to refute?"

Cole seemed oblivious to Daniel's tone.

"I seek only to refute Sedgwick's account of the creation of the world, of man, and all the creatures therein, and the infidel tendency of geological speculations to subvert the revelation of God. I'm in no way opposed to the legitimate science of geology, but I must speak against the speculative theories of origins and earth history which are perverting science and are contrary to scripture."

This man's words seemed to come out from a rehearsed sermon. But he spoke with a passion even greater than Ure's. What would Cole do if he knew Sedgwick was one of Daniel's mentors? A mentor who apparently conspired to kill him.

Daniel shifted in his chair and looked toward the kitchen. He could hear his mother handling pans and dishes. He turned to Cole.

"Now you've made me curious, Mr. Cole, because I'm an amateur geologist and quite familiar with Sedgwick's writings. Please tell me exactly what you find so subversive about Sedgwick's theories."

"Why, old-earth geology of course. Isn't that obvious to you as a Christian?"

Taken aback, Daniel shook his head. "Why would it be obvious?" Best not to mention the poor state of his Christianity.

"Because it contradicts scripture!" Cole said. "God's own finger inscribed the fourth commandment in the stones given to Moses: 'For in six days the Lord made heaven and earth, the sea, and all that in them is, and rested the seventh day.' The Lord used this parallel to establish man's work week. If God made everything in six days, how can the earth be millions of years old? Yet some truth-deniers affirm that the beginning of Genesis 1 occurred millions of years before the six days of creation. If this is so, then the Lord Jesus Christ was mistaken when he said that 'from the beginning of creation God made them male and female.' If Adam and Eve were present at the beginning of creation, how can the earth be millions of years old? Sedgwick must either deny the truth of his geological doctrine or deny the truth of the word of God! By saying the fossils of dead animals are older than man's creation, Sedgwick is denying what the gospel teaches: that death and sin came into the world through the first Adam. If millions of animals had been buried in the rocks before man was created, why then did God say that his creation was 'very good'?"

Daniel stared at Cole's throbbing veins as he spoke. What a conviction. What a shocking argument. What could he respond? He had rejected the Bible in favor of geology because he was taught that geology contradicted the story of the flood—he hadn't considered these other contradictions. That only served as justification: the real reason for abandoning his faith came down to vengeance against his father.

"What a pity," Cole said, "that a man of such distinguished learning, and with such eminently scientific, academic, and sacred stations as Sedgwick, would fall into the deepest folly of denying the Eternal Truth."

Cole's speech against Sedgwick sounded peculiar, but its insight rocked Daniel's soul. Cole had in fact seen in Sedgwick's writings what took Daniel a murder investigation to discover: that the Geological Society had undermined the authority of the Bible. What Cole didn't know was that Sedgwick had a political motivation.

"Daniel!" his mother cried. But her voice came from his father's room, not the kitchen. When had she slipped past them? "Daniel!" The urgency in her voice chilled his bones.

Daniel ran to the room. He heard Cole coming behind him.

He found his mother bent over the bed, tears running down her face.

"When I didn't hear his snores, I came to check on him." She was caressing, ever so gently, the still face of her husband. She let out a sob.

Daniel's hands fell to his sides and he stood there gaping. He blinked and felt his chest compress. Why so soon? Why now that he'd come back home? There were so many more things he wanted to say to his father. He wanted to—

"He's in a better place now," Cole whispered in his ear. "You *will* see him again."

He wanted to believe that.

TWENTY

LONDON - TUESDAY, 1 MARCH, 1836

7:30 A.M.

Daniel's heart ached for his mother. He wondered how she was holding up beneath her outward calm.

"I must tell Mrs. Nelson," she said, pulling a shawl tight around her shoulders. "She'll bring the news to the rest of the parishioners. And I must prepare—"

"No need to worry, Mama," Daniel said. "Mr. Cole went out an hour ago to take care of everything. The coffin, the undertaker, the flowers."

"Your father always wanted a simple ceremony on the church's courtyard. Nothing fancy."

"I know, mother, I know. Mr. Cole wants to officiate at the funeral. Is that all right?"

She nodded. "Your father would approve. Who better than Henry Cole?"

Daniel thought that despite his eccentric talk, Cole was a good man. He wished he had his passion and conviction.

"Did Dad call for Mr. Cole too?"

His mother smiled wryly. "Not really. He only asked for you. It was my idea to ask Henry to come—just in case you didn't. At least he would have an old friend by his side." She kissed Daniel goodbye and went on her way to Mrs. Nelson's.

Daniel glanced at the memories filling every corner of the house and felt a lump in his throat. It had become increasingly hard for him to control his emotions these last two days. He picked up his coat and stepped out of the house. The front yard carried memories also. Daniel shook his head and looked up the road. Cole came running in his direction.

"Daniel!" he said. "Bad news!"

He drew near to Daniel, panting, and bent forward, resting his hands on his knees. "I'm not made for this—"

"What is it?" Daniel said.

"Ah, yes." Cole wiped his forehead. "The undertaker is ill. He wants us to wait until tomorrow to bury your father."

Daniel thought about all the troubles that awaited him in London.

"Tomorrow? But my mother—"

"Unless we dig the grave ourselves," Cole said.

Daniel frowned. "Are you serious?"

Cole stared at him with a stern face. The pastor didn't seem to be joking.

9:10 A.M.

Five minutes had passed since Oatts first knocked on Scrope's door, but there still came no answer, not even the butler. Where were they? Hiding, for sure, but where?

"You stay 'ere, Willy, while I go check on the back with Peter," Oatts said, but immediately recognized his mistake. Willy could never detain Lloyd by himself. Even he felt uneasy. Who knows what the man could do now that Oatts had infuriated him? Hopefully the broken thumb would at least slow down his fist. Between Peter and Willy they could stop him long enough for Oatts to bring him down. "On second thought, Peter will stay with you."

"Aye, sir!" William said, placing a hand on his baton.

Oatts rounded the house. They were probably expecting him. Were they observing him right now? Oatts glanced at every window but the draperies were as still as the glass. He came to the servant's entrance, a damp passageway leading to an ancient green door. Oatts inspected the area, hoping someone would let him in. Nobody. He returned to the green door and forced it open with his shoulder. The door cracked open.

Inside, he could hear the low murmur of voices from another room. The hallway was dark and the damp dust smell penetrated his nostrils. He walked forward and bumped into some sort of clay vessel. It turned over with a loud thump and spilled water all over the floor. The murmur in the distance ceased.

Oatts muttered under his breath. He could bet that Lloyd wasn't here, much less Scrope. He strode down the hallway past four terrified-looking maids, who stood frozen in the middle of their duties.

"G'day," Oatts said and kept on going.

A spiral staircase led to the ground level. Oatts climbed up in long hops, his eyes focused on each step. From the state of the stairs, he could tell that the house—

Oatts halted and held the walls to keep his balance at the sudden appearance of a body in front of him. From the looks of it, it was the butler, slumped against the walls. Oatts put two fingers under the butler's neck and felt the pulse. Alive. He shook him but the butler only emitted a low mumble. Oatts stepped back and looked at the angle at which the butler lay on the floor. He'd probably sat on the stairs first, then fallen asleep. Strange—unless he'd been drugged.

The butler's wide figure blocked the way to the top. Oatts put one foot on the butler's round belly and pushed himself forward.

The ground floor seemed deserted. He checked each of the rooms on the first story—just quick glances—and found no one. Then he remembered Peter and Willy and walked to the front door. "Come in, Willy, Pete," Oatts said, swinging the door open. The two bobbies looked at each other, then followed their boss inside.

"Go upstairs and see if the master of the house is hiding."

"Yes, sir," Willy said.

Oatts walked back to the study, where he'd seen a half-empty glass and a folded newspaper. That had to be the place Scrope spent most of his time—a good place to find information.

He took the glass and sniffed. Whiskey. He looked around. Except for the newspaper resting on a chair, all the tables and chairs were empty. None of the books seemed to have been taken off the shelves in a long time—they all had a uniform layer of dust on them.

Just as he decided to leave, he noticed a lone crumpled paper in a wicker basket at one corner of the study. He reached for the paper and opened it. A letter with no date or addressee.

> You know what I'm capable of, traitors. So I warn you to keep your mouths shut. If you send the police after me, I'll tell them all about your plans against the king and your secret conspiracy. Leave me alone, Sedgwick, or you'll be next.
>
> A.S.

Oatts cocked his head and narrowed his eyes. Interesting. He rubbed the letter with his fingers. The paper was cheap and obviously fresh. The infamous "A.S." had threatened Sedgwick and his friends—even called them traitors. It seemed there were more than two sides in this plot.

He folded the letter and put it in his pocket. Then he remembered the note he took from Lloyd.

10:00 A.M.

"Two feet more," Cole said, drenched in sweat. "Just keep digging, my lad."

Daniel paused to breathe deeply. Digging for fossils was something he found exhilarating, but digging his father's grave was another matter indeed. Heartbreaking. But he couldn't refuse. It was the least he could do.

Cole apparently sensed Daniel's distress, because he hadn't stopped talking since they grabbed the shovels two hours ago. From the looks of the hole it was obvious neither of them was a laborer nor had either ever dug a grave before.

Daniel tried to numb his mind with the repetitive movement of the shovel and the indistinct noise of Cole's voice. Another hour slipped by.

"I think that's it!" Daniel said.

"You know, Daniel," Cole said, "many of the living today are digging their own spiritual graves with their sinful ways."

Oh, my, now he's going to preach.

Cole clasped his hands on top of the shovel. "And some of the living already look like the dead. Such a man came to my church on Sunday. I bumped into him the night of the anniversary of the Geological Society. He—"

"What did you say?"

"That some of the living—"

"No, no, about the Geological Society," Daniel said. "How do you know about the anniversary?"

Cole gave a nonchalant shrug. "My intention that night was to confront Sedgwick in an open debate about the Eternal Truth of the Divine Revelation, and I knew from the newspaper that he would be attending the anniversary meeting. So that's where I was going—"

"You weren't there," Daniel said. "I was with Sedgwick that night!"

Cole widened his eyes. "You were with—but why?"

"Because…it doesn't matter! The fact is, you weren't there, I know."

"That's what I was about to tell you," Cole said. His voice had become somber. "I never made it to Somerset House."

Cole narrated his walk across The Strand, the noises that stopped him in the middle of the street, the panting, and the encounter with the man with dead eyes. Daniel felt a chill creep up his arms.

"At what time did this happen?" Daniel said.

Cole sighed. "I couldn't say. An hour or two after dark, perhaps."

Daniel closed his eyes and pictured that night in his mind. Could it be the man who threw the rock? Could it be Lloyd? It seemed unbelievable that Cole had seen the man. This was an amazing coincidence. All of a sudden it didn't matter that the letters were gone. He trembled with excitement. They now had a witness who could identify the killer.

Daniel opened his eyes and found himself alone. He looked up the wooden ladder his mother had brought and saw the soles of Cole's shoes disappearing at the top.

"Wait!" Daniel cried.

"There's much to do, my lad!" Cole's voice came back. "Let's get washed up."

Daniel hurried up the ladder and ran to catch up with Cole. "Wait, Mr. Cole!" He stumbled on a rock and fell face down on the ground. He spat out the mud and jumped back on his feet. No time to lose. He couldn't believe how close he was to discover the identity of the killer.

Cole walked too fast for his age, it seemed to Daniel. The pastor had reached the far corner of the church building and turned to cross the path to the house. Daniel reached him at the door.

"Please, Mr. Cole," Daniel said, panting. "Tell me about

this man with the dead eyes. Describe him to me now!"

Cole frowned. "I don't know, my lad. I sense you haven't been forthcoming with to me. How is it you know the infidel Sedgwick? When you told me you were familiar with his writings I assumed you were simply a widely read young man. Now it turns out you're a friend of his."

Daniel sighed and put both hands over his face. He didn't have time for this. He heard the door open and withdrew his hands from his face. Cole had walked inside.

How frustrating. You couldn't lose him out of sight for a second or he'd vanish.

"Please, Mr. Cole!" Daniel said, storming in the house.

Half a dozen people turned to look at him. Some were familiar, others he didn't know—or perhaps he just didn't remember.

He smiled nervously. "Good morning."

"Daniel!" his mother said, coming out of the kitchen. "Do you remember Mrs. Nelson and her family?"

"How do you do?" the teary Mrs. Nelson said.

"Er—all right, I think," Daniel said.

"He's shocked," Cole said, coming to his rescue. "Like all of us."

The visitors nodded.

"You must be exhausted," Daniel's mother said.

"We are," Cole said. "Please excuse us."

Daniel followed Cole, who walked to the back of the house. Cole handed him a wash basin.

"Tell me the truth, Daniel Young, if you want me to speak more about this man."

Daniel felt as if his story with Oatts were occurring all over again. But that was the lesson—honesty and trust will get better results.

"It's a long story."

Cole grinned. "It's a lot of mud you have on you."

217

"All right. I'm a member of the Geological Society." Daniel waited for Cole to drop to his knees, praying for fire to fall down from heaven and consume the infidel, but he just nodded. After all, he'd been an Anglican clergyman before becoming a Methodist minister, right? He'd have heard confessions before.

Daniel said, "For a long time I have believed those revelation-denying doctrines, as you call them, but not like Sedgwick. He's different, because he has an ulterior motive. I have done it all in good faith."

It dawned on him that he was defending himself even though he wasn't being attacked.

"Where do I begin?" Daniel said.

"Your hands," Cole said.

"Pardon me?"

"You can begin by washing your hands, otherwise you wouldn't be able to clean the rest of your body. Wasn't that what you were asking?"

Daniel shook his head. "I meant where to begin my story."

Cole shrugged. "From the beginning, of course."

By the time Daniel told Cole about Alex's murder and the conspiracy, they were both clean and dressed for the funeral.

"I'm worried for your soul, my lad," Cole said. "God has spared your life so you would repent and come back to him. Of that, I have no doubt."

Daniel wanted to roll his eyes or laugh but didn't want to offend Cole. Besides, he'd thought as much himself.

"Now you understand my interest in this man you bumped into."

"Of course, I do," Cole said. "Now I see it was by God's design we met here today."

Daniel felt uneasy with the thought. Was his father's death also God's design? Every word from Cole had the power of stirring something within Daniel—and he hated it.

"So, tell me about this man," Daniel said and tried to picture Lloyd in his mind. "Was he a tall blond man with a square face, mid-thirties?"

Cole scratched his head. "Well, now, actually—"

Daniel turned to see why Cole had stopped talking and saw his mother.

"Daniel, it's time now," she said. "Mrs. Nelson's boys took the body and placed it in the coffin. I want you by my side, son, while Mr. Cole leads the procession to the burial place. All the parishioners are outside waiting."

"Indeed." Cole headed to the front of the house.

12:00 P.M.

Daniel couldn't shake off his annoyance. He'd tried to find a moment during the procession to speak with Cole, but his mother had clung to him, sobbing on his shoulder all the way to the graveyard.

About fifty people gathered around the hole he had dug with Cole, who now recited Psalm 23. "Yea, though I walk through the valley of the shadow of death, I will fear no evil: for thou art with me; thy rod and thy staff they comfort me."

Guilt made Daniel cringe. He was supposed to mourn his father, but all his thoughts were on the man with the dead eyes. Daniel realized that apart from Cole he was the only one present not crying. But hadn't he cried enough last night?

He stared down and tried to shed some tears but kept returning to Lloyd's eyes. Did they look dead? What do dead eyes look like, anyway? He should think about his father. How did his eyes look after he died? Dead eyes have an empty, lifeless quality that can't be explained. Was that how Lloyd's eyes—

Daniel felt his mother pulling his arm. "I'm so glad

you're here with me today," she whispered. "You will stay, won't you, Daniel?"

He smiled at her, but his chest filled with anxiety. He couldn't stay in Norwich, he had to finish his talk with Cole and return to London as soon as possible. Lives were in danger as long as the killer was loose. If Oatts hadn't caught him, Daniel would.

12:22 P.M.

Oatts read Lloyd's note one more time: Grey's Inn, 12. The old inn was right off a busy street in Islington.

What would he find there today? He rubbed the bruise on his cheek and scanned the area. Would Lloyd dare attack him again? He'd shown him what he was made of.

Oatts pushed his way through the street crowd, elbowing bums and off-duty soldiers. The inn's gray facade went well with its name. A bell rang when he pushed the door open.

"G'day, mister," a girl said from behind a counter. "Lookin' for a place to stay?"

She couldn't be older than thirteen, but she seemed to be running the place by herself at the moment.

Oatts grinned. "I'm actually lookin' for the guest in room twelve, young lady."

"A friend, are you?"

"You could say so," Oatts said.

"I could say so? Are you 'is friend or not?"

Oatts looked down on the girl. She was playing the smart one with him.

"I'm a policeman, chavy," Oatts said, narrowing his eyes.

The girl gasped and ran through a door behind her. "Dad, a p'leeecman!"

Oatts cringed. The girl would alert whoever was in room

12 of his presence. He looked down the hallway to a line of doors and strode quickly towards them. They were numbered 1 through 6, with black paint on the frames. Oatts cursed. Perhaps 12 was on the second story—but he would have to walk back to the counter and climb the stairs.

A greasy wide-eyed man stood behind the counter. "M-m-may I 'elp you?"

"Is room twelve up there?" Oatts said, pointing.

"A-aye."

Oatts left the stammering innkeeper and climbed up the stairs. A lone window at the end of the hallway provided the only light, so he couldn't see the numbers until he stood in front of the doors. Seven. Eight. Nine. He counted the number of doors left: room 12 had to be the last door by the window. He passed a hand over his mustache and popped his neck. This was it. He let the thrill of the moment take him. He might finally catch the killer. He was ready.

He tried the bolt at number 12. Locked. He knocked twice and waited. A whole minute passed. Whatever he was going to do, he had to do it now. Lloyd planned to come to this room for a reason—and he wanted to know why.

With a kick to the bolt, the old wood cracked and the door swung open to total darkness. A strong odor hit Oatts's nose. How could it be so dark at noon? Unless this was a windowless room. He waited for his eyes to adapt. The dim light from the hallway picked out a few objects near the entrance: a pair of shoes and a dozen bottles—liquor bottles, it seemed.

Oatts put the palm of his hand against the wall, feeling his way toward the side of the room where the window should be. He reached the corner of the wall and touched something that felt like a window frame, then a flat hard texture, like wood. This was no drapery. He pushed the wood and a thin stream of light entered the room for one second. He pushed again—the same result. The third time he kept the pressure in the middle and slipped his fingers through the space between the frame and the wood. Then he pulled hard. The light of day burst into the room, making Oatts blink. He held the top of a table in his hands. He dropped it on the floor and looked around. The place was a mess. Trash covered the floor and even the mattress.

Oatts kicked empty bottles and leftovers and cockroaches fled from the food to take refuge below the bed. He cursed. What could he find among all the trash?

Then he noticed something familiar about the mess in the bed. Yellowish sheets of paper.

12:40 P.M.

Daniel stepped forward to help fill in the grave, but his mother held his arm.

"Let the Nelson boys do it," she said. "Please stay with me."

Daniel nodded and glanced at Cole. The preacher stood five feet away, surrounded by parishioners who embraced him. Old friends, perhaps.

After a few minutes they walked to the house, Daniel's mother speaking words he heard but didn't take in. He glanced back at the gravesite but Cole had gone. Daniel looked around frantically. Cole was walking toward them at a quick pace. Daniel took his mother's hand off his arm.

"Excuse me, Mama, I must have a word with Mr. Cole."

He didn't wait for an answer but took long strides to meet up with the minister. Cole smiled at him but didn't stop walking, so Daniel grabbed him at the shoulders.

"Please, Mr. Cole, tell me what you were going to say."

Cole's face seemed lost for a moment. Daniel felt a surge

of anxiety and tightened his grip. Cole recoiled and gently pushed Daniel's hands away from him.

"You're really troubled, my lad," Cole said. "These thoughts about your friend's murder are consuming you. You forget it's time to mourn for your father."

Daniel clenched his fists and felt the blood rush to his face.

"But I will tell you," Cole said, putting a hand over Daniel's shoulder. "You asked me whether the man I bumped into was young and tall. That night I only saw his eyes—those horrific dead eyes. But the next time I saw him at my church, I imprinted his face in my mind so I could pray for him."

"And?"

"He's not a young man, Daniel. I would say he's closer to my age."

"Are you sure?"

Cole nodded, lips pursed. So it wasn't Lloyd who threw the stone after all. Oatts had been right all along.

"And what about his face?"

Daniel focused his eyes on Cole's mouth. It was vital he see every word coming out so he missed not a syllable. Daniel repeated the words in his mind and formed a mental image of the face Cole described, feature by feature, until the face matched something in memory. Then he gasped.

"I know who he is!"

12:47 P.M.

Oatts bent over the bed and picked up one of the papers. He couldn't understand what he read, but his best guess was that it was French.

He picked another one, a letter signed by some Comte. It talked about science.

But there was no doubt in his mind—these were the stolen letters.

He reached into his pocket for the note he'd found at Scrope's house, the one signed A.S. He compared it with the writing of the French letter. They could definitely be from the same hand. Unfolding the bottom of the French letter, he saw the initials again: A.S.

He felt his hands sweating, ruining the old letters. He had to figure something out soon. Who was this A.S.? He scrambled through the other letters, searching the names. Sooner or later he was meant to find it. After ten minutes of tiresome reading he found a name: Ananias.

Oatts bit his bottom lip. Ananias. The name sounded familiar somehow. He closed his eyes, reviewing all the places, conversations, and inquiries in the last two weeks. There came a vague memory of one Ananias he'd read about. Where? On a newspaper—the letters in the name were printed on a newspaper. But he never read the newspaper. Willy would tell him the news every morning. He hardly ever read—not his habit.

Where then? The image in his mind became clearer: A wall. A frame in the wall. A newspaper clipping inside the frame. A name in the clipping.

Oatts spoke the name. "Victor Ananias Shaw."

"That would be me," a voice said behind him.

A shattering blow hit his skull and again the room was engulfed in darkness.

1:30 P.M.

Cole muttered a prayer under his breath while Daniel spoke to his mother. The young man seemed determined to leave for London right away. "Gracious Lord, protect him...."

Cole felt an ulcer forming in his stomach. Daniel's life must be in danger. He'd told him about the inn where he saw the man with dead eyes, and Daniel pledged to go there with the police. But something didn't feel right.

Moved by this sense of dread, Cole approached Daniel. "I'll go with you."

Daniel looked at him and raised an eyebrow.

"I don't understand why you must leave," Mrs. Young said.

"I'll return as soon as possible, Mama," Daniel said. "I must take care of this—this issue. Then I'll be back. I promise."

"But why is Henry going with you?" she said.

Cole smiled. "To make sure he comes back."

He waited, no doubt for Daniel to say something to calm Mrs. Young. Instead, he turned away and went to pack his things.

"He needs some spiritual guidance," Cole said. "The long trip will give me an opportunity to minister to his soul."

She sighed. "I was looking forward to my son's company. But I guess he must do what he must, whatever it is."

6:05 P.M.

Susan's belly hurt from laughing. "You're incredibly funny, Richard. How do you come up with so many stories?"

"But they're all true, my dear Susan! Every single word!" Richard laughed, setting her off again.

Susan covered her mouth. What would her father think? She knew her father disapproved of Richard's visits these last two days, but his mind was so occupied he hadn't bothered lecturing her. She felt relieved. The truth was she liked Richard. He could take her mind off her worries.

"The strangest things happen to me," Richard said. "During my last trip to Switzerland I met a German fellow with a large beard who believed he'd killed God."

"Killed God?"

"That's right!"

"And how can he do that?" Susan said.

"That's exactly what I said! But he had the strangest ideas I couldn't understand."

Susan frowned. This story wasn't funny.

Richard opened his arms. "So I said, how do you know God is dead? And he looked at me very somberly and said, 'You will see his remains rotting across Europe very soon.'"

"Oh my, what a repulsive thought!"

Richard nodded. "That's only one of the strange characters I've met. Although I must admit, for the most part, my trips are entirely pleasant—albeit lonely."

She felt the heat in her face. Was he interested in her romantically? Didn't he care about his cousin's feelings? She tried to put that thought aside, but it felt good to have two handsome men competing for her affection.

She looked away from Richard's eyes and around the drawing room. She felt dampness at the back of her neck and on her upper lip.

"It's unusually hot, don't you think, Richard?"

He shrugged. "Doesn't bother me. I hate winter and love summer."

"But it wasn't as hot a few minutes ago."

Richard stood and walked to her. "Maybe you're running a fever, my dear." He took her hand. "But you're not warm."

Susan felt uneasy and withdrew her hand. "Of course it's not a fever. Wait—listen to that."

Richard moved his head from one direction to the other. "What?"

"Listen to the crackling sound." She stood up.

"The fireplace—"

"No, this is different, listen, it's louder."

Richard made a face Susan decided to ignore. She walked to the window but saw nothing strange in the night outside. Then she heard a scream.

"Mother!"

Running steps pounded above the drawing room. The screams continued. A surge of panic tightened Susan's chest and she sprinted from the room. The screams became clearer as she reached the stairs, forming one terrifying word from several voices:

"Fire!"

6:10 P.M.

Daniel jumped off the coach to assess the damage. The carriage was tilted to one side, the two right wheels sunk in a pool of mud. He grunted and turned to Cole, who was half-asleep inside.

"Wake up, Mr. Cole, we need to push."

Cole opened his eyes and coughed. "What did you say, my lad?"

Daniel smiled. "Ready to get dirty again?"

"Is it really necessary?"

"If we want to get to London, yes."

Cole shrugged. "Oh well!" He held one hand out and Daniel helped him from the carriage. "May the Lord be glorified."

After they had unloaded the carriage, Cole and Daniel stood side-by-side in the mud and pushed the carriage up and forward while the coachman pulled the horses' reins. Daniel glanced at Cole's bald forehead and the white hairs splattered with dirt and couldn't help but grin. It was incredible he could feel like this, having just buried his father after burying his best friend not two weeks before. But Daniel felt healed from so many things. Here in the mud he could not care less about emulating the leadership of the Geological Society.

The wheels moved a few inches.

"I need to rest!" Cole cried. His face was burning red.

"Not now," Daniel said. "Don't let it drop again. Just keep pushing!"

"Oh, Lord, help us! We won't make it to London tonight."

"No, but there's a traveler's inn a few miles ahead," Daniel said, motioning for Cole to get with him behind the carriage. "We'll spend the night at the inn. But let's get the coach rolling again first."

Daniel bent his knees and, with a deep breath and a groan, pushed until the wheels rose above the mud and the horses pulled the coach forward. A splattering sound made him turn. Cole lay face down on the mud.

"Mr. Cole!" Daniel said, reaching for Cole's arms, and lifting him up.

"Thank you, my lad."

Cole's white face was now a plastered brown. Daniel chuckled. Cole swiped at the mud with a handkerchief and patted Daniel on the back.

"It's all right, lad, laugh all you want. The Lord is my justice." Then the pastor chortled too, and Daniel shook with laughter.

"I hadn't laughed so much in a long time," Daniel said. Only Alex could make him laugh like that. He covered his mouth. "But maybe I shouldn't laugh. I should be mourning."

The pastor watched him for a moment. "The Lord turns our mourning into dancing, Daniel. Our sorrow into laughter. Don't be surprised you can laugh now, because I prayed for the joy of the Lord to come upon you."

6:22 P.M.

Black smoke poured into the hallway from the back of the house. Susan choked and gasped for fresh air. The house-keeper came running down the stairs.

"It's gone up to the second story, miss," Mary cried. "Your mother is up there."

Susan rushed up the stairs and into the hallway, only to halt when flames licked the frame of a door right in front of her. What was she thinking? She closed the door with one fast pull and looked forward to her mother's room. She was locked in, and smoke escaped from the bottom of the door.

"Mother!" Her body was paralyzed. What could she do? Where was father? Where was Alex?

"Oh, my God, Alex!" Susan sobbed and fell to her knees. Why did she call her dead brother while her mother was as-phyxiating in her bed?

She felt herself pulled from behind. Through her tears, Susan saw Richard dragging her down the stairs.

"Please, Richard, my mother!"

"It's too late now," Richard said.

"Please, help her, please!"

She knew she couldn't ask this virtual stranger to risk his life, but who else would?

"Where's my father?"

6:23 P.M.

"I see no man, sir," the bobby said. "Are you sure he came this way?"

Lord Bold rolled his eyes and decided not to answer. He knew it was Scrope's henchman when he saw him through the window. But it was true that the streets were deserted.

Lloyd had either run too fast or hidden somewhere.

"We should go back, sir. The superintendent ordered me to stay put at the house."

Lord Bold sighed. "Precisely because of the threat of this man we are chasing. If he's on the run, we have nothing to fear."

What was Lloyd planning, anyhow? Lord Bold kept walking, but the bobby seemed to hesitate.

"What is it?" Lord Bold turned back to the policeman, who looked mesmerized by something behind them. Lord Bold lifted his eyes. Above the trees, a smoky glow painted the night sky. He gulped. The smoke rose half a mile southeast from them. "My house!"

6:33 P.M.

The suffocating heat poured like a wave down the stairs.

"Come, quick!" Richard said.

Susan shook him off. "I have to save Mother." She looked up from the middle of the steps and saw the hallway filled with smoke.

She started up, but Richard held her arm.

"No! I'll go."

He pulled out a handkerchief, wiped her tears, put it over her mouth and nose, and plunged into the smoke. Half a minute passed.

"Richard!" she called. Oh, no, what had she done? "Richard! Answer me!"

She heard a crackling sound. Richard breaking the door, or the fire destroying the house?

"Miss Susan! Miss Susan!"

Mary called her from somewhere—maybe from outside. She kept her gaze on the smoke. Her eyes began to burn.

"Carry 'er out, Christian!" Mary said, closer than Susan had thought she was. She felt an arm around her waist as she was lifted. She had no will to struggle. Black smoke consumed her breath, her eyesight, her hope.

They were almost out the front door when Susan saw a charcoal-like figure emerging from the smoke. Richard trotted down the stairs coughing. Just him. He wasn't carrying her mother.

Susan sobbed as Christian carried her away and put her down on the ground, about sixty feet from the house. Richard fell to the ground.

"I tried to save her, I truly did, Susan, but the flames—they were all around her...." He looked at her with desperate, bloodshot eyes. "I'm sorry, Susan. I'm so sorry."

6:44 P.M.

Lord Bold slowed as the flame-enveloped house came into view. A group of people gathered a safe distance from the house, not too far from where he stood. His family and servants were surely there, along with curious neighbors.

"Sir!" the bobby called behind him. "The Jimmy Braiders are coming!"

The London Fire Engine Establishment's four-wheel wagon rushed past him. Lord Bold trotted behind it and observed the water pumper on the wagon. The machine's tub was connected to a long, parallel handle that the firefighters would move up and down. A dozen firefighters rode or trotted along—they were younger and faster and reached the house before Lord Bold.

Whoosh!

A wall collapsed. Lord Bold covered his face as a bright set of flames replaced the wall.

The house had insurance, but not his family. Where were they?

"Father!" Emily ran toward him, the nanny behind her.

Emily hugged him around the waist and he patted her head.

"Is everyone safe?" Lord Bold asked the nanny.

She couldn't look at him. "All are safe but Lady Bold, milord. She… remains in the house."

Lord Bold thanked her and put his fingers to his eyelids. Had Scrope been before him, he'd have killed him on the spot.

TWENTY-ONE

LONDON, 1806

Jacques-Louis stared at the pool of blood forming on the ground near his flowerbed. He was glad blood didn't run in London as it had in Paris when he fled the revolution, but sometimes he couldn't help it. A kingdom couldn't be brought down without force.

"That's enough, Ananias," Jacques-Louis said. "I think our guest has learned an important lesson."

The beaten man tied to the tree moved his head in what seemed a nod. Blood dripped from every orifice in his face.

"No one steals from me!" Jacques-Louis spat in the man's face. "Much less my diamonds." He raised the bag with the three diamonds presented to him by the Earl of Bridgewater and held it before the man's eyes. Then he offered the bag to Ananias. "Take the diamonds and place them in my minerals cabinet. Then show our guest the exit."

Jacques-Louis crossed the garden, entered the house, and went to his office. The open inkbottle reminded him it was time to work on his monograph. He sat at the desk and read the few pages he'd already written. What now? He found it hard to concentrate. After ten minutes of fruitless thinking, he decided his mind was too agitated to write. His thoughts were on his stones.

He walked down to the library to see his cabinet and found Ananias with a book.

"What are you reading?" he asked.

Ananias looked up and showed him the book's spine.

"Rousseau. Interesting choice." Jacques-Louis said, drawing near to his cabinet. "Do you know Askesis will adopt the British Mineralogical Society?"

"No, sir," Ananias said.

"Indeed. Many changes are ahead of us, Ananias. Soon the Askesian Society will cease to exist as such."

Ananias jumped from his seat. "Impossible! How could—"

"No need to worry, my friend, it's all for the good. Sit down."

Ananias sat back with a deep frown on his forehead. Jacques-Louis sat across him.

"The Askesian Society isn't having the impact we expected. And one of the reasons is that its mission is too broad to attract the attention of the minds we want to recruit. We're no match for the Royal or the Linnean Societies. So we're planning to disband this particular society and form others with more specific areas of interest."

"Like what?"

"Like a geological society, for example. Or a mineralogical society. We'll establish them as formal societies with open membership."

Ananias was still frowning.

"What is it?" Jacques-Louis said.

"What about the cause?"

"We will keep working for the cause, my friend!"

Ananias put the book aside and passed a hand through his hair.

"Open membership?"

"That's right."

"What about me? I have no expertise in science."

Jacques-Louis leaned forward. "You're important to the cause, my friend. We'll find the right place for you to fit in."

Ananias mumbled and took his book again, sparking an idea in Jacques-Louis's mind.

"The Geological Society will probably need a curator for its museum and a librarian for its book collection. And you, my friend, feel at home among books."

PART III

"See to it that no one takes you captive through hollow and deceptive philosophy, which depends on human tradition and the basic principles of this world rather than on Christ."

Colossians 2:8

"The [Darwinian] revolution began when it became obvious that the earth was very ancient rather than having been created only 6,000 years ago. This finding was the snowball that started the whole avalanche."

Ernst Mayr, evolutionary biologist, Harvard University

TWENTY-TWO

LONDON - WEDNESDAY, 2 MARCH, 1836

4:36 A.M.

Oatts knew his eyes were open but he couldn't see any-thing. The room so dark, his mouth so dry. His head a ball of pain. His body too numb to do anything but close his eyes. So he did.

6:56 A.M.

A ticklish sensation on his nose stirred Oatts awake. He saw a cockroach under a faint light. He felt so weak he couldn't move. The nausea was insufferable. And the throbbing head-ache. What had happened to him? His eyes hurt—better to close them again.

11:10 A.M.

The dampness on his mouth pulled Oatts from the gloomy place he wandered in his dream. His tongue reached out for more but then retracted when the liquid burnt the back of his throat. His head spun with intense dizziness and he felt like he was falling—but he already lay on the dirty floor.

"Wake up, dog!"

Oatts breathed in with pain. His face was wet and stank

of cheap liquor. He was sure he would vomit any second now.

"That's it, dog, listen up!"

Oatts tried to look up without success. He felt something like a boot sticking in between his abdomen and the floor. The boot pushed him over onto his back—his head banged against the wood, sending a bolt of pain through his body. On the verge of passing out, he breathed in. The breath hurt, but the oxygen seemed to clear his head. His hands were tied behind his back. He tried to move his feet—also tied.

A scarred man stared at him. Victor Ananias Shaw. The librarian.

"Who sent you?" Shaw barked, his lips twisting awkwardly. "Sedgwick? Lyell?"

Each word trailed in his mouth and ended with a hiss. The speech of a drunkard. Shaw began to pace, coming in and out of Oatts's sight.

"They all want to get rid of me."

Not only was he drunk but he spoke like a madman. His hands flapped around, out of control.

"Since they got that idiot Lloyd they don't need me any more. Think I'm too old to protect the interests of the society. But I proved them wrong! And what do they do? I ask you! They spat on my face and threw me out! Ha! Lyell was furious, said the boy was harmless. But he knew too much and wouldn't stop. Yes, I saw him. Reckless kid."

He continued pacing and moving his chin up and down as if nodding at some interior voice Oatts couldn't hear. He put the bottle to his mouth and gulped.

"That viper Sedgwick! Told me to get out and never come back. I swear I'll kill him next! He got lucky once, but his days are numbered! I'd like to see Sedgwick die slowly—just like you."

Shaw started laughing, but the laughter gradually turned into a violent coughing spell. The spell paused and Shaw spat a large ball of phlegm to the floor that made Oatts wince.

"Agh!" Shaw bellowed at the empty bottle and cursed profusely. He kicked and shuffled things around, raised every bottle he found and reached with his tongue for any drop left. After a few minutes, he broke the last bottle against a wall, lifted the mattress and pulled a bill from under it.

"I'll be back later, dog!" Shaw said. "You're not dead when I come back, you'll wish you were."

12:36 P.M.

"Why did you tell the coachman to go by Somerset House, my lad?" Cole said.

"There's something I must look into. It occurred to me last night at the inn. If I'm right, we'll find strong evidence that the librarian killed my friend."

Cole shrugged. "I trust you know what you're doing."

"Thanks."

Daniel glanced at the street. The coach rolled down the Strand. Uneasiness gripped him as he realized he was heading into harm's way. If the superintendent was keeping a close watch on Lloyd, then Shaw had to be the man who tried to kill him at Hyde Park. But for all Daniel knew he could be following orders from the society's leadership. With Shaw now in the scene, Lloyd's role in all this had become a mystery. That's why he had to go to Somerset House and find out.

The coach halted.

"Come with me, Mr. Cole."

Daniel led Cole to the modest museum of the Geological Society. Other than the beak-nosed clerk, they didn't see anyone around.

"Is this your first time here?"

Cole looked around. "It is, my lad."

Daniel walked to one of the cabinets that held the society's rock collection and looked through the glass.

"See this, Mr. Cole."

Cole stood besides Daniel.

"There," Daniel said, pointing inside the cabinet. "Just what I thought. Some of the volcanic rocks are missing. You can see where they used to be. And besides the curator, only the librarian had easy access to the keys to the cabinet. Shaw took the rocks and used one to kill Alex. Then he threw another one through the window the night of the anniversary. So it wasn't Lloyd after all."

Daniel began pacing around the museum.

"But Lloyd was smuggling documents out of the library while Shaw was gone. Then Lloyd asked Greenough about Shaw and Oatts saw Lloyd at Shaw's place." He looked at Cole. "Why would he ask Greenough about Shaw if they were working together? It doesn't make any sense to—"

"Daniel?"

They turned to see Sedgwick standing by the door.

12:51 P.M.

Cole followed Daniel's gaze. A refined gentleman had entered the museum.

"Reverend Sedgwick!" Daniel said.

So was this Sedgwick? Something stirred inside Cole's body. At last he was meeting the enemy of the Christian faith. An impeccably dressed enemy. But appearances could be deceiving. Scripture says the devil disguises himself as an angel of light.

"What are you doing?" Sedgwick said.

Daniel narrowed his eyes and stared at Sedgwick. Sedgwick frowned when Daniel didn't answer and turned to Cole.

"And who are you, sir?"

"I, sir," Cole said, thrusting his chest forward, "am the enemy of your impious doctrines, the denouncer of your false teachings regarding the scriptures and geology."

"A religious fanatic. Daniel, what is this man doing here?"

Cole saw Daniel's lips trembling. "He's my friend and I brought him here."

Sedgwick raised his brows. "And since when do you mingle with such perverse friends?"

Lord, what a selfishly proud man.

Daniel took one step forward. "I'd rather mingle with him than with murderers and conspirators!"

Sedgwick's face twisted with incredulity, then changed to contempt.

"Very well, then. You've chosen your friends and your foes poorly. It will cost you."

Cole gaped at them. He could hardly believe what he was hearing.

"What now? Will you try to kill me again?" Daniel said.

"Don't be a fool! Nobody's trying to kill you. But you're playing with fire, just as the Bolds did last night."

"What?" Daniel said.

Sedgwick radiated pure evil. Cole felt a heaviness just being in this man's presence. What could poor Daniel do against him?

"You don't know, do you?" Sedgwick said. "A tragic fire consumed their house last night. I heard there were hardly any survivors." He gave Cole a hard look, spun, and left.

12:53 P.M.

Oatts's wrists hurt from struggling against the rope. He wouldn't be surprised if they were bleeding. The bump on his head was tender, and pain struck him whenever it touched a hard surface. In the last hour he'd tried to stay awake and remember all that had happened before he lost consciousness, but there were definitely missing parts. His last encounter with Shaw, however, was vivid in his mind. He felt certain the man intended to kill him.

How was he going to get out of this one? He'd escaped danger more than once, but he didn't feel he could do it himself just now.

His right hand went numb and his feet tingled. Perhaps it was the position of his body, but perhaps it was something worse. One of the first Bobbies to join the Metropolitan Police, John Harris, hit his head with a treadmill stone and ended up paralyzed. Oatts just hoped his limbs would work when the time came to beat down the librarian.

He needed help. He glanced at the door. It couldn't be locked, he'd cracked the lock when he broke in.

Oatts rolled toward the door, trying to keep his head from touching the floor. The trash and empty bottles were in the way of his sides and legs. He twisted like a snake, trying to knock them away, and hit his bump against the floor. He winced and groaned. This ain't working.

Circling around, Oatts put his feet around a leg of the bed and pushed his torso up. He was almost in a sitting position when the door opened.

"Where do you think you're going?" Shaw bellowed.

A kick on his back made Oatts arch his torso—his head hit the floor again. Then came more kicks to his side and stomach. Shaw grabbed him by the coat and shoved him to the back of the room. The drunk attacker lost his balance and fell over Oatts, who began to lose consciousness again.

Shaw opened his mouth and Oatts closed his eyes at the sight of the vomit that washed over him. He wiggled his hips to break free from Shaw's weight. He managed to stick his head and gasp, but the librarian encumbered the rest of his body.

Great. Shaw had passed out, but Oatts knew damn well he himself couldn't move an inch.

2:10 P.M.

From the distance, Daniel could see what was left of the Bold's house—barely a fourth of the structure remained standing. The cruel Sedgwick had not given him details, and dread filled his chest. Although Cole had offered to come, Daniel refused. For whatever reason he'd decided to face this alone.

When the cab halted before the pathway to the house, Daniel realized he had been biting his nails. "God, don't let her be dead."

The acrid smell of burnt wood hung in the air. Daniel walked down the path, avoiding men carrying objects back and forth. They were probably from the insurance company, inspecting what could be salvaged from the fire.

Once in front of the blackened ruins, a grim mood overcame Daniel and his shoulders felt heavy. Unbelievable. The honor and pride the Bold family drew from this mansion had been destroyed with the building. He shook his head, then noticed Lord Bold contemplating the same scene from one corner of the front yard, arms crossed over his chest.

"My lord!" Daniel called.

Lord Bold looked back with his usual impassive expression, but Daniel could tell there was something different in his eyes. He nodded and turned back to the house.

Daniel stood by him. "What happened?"

"What do you think? Scrope's vengeance."

Daniel grimaced. "Is everyone all right, my lord? What about Susan? Emily and Lady Bold?"

"I thought you knew," Lord Bold said, raising one brow. "My daughters and their companions are at your cousin's house."

Daniel suddenly felt free of an unbearable burden. Thank God, Susan was alive. But—

"My wife died in the fire."

A dozen images of Lady Bold passed through Daniel's mind in one second.

"I'm deeply sorry, sir. What a terrible loss."

Although his voice sounded almost neutral, it hadn't carried the same sense of detachment as when Lord Bold spoke of Alex's death a few days ago.

Lord Bold stared at the burnt house with an unreadable expression.

"They will be sorry," he said.

Daniel blinked. At last he saw some emotion in that face—raw anger.

"I saw him, Daniel."

"Who, sir?"

"Lloyd." Now his voice was deep and raspy, as if he were speaking from some dank cave deep within him. "I saw him and chased him away but didn't realize he'd already started the fire."

Daniel pressed both palms against his temples. "We must tell the police. Does Superintendent Oatts know? He—"

"No," Lord Bold said. "The superintendent's job was to keep something like this from happening. He failed and is not to be trusted. I'll take care of this myself."

Daniel raised his brows. "How, my lord? These men are dangerous beyond—"

"I know, Daniel. There are ways to deal with them, ways only I can accomplish." His tone was now the one Daniel knew so well. "Please, just watch over my daughter. Prove you are worthy of her."

3:25 P.M.

Daniel's body trembled with anticipation as he knocked at his cousin's door. Now more than ever he was convinced that he and Susan were meant to be together. Even in their trials they could identify. They both had brothers who'd died unjustly. She had lost her mother and he his father. No one could understand what she was going through better than him. They would be drawn closer together now.

Mr. Welsh opened the door with a somber face. In fact the whole house seemed invaded by a gloom. The hallways, usually empty but well lit, were eerie.

"Where's my cousin?" Daniel asked Mr. Welsh.

"In the study, sir."

Daniel had thought about asking for Susan but decided to speak with Richard first—he wanted to find out why Lord Bold had sent Susan here.

Richard had built a study in a peculiar place in the house, so Daniel had to go around the stairs and into a hallway on the back, then exit the building into the garden and walk back into the study through another door. Richard wanted to see his garden while in the study and had designed his home accordingly. When Daniel came to the door Richard sat staring through the window.

"Daniel! You're back so soon!" Richard came to Daniel and gave him a hug. "How's your father?"

"He died. Very soon after I arrived."

Richard gasped. "Oh, cousin!"

"But I had the chance to talk to him, and—well…" Remembering that night brought tears to Daniel's eyes. He surprised himself when he spoke again. "I believe he's in a better place now."

Richard nodded and sat back by the window, having waved Daniel into a comfortable chair.

"These are difficult times," he said. "Not that saying so covers it."

"I spoke to Lord Bold today," Daniel said. "He told me about the fire."

Richard said, "Another tragedy."

"Lord Bold said Susan is staying here, how did that happen? Did she come looking for me?"

Daniel didn't like the smile that formed in Richard's face.

"Not exactly," Richard said. "I happened to find out about the fire and offered them my house."

"How?" Daniel said.

"How what?"

"How did you know about the fire? Who told you?"

"Oh, for goodness sake!" Richard raised his hands, palms out. "I was there, all right? I was there through the whole thing. I damn near suffocated trying to save Lady Bold!"

Daniel stared at him. Of course he almost suffocated. He was a hero.

"So why didn't you say so from the beginning?"

"Well, I didn't. Save her." Richard said this staring out the window.

Daniel frowned. His cousin was acting strangely. What was his business at the Bold's house, anyway?

"I must speak with Susan," Daniel said.

"I'm afraid that's not possible now."

"What?" Daniel stared at him. Unbelievable. "Why not?"

"She's resting. Went to bed a few hours ago and doesn't want to speak to anyone. That's what Mary said."

Daniel eyed his cousin. "Is that so?"

"It's true," Richard said. "Won't even speak to me!"

"And what's that supposed to mean? You barely know her. Why would you assume she'd prefer to speak to you over anybody else?"

"That's not what I said."

Daniel sighed. "Tell me the truth, cousin."

Richard stood up, and Daniel followed suit. He leaned his torso backwards as Richard's face came too close to his. "You don't want the truth, cousin," Richard said and walked away.

4:40 P.M.

As the sun set, the crowd at the Metropolitan Police headquarters thinned down. Daniel leaned against the wall outside Oatts's office, tapping his fingers and trying to remember a tune to whistle—anything to keep his mind from thinking about Richard and Susan.

He peered down the hallway. Where could he be?

To pass time, he checked his moneybag. Almost empty. He should stop taking cabs everywhere.

A bobby who had come by a couple of times before walked up to the superintendent's office. As he had the last few times, the bobby slowed down, glanced at the closed door, and walked away without saying anything. This time Daniel called him.

"Hey, sir!"

The bobby turned around. "Huh?"

The towering man had some quirkiness about him that made Daniel smile.

"Are you looking for Superintendent Oatts?"

"Aye, sir."

"I am too," Daniel said. "Do you have any idea where he might be?"

The bobby walked closer to him. "I 'aven't seen 'im since yesterday, sir. This isn't like the boss. You can count on 'im to always report to the chief every day."

The bobby had genuine concern in his face. How intriguing. If Oatts had gone chasing Lloyd, anything could have happened to him.

"Do you know where he was going the last time you saw him?" Daniel said.

"Yes, sir, but why should I tell you?"

Daniel looked at the bobby in the eyes.

"My name is Daniel Young and I've been helping the superintendent with the murder investigation of Alexander Bold, who was my best friend."

The bobby grinned and his eyes lit up. "Aye. The boss did mention you! I'm William, but the boss calls me Willy."

"Pleased to meet you, Willy."

Willy shook Daniel's hand. "The boss said 'e was goin' to Islington."

Islington? There was only one reason Daniel could think for Oatts to go to Islington.

5:15 P.M.

George Scrope passed a hand over his coat and straightened his cravat before resuming his walk. He turned left through one of the passageways in Westminster Hall that connected the burned down section of the building with the temporary quarters of the House of Commons. He hated to walk through the ugly passage but it was the fastest way, and he didn't want to be late for that evening's session.

As he emerged, three men in dark clothes stepped out from behind columns.

"In a rush, are you?" one of them said. The shadow of the man's hat covered most of his face, but Scrope could see a thin mustache and a small scar under his chin.

Scrope frowned and kept walking. "Excuse me." He tried to squeeze between them but they stood one against the other, blocking his way. Scrope gulped. Why did this happen precisely when Lloyd wasn't with him?

"Come with us," thin mustache said, grabbing Scrope's shoulder and pushing him back. The two other men surrounded him under the dim light.

"No! Leave me—"

A gloved hand covered Scrope's mouth. He felt his arms pulled backward and a fist—from thin mustache—punching his stomach. He gasped.

"We have a message from a friend in the House of Lords," thin mustache said.

Scrope widened his eyes. A *friend*? He took a deep breath and spoke despite the pain in his belly.

"What message?"

"This one."

Another, harder punch to his stomach. Scrope felt the pain run all the way to his back. His abdomen burned. The men dragged him back through the passageway to an unused section of the building and blindfolded and gagged him. Panic took hold of him. What would they do to him next?

"Don't worry," a voice said. "We'll spare your noble face."

Scrope heard laughter. Then followed the worst pain he had ever felt. A blow—it felt like a kick—to his testicles. He only had time to cringe for a second before he was thrown onto the dirty floor and kicked like a football, again and again.

Unable to scream because of the gag, Scrope moaned and cried. Whoever sent these men would surely pay with his life.

After a whole minute, the kicking stopped. Every inch of his body screamed with pain. He felt a warm stinking breath near his ear.

"Your friend sends his condolences," thin mustache whispered, "for the death of the Republic."

I curse you, Lord Bold!

5:35 P.M.

The pain subsided enough for Scrope to breathe regularly and try to get up. He took off the blindfold and struggled to untie the knot of the gag. When it came off, he threw it away, cursing.

He pushed himself to a sitting position. The pain in his sides made him scream, and the sound echoed in the dark chamber. A hole in the outer wall let the light of a gas lamp enter, revealing a few masonry tools lying on the floor.

Scrope crawled to the nearest wall and inched his way up. Every muscle below his neck ached horribly. The suggestion that the Republic was dead infuriated him.

Groaning, he limped toward the passageway. Soon the pain in his muscles made him dread every next step. But perhaps there was still a chance to catch up with the imbeciles who'd battered him. He'd have the police arrest them in no time.

The deserted alley seemed miles, but Scrope reached the other end after ten minutes. Instead of turning left toward the House of Commons, he walked down through another hallway that led outside. There were usually a couple of bobbies stationed there.

Scrope quickened his pace. The evening wind blew on his face. He was near the exit.

At the distance, Scrope saw three helmets. The bobbies stood chatting by the stairs.

"Officer," Scrope called. His voice came out like a little girl's cry. He cleared his throat and tried again. "Officer!"

The bobbies turned to him and one of them walked over. "Sir?"

Scrope breathed deeply, but even that hurt, and he moaned. He put his hands on his waist, exhausted.

"I've been attacked by three men in dark clothes.."

252

"Three men, you say?" the bobby said. "No one's entered or left except for MPs, sir. Are you sure?"

Scrope grunted. "Of course! They—"

He looked up. The bobby had a thin mustache and a scar on his chin.

5:55 P.M.

Oatts's eyes popped open. He'd fallen asleep again, but the odor of vomit and the suffocating weight of Shaw's body woke him. His head throbbed and his right arm had gone completely numb.

He groaned and tried to shake Shaw off. His body hardly moved. He tried with his legs, bumping his knees against the gross librarian, who snorted and woke. In the scant white light that filtered through the window, Oatts saw the large figure sit straight. His tormentor was sober.

Shaw glanced around him and cocked his head when he saw Oatts lying on the floor next to him. He frowned and bent over Oatts, examining his face. Few people ever scared Oatts, but the librarian's eyes were vicious.

"You're a goner," Shaw said between clenched teeth.

5:56 P.M.

"Thank you for coming, Mr. Cole," Daniel said. "It was easier to find your church than to find the inn."

"Glad to serve, my lad."

From his vantage point at the corner of the street, Daniel could see everyone coming in and out of Gray's Inn. In the past twenty minutes they hadn't seen anyone enter or leave.

"Are you sure the superintendent came here?" Cole said.

"Where else? I don't know how he found the lead about Shaw, but he's very smart."

"What's your plan?"

Daniel bit his upper lip. "I don't know," he said. "I'll trust my instincts."

"Trust the Holy Spirit instead," Cole said.

"Huh?" Daniel said.

"Just pray and believe you'll receive what you ask for."

Pray? Easier said than done. But one way or the other, Cole would push him to it.

Daniel muttered, "God, I need your help tonight. Show me what to do."

Cole nodded with a wide grin. Daniel turned back toward the Inn and saw a girl at the entrance. She was waving them over. What could she want? Had Oatts sent her?

Cole patted Daniel's back. "You see? God is showing you the path."

Daniel felt the hairs of his arms rising. Was God really guiding him?

The pastor pushed him gently. "I'll wait here and pray."

Daniel approached the hollow-cheeked girl.

"Lookin' for a place to stay, mister?" she said in a high-pitched, sweet voice.

"Do you know if a man called Victor Shaw is staying here?"

The girl eyed him from head to toe. "Are you p'leec'man too?"

Daniel raised his brows. "No, why? Did a policeman come by asking for Mr. Shaw?"

The girl nodded. "I think that's the nasty man at number twelve. The p'leec'man went up yesterday but I ain't seen 'im leave."

Daniel widened his eyes. "Is Mr. Shaw up there?"

"The man in twelve? Aye."

"Oatts!" He felt frantic. "Where is twelve?"

The girl's lips trembled and she stepped back.

"Where?" Daniel raised his voice.

The girl pointed. "Second story, sir."

Daniel swung the door open and stepped inside. The foyer was shadowed but he could see the stairs by the innkeeper's counter. He climbed the steps two at a time.

At the top he waited a moment, slowing his breath, feeling the sweat in his hands and the tingling in his legs. He thought about Shaw's scarred face and the strength he'd displayed carrying heavy books at the library. If Oatts had been overpowered, what chance did he have? He'd never picked a fight in his life, though he'd witnessed many.

A lone candle lit the landing. Daniel took it and walked down the hallway. When he reached 12, he blew out the candle and dropped it behind him. He crouched and moved his ear to the door.

"Ready to die?"

Daniel gulped. It was Shaw's voice but with a harshness he'd never heard before, full of hatred. The door swung in a few inches as he laid a hand on the knob. Daniel heard a gasp. Then heavy steps, increasingly close. He stood fast and his knees popped. Right before the door opened he slid back into the shadows of the hallway.

Daniel leaned against the door of 10, holding his breath, tensing his muscles till they hurt. Shaw stuck his head out like a tiger smelling prey. Only his profile was visible against the backdrop of a window at the end of the hall.

God, don't let him see me.

After five excruciating seconds, Shaw's head disappeared. The door slammed.

Daniel sighed. He had to go in. There'd been enough deaths already. But how would he face the big man? He needed a weapon.

He grasped the knob of 10. Locked.

A new sound from 12 stopped him cold. It sounded like furniture being moved. What was he doing? Daniel crouched and pushed his palm against the door of 12. It didn't budge.

He must have put the bed against the door. Now what? Knock?

Thump, thump. Faint moans. It had to be Oatts.

Daniel bit his upper lip. No time to waste. He pushed with his body against the door, but it still didn't move. The thumping continued. He looked at the window. Maybe.

He searched for the candle on the floor and plucked it out of its metal base. Dropping the candle, he tucked the base in his pocket and walked to the window.

With the soft pull of a latch, the window swung open in two parts. Daniel looked down to the lower roof of the contiguous building and winced. The window to Shaw's room was three or four feet away to his right, but there was no ledge he could use to get to it.

Daniel scowled and considered the window. Each section consisted of a single glass panel in a wooden frame. He pulled the right mid-section toward him and broke the glass with the candle's metal base. He didn't care about the noise any more. Oatts didn't have much time. The broken glass fell on the roof below.

Daniel pulled hard on the window frame—it felt sturdy enough to hold his weight. Another moan from 12. He climbed out onto the frame, putting his right foot where the glass used to be and the left on the wall's edge. He curled his right arm around the top of the wooden frame and held the candle's metal base in his left hand. He only had one chance to make this right.

"God, let this work."

He pushed himself forward with a kick from his left foot. The window frame swung on its hinges, propelling Daniel toward Shaw's window. The candle's metal base tapped against the glass, shattering it with an ear-splitting noise. The momentum brought Daniel back to his original position at the hallway window. He pushed himself outward again and the window frame swung with a crackling noise. Daniel's weight was loosening the hinges. He saw the broken window approaching fast and lowered his head, aiming for a dive into room 12.

The remaining pieces of glass in the window cut through Daniel's coat, stinging his arms and upper back. His body landed on the floor with a loud thump, but the pain of the fall paled in comparison with the sting of his cuts. A flickering candle reflected on the shattered glass.

Groaning, Daniel lifted his head and saw Shaw staring at him. Oatts lay on the floor, bleeding from his mouth and nose.

"I—I killed you!" Shaw shouted.

Without thinking, Daniel charged full strength against the librarian, grabbed him around his waist, and smashed his body against a wall. Shaw's head bounced, his body jerked, and his legs gave way. Daniel released him. Shaw slumped on the floor, his back still against the wall. He moaned and shook his head as if to clear it.

Daniel stepped back. He looked at Oatts and knelt beside him. "Superintendent, hold on. I'll get you out of here alive." Oatts eyes were half closed and his body stiff. "You hear me, Oatts? Stay with me. You're not dying tonight!"

Daniel looked up. Shaw was bent over on his hands and knees, breathing rapidly. He straightened up like a waking lion.

"I'll kill you this time!"

Seeing the librarian like this was hard to fathom. When did poor old Shaw become such a beast?

Oatts moaned and Daniel glanced at him again. An empty glass bottle lay besides his head. Daniel took the bottle by the neck and jumped to his feet. In two swift steps he was at the bed blocking the door. He smashed the bottom of the bottle against the headboard.

Shaw halted when he saw the weapon in Daniel's hands. "You won't dare," Shaw said. "Have you ever killed anybody, Mr. Young? Bet you don't have the courage."

"Then bet your life if you please," Daniel said. "You killed my best friend and tried to kill me twice. I have plenty of motivation."

Shaw hissed. Daniel held the broken bottle before him like a sword. His fear was gone. Cole must be praying.

With one eye fixed on the panting Shaw and one on the door, Daniel pushed the bed before him with his legs. It moved barely a couple of inches. But he had to clear the door somehow.

Just as Shaw dove for a bottle, Daniel grasped the bed's headboard and shoved the bed hard in his direction. It slammed into Shaw's head. Daniel took one step and kicked the bottle from Shaw's hand—it flew across the room and shattered against the wall.

The librarian growled and charged Daniel, who shifted to one side and swung the bottle in front of him. He felt the glass slicing flesh. Was it a death wound?

Shaw bumped against the door and turned, one hand on his bloody face. The glass had cut him forehead to cheek. His right eye bled in torrents. The librarian hesitated for a second, then opened the door behind him and ran out.

Daniel exhaled and slumped to the floor.

6:33 P.M.

Cole's heart drummed within him when the man with dead eyes bolted out the inn, his face and shirt drenched in blood.

Was the blood his or Daniel's? In the poor light of the street lamps Cole couldn't tell if there were serious wounds, though the man kept a hand pressed to one eye. He knew he should run and see what had happened to Daniel. But concern for this other man stirred his soul and robbed him of any peace.

The man was a murderer, wasn't he? If so he was even more in need of God's mercy. Then again he seemed dangerous, and it would be wiser to stay away. No, his duty called him to minister to every man and trust in the Lord's protection.

Cole shook his head to silence the conflict in his mind and followed the man with his eyes. He remembered his name: Shaw.

"Lord, have mercy on his soul."

He watched Shaw walk over to a tramp sitting on a bench in the street—an old lady—and snatch her shawl. The woman started to protest but screamed and fled after seeing Shaw's face. Shaw wrapped the shawl around his head and trotted away.

Cole rushed into the inn and instinctively moved up the stairs. All was dark but for the moonlight at the end of the hallway. He walked toward the light, found an open door, and stepped inside. Daniel was bent over a man on the floor. Cole knelt beside him.

"Dear God!" Cole's heart sank at the bloody grimace of the poor man before them.

"We must help him, Mr. Cole."

Cole nodded. "Let's take him to my place. I'll care for him."

7:00 P.M.

Scrope took the cup Sedgwick's butler offered him, then shifted in his chair and sipped the tea. He was sure the soreness would drive away all sleep tonight. "We must finish him, Adam," he said. "We must finish him now!"

"Patience, George," Sedgwick said. "If Lord Bold has decided to retaliate like this, he must be quite confident. We must finish him when he least expects it. He may think he's intimidated you and that we'll stay away from him."

Scrope said, "I'm not so sure about that."

"Let us just wait and see," Sedgwick said. "My concern is now with Daniel Young."

"Who?" Scrope frowned.

"Young Bold's friend, the one who survived the librarian's assault."

"What about him?" Scrope took another sip of tea.

"He's been inquiring about the murder. It seems he knows more than we thought. I'm sure he's Lord Bold's ally in all this."

Scrope sighed. "So we have another subject to eliminate? We're seeking a revolution without blood. The occasional casualty doesn't bother me if it's for the sake of the republic, but we must be careful not to start a bloodbath."

"I know," Sedgwick said. "Many who sympathize with our cause might frown upon our recent tactics, even distance themselves from the society. Nonetheless we must do something. Don't you agree?"

Scrope nodded. If the pain weren't so bad he might be able to think more clearly. He gulped the rest of his tea and turned to speak over his shoulder.

"What do you say, Stephen?"

"I'll kill the peeler," Lloyd said.

Scrope had forgotten about the superintendent. "What about Daniel Young?"

Lloyd shrugged. "I'll kill him too."

Scrope smiled and gave the empty teacup to the butler.

TWENTY-THREE

LONDON - THURSDAY, 3 MARCH, 1836

4:07 A.M.

Shaw woke up drenched in cold sweat, disoriented, wary of his surroundings.

Where was he?

A familiar smell, humidity stains on the ceiling. His flat. Did the landlady see him come in? He tried to remember how he got here. No, there was no way she could have seen him.

"Agh!" He'd done his best to clean and stitch the wound but had nothing to treat the pain. It only grew worse.

He touched his forehead and was relieved at its coolness. At least he wasn't running a fever.

He stared at the ceiling, thinking of better times. If only he could go to the library and work again as before. But too much blood covered his hands now.

Drowsiness settled in. Weakness numbed his limbs. His eyelids closed.

No, no, no!

He grabbed his hair and yanked so he wouldn't fall asleep. He dreaded dreams of his drunken stepfather beating him, then dragging him to church—sinning and praying to get even. Or dreams of the comte and his guillotine.

He hated sleeping sober. Only alcohol running through his veins would drown those dreams in oblivion. And only alcohol would give him the courage to smash his enemies.

He sat up. The landlady must have some liquor in her flat.

7:52 A.M.

"I really 'ope Pastor Cole comes to see you today, my man."

He looked at the ugly, heavy woman with half-opened eyes. The nausea wasn't as bad this morning, and breathing had become easier. But his head still throbbed if he moved even a little.

"I ain't got no more food for you," the woman said. "And I don't know if you'll live. But the pastor can prepare you for 'eaven."

The poor hut shook with her every movement, and he feared it would fall on him at any moment. This place was so strange, so not-like-home.

He tried to talk but his mouth was so dry his lips wouldn't even separate. Who are you? He wanted to ask her. Why am I here?

9:00 A.M.

Sedgwick was uneasy when he saw two redcoats stationed at the north entrance to Somerset House. But after all, Somerset House hosted more than the Geological Society.

He quickened his pace and entered the society's apartments. The sooner he finished his businesses with Lyell the better. Much had to be done before his return to Cambridge. His stay in London had been long and turbulent enough already.

Sedgwick's muscles tensed. Two more redcoats stood at the door to Lyell's office. One approached him.

"Are you Mr. Lyell, president of the society?"

"I'm Reverend Adam Sedgwick, immediate past president. Mr. Lyell should arrive soon. Is everything all right, officer?"

"Sergeant."

"I'm sorry, Sergeant. Is there something I can help you with?"

"I must speak with Mr. Lyell," the sergeant said, eyeing Sedgwick from toe to head. "But you may stay and answer our questions as well."

What a hateful man. Sedgwick despised the king's army with all his might.

"Adam?"

Sedgwick turned to face Lyell, who strode toward them with a deep frown.

"What's happening?" Lyell said.

Sedgwick shrugged. "They—"

"Are you Mr. Lyell?" the sergeant said.

"Yes—yes, I am."

"Sergeant Wolfe. I must ask you some questions."

Lyell took his hat off and raised one brow at Sedgwick. "Of course, please come into my office."

The four men entered Lyell's small quarters. Lyell and Sedgwick sat, but the soldiers remained standing. Sedgwick's uneasiness mounted.

The sergeant stared at Lyell. "His majesty has been informed of the presence of dangerous political radicals among members of your society."

Sedgwick gulped. Lord Bold was behind this.

Lyell looked at Sedgwick and cleared his throat. "The Geological Society is a scientific organization, not a political—"

"You must provide—immediately—a list of all your members to be examined by the Army. And you must inform us of any member associated with the Friends of the People."

Sedgwick gaped at the sergeant. The Friends of the People? He hadn't heard about that political society in years, and as far as he knew, more than one group of underground radicals called themselves by that name.

"What is the basis of these demands?" he said. "Who made such accusations about the Geological Society?"

The sergeant looked at Sedgwick for one second and then faced Lyell again.

"Until this investigation is finished, you are barred from holding any public meetings or assemblies."

Sedgwick jumped to his feet. What an abuse! "You have no right to do this."

The redcoat ignored him. "Do you have anything to confess, Mr. Lyell?"

Lyell shook his head—his expression was one of complete astonishment.

"Very well, then." The sergeant nodded toward the other soldier. "Officer Gaines will take the membership records from you. An official investigator will visit you in a few days."

With that, the sergeant turned and left the office.

9:40 A.M.

Daniel woke to discover his back glued to bed sheets. He ripped the sheets from his skin and the pain made him scream. He stared at the bundle in his hands. The sheets were a mess of dried blood. Then he remembered. His wounds from last night. He'd forgotten about them in his anxiety to save Oatts.

Daniel felt the cuts with his hand. The one on his upper back still oozed blood—he probably tore the healing skin when he pulled the sheets away. The cut on his arm was scabbing. He grinned. He still couldn't believe he'd faced Shaw and rescued Oatts.

He hoped the superintendent was all right. Finding a doctor in Islington willing to see him had turned out to be a challenge—impossible, actually, since they found only an apothecary. Islington wasn't the best borough in which to get hurt.

He slid off the bed and searched for his pants. The shirt would have to wait until he washed off all the blood. He walked out of his room and heard a woman's voice coming from down the stairs. Of course. Susan was there. He rushed to the bathroom. Now he had a reason to get cleaned up.

9:45 A.M.

Sobriety was killing him. Shaw flapped his hands around his head as if trying to knock down the flock of thoughts in his mind, mumbling incoherencies.

He stumbled through the room, opened his wardrobe, and pulled out a mirror. His face was covered in sweat. The skin around the wound was turning red and felt painfully swollen.

"I called this curse upon myself."

He flapped his hands.

"My hands are stained with death."

He flapped his hands with greater vigor.

"I must act in penitence."

His arms swirled around his head.

"No! I must drink. I'll kill the one who cut my eye."

Shaw fell against the wardrobe. He felt warm. Perhaps he was running a fever.

Two knocks on the door and a voice. "Mr. Shaw, is that you?"

The landlady. Shaw cursed under his breath.

"Mr. Shaw? Who's there?"

The knob began to move. But she shouldn't see him like this.

"Yes, it's me," Shaw said in a raspy voice.

"Oh, thank God, Mr. Shaw!" the landlady said. "I was so worried! Are you well?"

Shaw stood behind the wardrobe door. "Yes."

"I 'eard you scream—"

"I'm all right."

"Good! Do you need anything?"

I need you to go away.

"Do you want to come out?" she said.

"No!" he said, perhaps too harshly.

He heard the landlady gasp.

"I'm not ready." He faked a cough. "Still recovering."

"Oh, poor Mr. Shaw. I was really worried about you. You're always so polite, I 'ate seein' you sick. I'll bring you some food, Mr. Shaw, don't worry."

Shaw was about to protest but the sound of her footsteps faded away quickly down the stairs.

10:00 A.M.

She wasn't in the drawing room, the dining room, or any of the guest rooms. Daniel slapped his leg. Was it possible she'd left already?

He examined each corner of the house one last time and sighed in frustration. He hadn't yet visited the garden. Daniel walked out the back door and peered around the green lawn. No one.

He tried not to think about Susan and instead focus on what lay ahead. He had to visit Cole and Oatts—

He heard Richard's muffled voice, coming from the study. Who was he talking with?

Daniel hesitated. After yesterday's confrontation he was uncomfortable with the idea of facing his cousin. But he knocked once and opened the door. "Hey, Rich—"

Daniel froze in his place by the door when he saw Susan sitting in his cousin's favorite chair. She lifted her sweet sad eyes. She didn't smile nor say a word. She just looked at him for two seconds, then lowered her teary gaze to her lap, where she traced the patterns of her dress with one finger.

Richard barely raised a brow in acknowledgement of his presence, and Mary, who seemed to be in charge of Susan, didn't even look his way. In one corner of the study Emily and her nanny sat reading a book.

"Good morning," Daniel said. "I didn't know you were here."

"You slept late, cousin," Richard said. "Were you out celebrating?"

Daniel gave him a cold look. "I wouldn't call it that. I—"

"Anyway," Richard said, "this afternoon is Lady Bold's funeral and perhaps you can help with some of the details. That is if you've finished whatever you were doing last night."

What was he insinuating?

Daniel looked at Susan, but she seemed totally absorbed by her thoughts. She must be really suffering.

"I am so sorry for your loss, Susan," Daniel said. "I can relate completely."

"Thank you," she said without looking at him.

Richard knelt beside her and took her right hand between his.

"Susan, dear," he said in a nauseatingly sweet voice, "is there something you want me to do for you?"

Daniel could hardly believe his senses. What an obvious and shameless way of courting a woman. His woman. His face flushed.

Susan pulled her hand back from Richard and shook her head with a slight frown. At least she wasn't responding to him.

Richard stood, apparently untroubled by Susan's reaction. "Don't worry, I'll take care of you."

Daniel felt like grabbing Richard by his shirt and setting him straight, but he needed to borrow a few pounds. If his cousin didn't lend him money he'd have to walk to Islington.

"You look tired, miss," Mary told Susan. "Do you want to go up and rest?"

Daniel stared at Susan, longing to hear her voice again. Susan nodded and let Mary lead her out of the study. Daniel sighed as he saw her disappear.

Emily's nanny ushered her charge to the door.

"Can't we read some more?" Emily said.

"Let's read in the garden," the nanny said.

"So," Richard said once they were alone. "Where were you last night?"

Daniel smiled, reminding himself to be polite with Richard. "It's a long story. I went looking for Alex's killer."

Richard raised one brow. "Is that so?"

Daniel hated that skeptical tone. "I found the police superintendent gravely injured and had to subdue his attacker, then take the superintendent to a safe place and find a doctor."

Richard flattened a wrinkle on his shirt.

"I must follow up with him today," Daniel said. "Make sure he recovers." Daniel smiled. "But I need to borrow some money for the cab."

"You're out of money already? It's only the beginning of the month!"

Daniel knew he was going to get chided about it. But he couldn't tell his cousin he hadn't collected the earnings—and his commission—from one of the factories. He averted his gaze and let Richard ramble on about responsibility.

"If you waste your monthly earnings so easily," Richard said, "how can I trust you not to lose this house to a creditor when I leave it to you?"

How unfair to bring that up.

"I promise it won't happen again, Richard."

"Anyway, in light of recent events, I'm postponing my move to Switzerland. Who knows? Perhaps I will find a wife to take with me to the Alps."

Daniel blinked. A wife? Where did that idea come from?

Richard walked to the door and said over his shoulder, "There's money in the box in the top left drawer of my desk. Take what you need, cousin."

10:20 A.M.

Cole felt his eye twitching again. It often happened when he was worried. The superintendent grew less responsive as time passed. His wounds were healing but Cole feared something had been damaged inside his head. At the least Cole knew Oatts couldn't move his limbs.

"Gracious Lord, concede this man the strength to recover and be healed. I pray this paralysis is temporary, in Jesus's name."

Cole sighed. There wasn't much he could do but wait for a miracle—and try to prepare the superintendent for death.

"I know you can hear me, good man," Cole whispered in Oatts's ear. "Hear the eternal gospel of salvation."

Opening his Bible, Cole began to read.

"For I delivered unto you first of all that which I also received, how that Christ died for our sins according to the scriptures; and that he was buried, and that he rose again the third day according to the scriptures. For since by man came death, by man came also the resurrection of the dead. For as in Adam all die, even so in Christ shall all be made alive."

Cole glanced at the still face before him. He shuffled some pages. "For all have sinned, and come short of the glory of God. But if thou shalt confess with thy mouth the Lord Jesus, and shalt believe in thine heart that God hath raised him from the dead, thou shalt be saved. For with the heart man believeth unto righteousness; and with the mouth confession is made unto salvation. For the scripture saith, Whosoever believeth on him shall not be ashamed."

A knock on the door. Cole grumbled. What could be more important than the salvation of a soul? He didn't have time for—

The knocking continued. Perhaps it was Daniel.

Cole put the Bible on his desk and crossed the room to open the door.

"Pastor Cole!"

A woman from his church. What was her name? Lettie?

Cole smiled. "Good morning, child."

She took his arm. "It's Lottie, pastor Cole. Please, you must come and see my man."

Oh, yes. She'd been insisting. "Is your husband ill?" Cole said.

"No, sir, me 'usband died many years 'go. This is the man I found by the river."

"The river?" Cole frowned.

"Aye, pastor," she said. "Many days 'go I was walkin' near the Blackfriars Bridge and sees these bloody kids stealin' the clothes off a man on the riverbank. I shoos them away and find the man near dead, bad 'urts on 'is 'ead. So I feels sorry and carries 'im 'ome."

Cole glanced at the thin woman. "Did you carry him by yourself, mum?"

"Aye, but just to the street. Then a cabby 'elped. I live in number twenty-two."

"You've done a very good deed, mum," Cole said. "Just as Jesus taught us with the story of the Good Samaritan."

The woman looked down. "I did what I could, pastor, even shared my food with 'im. But I can't take care of my man any more."

Cole felt sorry for her. He looked back and saw Oatts on the cot and sighed.

"I can't go with you now, but I'll come as soon as I can. I must care for another hurt man now."

12:02 P.M.

"How long has he been sleeping?" Daniel said.

"Three hours since he last opened his eyes," Cole said.

"What if he doesn't wake up?"

"God's will be done. Let's have faith."

"I think we should take him to a hospital," Daniel said.

"I have no money for doctors."

"I'll worry about that. Where's the closest hospital?"

"St. Bartholomew's."

"All right," Daniel said. "I'll go fetch a cab."

1:55 P.M.

Daniel watched with surprise as a slender boy parked in the front yard of his house. He walked past the boy, who simply nodded and whistled a popular tune. How strange. Even stranger, the front door to the house was open.

He thought about interrogating the boy but decided against it. No time for that. He had to make it to Lady Bold's funeral—what would Susan think if he didn't? The house was eerily quiet. It seemed everyone had left. He rushed to his room in search of his black suit. He checked his wardrobe, his bags, every corner of the room—nothing. The last time he wore it was at his father's funeral. He remembered packing all his clothes—but he could picture it now: the black suit hanging on a chair in Norwich. Just marvelous. Now what?

271

Daniel paced around the room. He'd look ridiculous in one of Richard's suits, which were too short for him. He had a black morning coat, but that was hardly appropriate. He had no time and no money to buy a new suit. The only other man in the house right now was the butler. Daniel walked down the stairs. "Mr. Welsh!"

The butler ran out of the kitchen toward Daniel, who almost stumbled. Mr. Welsh never ran.

"Mr. Young!" the butler cried. "I'm so glad to see you!"

"Well, thanks."

The butler cleared his throat. "I apologize for my behavior, sir, but let me explain—once you tell me why you were calling, of course."

Daniel's curiosity had been aroused. "No, it's all right. What is it you need to explain?"

"Thank you, sir." The butler bowed his head. "Both my grandfather and my father served as butlers for distinguished families in London. It's a bit of a family tradition."

Daniel nodded. The suit. The funeral. He had no time for stories.

"Hence my brother works as a butler in the house of Reverend Sedgwick."

"Sedgwick?" Daniel remembered. "Of course, I remember Sedgwick's butler. In fact I thought you two were related the first time I saw him."

"Yes, sir," the butler said. "That's my brother."

"All right. What about him?"

"On my recent holiday I met with him and he mentioned a strange incident with a guest who disappeared from his house: you, sir."

Daniel thought it a funny coincidence, but why was it important now?

Mr. Welsh pulled a paper from his pocket. "My brother sent me a letter just now. He says there are two guests at his master's house." Mr. Welsh opened the letter and skimmed over it. "MP George Scrope and his aide, Lloyd. My brother heard them plotting against your life, sir."

Daniel stared at the letter, amazed at the odd way this news had reached him. It didn't surprise him that Scrope and Sedgwick were planning to kill him. Hadn't they tried already and failed?

"So Lloyd and Scrope are staying at Sedgwick's house?" Daniel said.

"Yes, sir."

What a shame Oatts wasn't up and well. They could set a trap for Lloyd and arrest him. Daniel bit his lower lip. He had to do something before they tried to kill him again—with or without Oatts. A plan began forming.

"Mr. Welsh," Daniel said. "Do you think we can have a messenger take a letter to your brother's master?"

"Indeed, sir. The messenger was still outside not too long ago."

3:00 P.M.

I should have died, Susan thought as they set the coffin down from the carriage.

She buried her face in her scarf and let the tears soak her cheeks. She felt as if thick fog was clouding her mind. There was no distraction, no consolation left. She would let the fog of sorrow surround her, strangle her.

She felt a hand on her elbow and turned. Richard with his twisted smile. Susan glanced around. Daniel hadn't come. Daniel, the only one who really loved her—at least that's what she'd believed—wasn't there for her. Perhaps he'd fallen in love with someone else. Perhaps that was why he'd gone on a pleasure trip and didn't even tell her, but sent his cousin to say he'd be away for a while. But he'd returned, hadn't he? Yes, and gone carousing while she almost died in the fire!

"Be strong, Susan," Richard whispered to her ear.

Susan ignored Richard and looked at her father's stern face. He stared at the coffin through narrowed eyes. Not a single tear shed, not one. How could he be so stone-hearted?

Susan followed her father's stare to the coffin. She sobbed. They hadn't let her see her mother's charred body—they said it was too horrible. She hadn't seen Alex's body either—it was probably in the ocean now or eaten by big fish and crabs.

3:05 P.M.

The woman lived in an old hut in the south side of Islington. The smell of raw sewage filled the air.

The one-room hut was well lit thanks to a foot-wide hole in the roof. The woman hunched over a pail of water at a corner opposite the cot, where the still body of a man stared at the roof.

"May the Lord bless this home," Cole said.

The woman turned with a wide smile. "Pastor Cole!"

He walked to the cot and looked into the man's blue eyes. His blond hair was a mess. He seemed to be around Daniel's age.

"Hullo, my lad," Cole said. "What's your name?"

The man returned Cole's stare, but once he opened his mouth, his whole face winced in apparent pain.

"'Tis the strangest thing, pastor," the woman said. "My man is wide awake but 'ardly can speak. Sometimes 'e complains about the pain in 'is 'ead."

Cole scratched his neck and bent over the bed to examine the man's cranium. He had fading bruises in the face and scabs all around the head.

"I don't believe this was the result of an accident," Cole said. "Someone did this intentionally. You don't have to speak, young man, just nod if you understand me."

He nodded.

"Good," Cole said. "Do you know where you are?"

He shook his head.

"Do you remember what happened to you?"

He shook his head again.

Cole rubbed his face. "My lad, it seems you've lost your memory. We need to find your family."

The man's shirt was missing, his torso covered with a blanket, but he wore a pair of trousers. Cole examined them. Despite the dirt, Cole could tell the trousers were of good quality. The young man probably came from a wealthy family.

Cole turned to the woman. "I'll take him to St. Bart's, where they can see he recovers fully."

4:10 P.M.

Adam Sedgwick finished his tea. Mr. Welsh refilled his cup with trembling hands. "What is it?" Sedgwick asked him.

"Pardon me, sir?"

"Where is Buckland?" Scrope said from across the table.

Sedgwick looked at Scrope.

"Buckland returned to Oxford yesterday," Lyell said.

"Of course," Sedgwick said. "I should be back in Cambridge by now as well." He turned back to the butler but he was gone.

"These are special circumstances, Adam," Scrope said. "You had to extend your stay."

"Yes, but I can't explain the real reasons for my stay to the board—"

"Lie," Scrope said.

275

"Please, gentlemen," Lyell said. "Adam will get to Cambridge soon enough, but now that we're here, let's discuss the business of the society."

Scrope said, "I thought you wanted us to handle the issue with Lord Bold and—"

"Not *that* business!" Lyell said.

"What, then?" Scrope said.

Lyell rolled his eyes. "I meant *geological* business."

Sedgwick nodded. He would welcome anything that took his mind off murders and royal investigations.

"Good idea, Charles," he said. "You'd mentioned the small pocket of catastrophists remaining in the society. What should we do about them?"

"Kick them out!" Scrope said.

Sedgwick ignored him and addressed Lyell. "We should assimilate all the evidence they present for catastrophism and reinterpret it within a uniformitarian framework."

"Or we can simply ignore all evidence for geological catastrophes," Lyell said. "That's what I did in my *Principles*. I didn't use the word 'stratum' once."

Sedgwick smiled. "Now that we're in control, we can make sure the catastrophists will never publish in any respectable geological journal."

Lyell nodded. "We must reach the point where catastrophism and supernatural creation are scientific heresy."

"If we do this right," Sedgwick said, "it won't be long before Bible-believing geologists are mocked and even banned from the scientific establishment."

Sedgwick lifted his head when the butler returned and handed him a letter.

"An urgent message for you, sir."

"Who is it from, Adam?" Scrope said.

"I don't know." Sedgwick opened the letter and skimmed down to the signature. "Daniel Young."

"What?" Lyell said. "Isn't that—"

"Read it," Scrope said.

Sedgwick glowered at him, then began to read aloud.

> Rev. Sedgwick,
>
> Last night I had an encounter with the society's librarian, Victor Shaw. It seems he has a rather disturbing history with the Askesian Society. Yes, I know about the Askesian Society.
>
> I wonder what would happen if the political motivations of the Geological Society were revealed in the London *Times* tomorrow. Perhaps the press would be interested in knowing the Geological Society killed Alexander Bold and burned the house of Lord Charles Bold, killing his wife. The *Times* could also reveal the society's ties to exiles from the French Revolution and its intention of overthrowing the king and establishing a republic. I'm not sure whether they would want to know about your manipulation of geological evidence to fit your political agenda. Perhaps that discussion would be too technical. Perhaps not. What do you think, Reverend?
>
> Of course, every man has a price. And the price for my silence is 2,000 pounds. I will be at Somerset House tonight at six-thirty. Bring the money and I will make sure the letter I have written to the *Times* is never sent.
>
> Sincerely,
>
> Daniel Young

Scrope cursed. "Who does he think he is?"

"What is the meaning of this?" Lyell said. "When did Daniel Young become involved?"

277

Sedgwick ignored the question. He felt the blood rushing to his brain. Daniel was a fool.

"What are we going to do?" Lyell cried. "I knew Shaw was going to be a problem. Stephen was supposed to eliminate him."

"Apparently they found him before us," Scrope said.

"It doesn't matter," Sedgwick said. "Just tell Stephen where Daniel will be tonight. He'll take care of everything."

6:32 P.M.

Daniel rested his shoulder against the arch of one of the east wing windows facing the central courtyard at Somerset House. His heart pounded in his chest as he waited for Lloyd to enter the courtyard from the north. He was sure Sedgwick would send Lloyd—otherwise the plan would fail.

What if he entered through the open section on the west?

He shot a quick glance to the west side of the courtyard. Nothing but shadows.

A hand grasped his arm, and Daniel recoiled in terror.

"It's me, sir, Willy."

Daniel put a hand on his chest and gasped. "What's the matter, Willy?"

"We're all in position," Willy said. "But I saw a boat dockin' below the terrace. You think it might be our man?"

Daniel glanced back to the north entrance, then looked at his pocket watch: 6:36. Lloyd was late.

"I don't think so, Willy. I don't think he has a boat. Must be someone from the Royal Marines. Their offices are on the south wing."

"I can go and see."

Daniel nodded. He didn't want Lloyd to come and see a policeman talking to him. Daniel needed him to talk, to try something against him. Despite the cool breeze, he felt some sweat below the line of his hair. He couldn't believe that after all he'd been through he was now serving as bait.

He wished Oatts could be there. While staring at the north entrance, Daniel wondered how well Willy and the other three bobbies he'd recruited could protect him. Lloyd seemed strong enough to fight more than one man at the same time. Hopefully not strong enough to beat five.

He glanced back and saw Willy going toward the terrace—with the three bobbies following him.

Instinctively, Daniel stepped out from his hiding place to go after them, but the sound of footsteps from the north made him halt. Daniel's heart skipped a beat when he realized he was standing in the middle of the courtyard. He turned and saw Lloyd striding toward him.

Daniel faced him and thrust his chest forward. He had to show some courage, even if he had no backup. What a bad time for the policemen to leave him alone.

Now all the available lights—from the few lit windows on the north wing—were behind Lloyd.

"Mr. Young?" Lloyd said.

"Yes," Daniel said in the firmest voice he could manage.

Daniel saw Lloyd's arm in silhouette as he pulled something from a coat pocket. Lloyd leapt. Daniel saw the glint of a knife aiming for his chest and dodged.

Lloyd immediately regained his footing. With a sudden turn he smashed his elbow against Daniel's shoulder.

Lloyd loomed over Daniel. A faint voice called, "Hey, you in the boat!" Lloyd glanced south. Daniel sprinted toward the terrace.

He knew Lloyd's longer legs were gaining on him. The door to the terrace was right in front of him, fifteen feet away. A door to his right led to the Royal Marine offices. He veered right and ran through the door like a bull. The impact shook his bones but he was soon inside. He'd never been in this part of Somerset House, but it couldn't be that different from the Geological Society's apartments—to his left he would find stairs going up and down.

Lloyd came through the door. Climbing would only slow Daniel down. He dashed down the stairs and halted in the basement, holding the rail and listening. He was panting. Should he keep going down to the cellar? The pitch-black basement smelled like a damp cloth. He moved through the gloom and crouched behind a sloping desk.

Lloyd could be right in front of him and Daniel wouldn't see him. But if Lloyd was here Daniel surely would have heard him. Why didn't he chase him down? Perhaps Lloyd realized Daniel had nowhere to go.

A light descended from the ground floor and Daniel peered from behind the desk. He saw Lloyd's legs first, then his hands and face. He carried a lamp in one hand, the knife in the other. Lloyd put the lamp on a table near the stairs and began searching the basement.

Daniel's skin prickled. Lloyd would discover him eventually and this time Oatts couldn't come to his rescue. This had to end—he was tired of running. If he'd faced Shaw, he could face Lloyd.

Lloyd walked in his direction, examining each desk. Now or never. Daniel gritted his teeth, grabbed a stool by its legs, jumped to his feet, and brought the stool down hard on Lloyd's back as he bent to look behind a desk. Lloyd stumbled and moved his head as if trying to shake the pain off. He still held the knife.

Daniel grabbed another stool and smashed it on Lloyd's head. The knife fell to the floor, and Lloyd's face hit the wall. A trail of blood smeared the wall as Lloyd's body slumped. He killed him? But the man's chest rose and fell. Blood oozed from his nose.

TWENTY-FOUR

LONDON - FRIDAY, 4 MARCH, 1836

8:00 A.M.

Daniel washed his face in the basin near his bed and put on fresh clothes. The morning felt different, safer perhaps, knowing Lloyd was behind bars. But things were far from fixed. He'd missed Lady Bold's funeral and surely Susan was hurt and angry with him. He had to explain himself, tell her everything, and win her forgiveness.

He walked out of his room and found Richard in the dining room, eating breakfast.

"Good morning," Daniel said.

Richard raised one brow. Daniel sat at the table and took a slice of dry toast from the rack. He buttered the toast while the housekeeper brought him eggs and porridge.

"Where have you been, Daniel?" Richard looked down at him. "If you're not in Norwich supporting your mother—where you should be—at least be loyal to your friends and family here. I didn't know how to explain your absence at the funeral!"

"I can explain."

"Of course you can."

"When Susan comes down for breakfast I'll tell you all what happened yesterday—and the night before."

"Don't bother, cousin," Richard said. "Susan's not here any more. She's with her father now."

Daniel widened his eyes. "What? Where?"

"I really think you should leave her alone."

"They can't be at their house, where are they staying?"

"Aren't you listening?" Richard said. "Susan is grieving for her mother. Leave her alone."

"Don't tell me what to do, Richard! Where is she? I must speak to her!"

"Mind your words, cousin! This is my house and you're a guest. Don't forget that!"

Daniel pushed his chair back with a sudden move that shook the plates and cups. He stood, feeling his face flush.

"You may own this house, but you don't own Susan."

Richard smiled. "Not yet."

"I know of your intentions," Daniel said. "But she loves me. Don't forget that!" He left the table.

8:42 A.M.

Daniel kicked a stone as he walked away from the house. How was he supposed to win Susan back if he didn't know where she was?

Sunlight filtered through the sides of the Kensington mansions as Daniel mulled over his frustrations. If only Alex were here—he could distract him with his high wit and low comedy. How he missed his friend.

Friends. Oatts and Cole came to mind. Two men totally different from him and from each other. Perhaps he should go visit the superintendent.

9:50 A.M.

Daniel crossed the gate under Henry VIII's statue and made his way through the oldest hospital in England. He walked

past the mural of Christ at the Pool of Bethesda and headed to the east wing, then quickened his pace and zigzagged
through the ancient hallways to the ward where he and Cole
had left Oatts. The superintendent drowsed in his bed.

"Good morning," Daniel said.

Oatts's eyes flickered and he looked around until he
found Daniel. The superintendent's expression reminded
Daniel of the moment he woke his father the night he died.

"How do you feel?"

Oatts cocked his head and winced. "Been better, Mr.
Young." His voice sounded weak, yet harsh.

"But you're alive," Daniel said. "I thought we'd lost you."

"Aye, alive thanks to you."

Daniel smiled. The diminutive Irishman looked even
smaller out of his dandy clothes and dressed in a hospital
gown.

"The doctor says me legs may not work like before. Something got broke in me 'ead that may 'ave caused a…"

"Paralysis?" Daniel said.

"Aye. We don't know yet. Best case, I'll walk out of 'ere
with a cane."

"At least you won't have to worry about Lloyd."

Oatts raised his brows.

"We set a trap for him," Daniel said. "Willy and his
friends took him to jail."

"Willy? Me Willy?"

Daniel nodded.

"Then I really 'ope Lloyd was unconscious."

"I made sure of that," Daniel said.

The superintendent cocked his head.

"You, Mr. Young? You put the big Lloyd out of commission?"

Daniel grinned and told Oatts about last night.

"Not bad," Oatts said when Daniel finished the story.

"You should consider joining the force."

Daniel laughed. He was no policeman—although lately, his futures in both geology and business were looking grim.

"Your friend the pastor was 'ere not too long ago," Oatts said.

"Mr. Cole?"

"Aye. 'E said 'e had to visit a man and would be back. Will you wait for 'im?"

"Oh, I don't know," Daniel said. "I must find Susan—"

"Daniel, my lad!"

Daniel turned to see Cole hurrying toward him. It surprised him how glad he was to see the pastor.

"It seems I just can't get rid of you, Mr. Cole." Daniel smiled.

"I just pray every day to be in the right place at the right time," Cole said. "Wherever God needs me."

"It seems the superintendent is doing better," Daniel said. "I was just ready to leave."

"Wait for me, we can walk out together. I just came to see if Mr. Oatts wants to say a prayer with me."

Oatts cleared his throat. "Not today, sir, thanks."

"Do not delay the day of your salvation," Cole said, waving one hand in the air. "The Lord is near!"

Daniel lowered his head and looked around. He really hoped nobody was watching.

"I will keep praying for you," Cole said and patted Oatts's shoulder. "Do you need anything?"

"Aye," Oatts said. "A new head."

Cole smiled and looked at Daniel. "Let's go, lad." They walked side-by-side out into the hallway. "Oh, my," Cole slapped his leg. "I didn't share the gospel with the young man who has lost his memory!" He faced Daniel with wide-open eyes. "I was so busy asking the doctor about his health I totally forgot about the purpose of my visit."

"What young man?" Daniel said.

"I must go back," Cole said. "You may come if you want, this will only take a few minutes."

Cole began to walk away. Daniel hesitated. He had no interest in preaching to a stranger. But he had nowhere to go, and he was curious. He ran after Cole.

10:58 A.M.

Scrope stretched his neck and walked into the Metropolitan Police Building, tapping the folded note against the back of his left hand.

Once inside, Scrope signaled a clerk to approach him. "I'm looking for the chief superintendent's office."

"Right this way, sir." The clerk led Scrope down a long corridor, then stopped at a large oak door. "The chief's inside, sir."

"Thank you."

Imagining he was about to take his place in Parliament, Scrope breathed in, fixed his eyes ahead, and knocked.

"Come in."

He slid the summons in his pocket and stepped into an imposing office.

The white-haired superintendent rose from his chair and moved to shake Scrope's hand. "Mr. Scrope, sir. Thank you for coming." The warm reception eased Scrope's tension.

Scrope nodded. "I'm pleased to see you again, Chief Superintendent."

"Please, sit down," the chief said.

With the corner of his eye, Scrope saw something move in the back of the room. He turned his head. Two bobbies stared at him and uneasiness stirred again. Scrope smiled at the man across the desk.

"So, what is this about, Chief Superintendent?"

The superintendent sighed and pursed his lips. Not a good sign.

"We arrested your aide, Stephen Lloyd, last night. He was trying to kill a man. He had previously attacked one of my superintendents and bribed a guard to escape from jail up in Islington. He's been doing quite some damage."

Scrope let his jaw drop. "I—I had no idea, Chief Superintendent. Stephen left my home several days ago and never returned. I had no knowledge he was involved in criminal activities. Why would he try to kill a man?"

The chief superintendent looked skeptical. Scrope knew he wasn't buying this story. They'd had a good relationship in the past. What would he do now?

"So Lloyd was acting by himself?" the chief superintendent said. "And you were never involved in this?"

Scrope gulped. "No, sir, I was not involved. These are shocking crimes."

"Very well. I'll pass that information to the commissioner." The chief looked up, past Scrope's head. "Willy, Peter, you may leave now."

Scrope watched the bobbies leave and sighed in relief. He turned to find the superintendent's face stern—angry, even.

"Let's stop pretending, George," the chief said. "I know your aide was working under your orders. Be that as it may, I owe you a favor."

Scrope nodded. The chief superintendent had him, among others, to thank for his position in the police force.

"This time, Lloyd takes the fall and you walk away," the chief said. "But now I owe you nothing else. So if they catch you being naughty again, I won't step in for you. You'll have to answer directly to the commissioner."

Scrope narrowed his eyes and said nothing.

"And one more thing," the chief superintendent said,

leaning back in his chair. "We've heard rumors you have a quarrel with Lord Bold, *the Earl of Devon*. Whatever happened in the past, we can blame Lloyd. But if something happens in the future?" The chief pointed a finger at Scrope's chest. "The blame will fall on you. Do you understand?"

Scrope felt his cheeks burn. Not knowing what to say, he simply nodded.

11:00 A.M.

Daniel kept a respectful distance from Cole. He'd always felt preaching was fine within the walls of a church, but in a hospital?

Of course, as his father would probably say, what better place than a hospital?

All he could see of the man Cole was ministering to was a head of wild blond hair. Daniel smiled. How curious to see someone with Alex's hairstyle. Daniel leaned against a wall and stared at the ceiling. A lump formed in his throat. Alex did it on purpose—he never tamed his hair, despite professors making negative remarks about it. Those times—

"You're here." Cole's voice brought him back from the past. "Thank you for waiting. We may leave now."

"All right." They walked off.

Cole pursed his lips and shook his head. "Poor lad. He doesn't remember what happened to him and finds it hard to speak. Although he's able to say a few words."

Daniel glanced at Cole. He seemed to really pity the injured man.

"I told him what the woman told me," Cole said, "to see if he remembered anything—but the poor lad was hit so hard in the head, then thrown in the river... I don't blame him for forgetting."

Daniel's head wound tingled and he thought about Oatts. Blows to the head were abounding in London.

"But he must come from a good family," Cole said. "The few words he said show education."

Daniel stiffened. The hair. The head wound. The river. The family. His hair. Daniel's heart raced.

"What is it, Daniel?"

Daniel looked at Cole. It couldn't be.

He sprinted back to the ward, searching every sick face. And there, six beds away from him, lay the man with the wild blond hair.

With a sudden fear it might not really be his friend, he inched forward. A blanket covered half the patient's face. His hands trembled.

Daniel took a deep breath and pulled the blanket back— just enough to uncover the man's face.

Alex!

Behind the bruises and the confused stare was Alex.

Thank you, God.

The atmosphere surrounding him seemed surreal. Alex alive. How? Dead one moment, alive the next, here in St. Bart's. How was this possible?

Alex grabbed his blanket with both hands and pulled it up, just below his chin. Daniel saw fear in his eyes.

"Alex, it's me, Daniel."

Alex blinked and Daniel's heart faltered—did his friend not recognize him? But what mattered was that he'd found him.

Alex opened his mouth and mumbled something. Daniel drew closer. Alex tried again, wincing.

"Da—Dan—" He gave up, apparently exhausted. Happiness washed over Daniel.

"Yes, Alex, it's Daniel. No need to talk now. I'm here to take care of you."

11:40 A.M.

Shaw trembled in his bed with fever chills. He touched his swollen face. The skin felt warm and hard and hurt like the dickens.

He staggered out of bed, searching for the mirror. He blinked with his good eye and stared at the reflection: one side of his face looked like a burning red football.

He searched in his wardrobe for his pocket knife—the old Barlow knife he'd taken from an American exile twenty years ago. He took the knife and the mirror and put them on the bed. Then he brought the wash basin and placed it besides the mirror.

Shaw bent over the basin, eyes focused on the mirror, and clenched his teeth. He grabbed the knife and slit his swollen wound. He groaned, although he knew the worst was yet to come. He took a deep breath and closed his eyes as he squeezed his face. Pus dripped on the basin.

Despite the pain, he squeezed harder and without pause. The pus began filling the basin as fast as pain filled his head. He felt dizzy but the rigidity in his face was giving way, so he kept squeezing. Nausea. Lack of air. Numbness overcame him and he released his grip just seconds before passing out.

3:12 P.M.

Alex's head throbbed. Daniel had been talking for hours about the events of the past two weeks—during which he'd escaped death and come back to life. The last thing Alex remembered was going to work to the library one morning, just like every other morning—except that on this particular morning he had decided to sneak out a few more letters. The next memory was an old, dirty hut and a thin, ugly woman.

Some of the details in Daniel's story made sense, like the people from his letters. But some feats seemed impossible. Daniel taking risks and fighting villains? He wanted to laugh. But then the overload of information turned into a black cloud in his brain, worsening his headache.

"Stop, please...." Alex muttered and grabbed his head.

"He must be tired, Daniel," Cole said.

"What he needs is to see a familiar place, like his hou—" Daniel put a hand over his mouth.

Alex stared at Daniel. *What is it?*

"There's bad news, Alex," Daniel said. "A fire burned most of your house."

Alex sat straight on the bed. "Wha—what?"

Daniel lowered his gaze. "Your mother died in the fire. I'm so sorry."

Alex shook his head. *This doesn't make sense.*

"No," he said, loud and clear. "No!"

But Daniel just nodded.

No. His life was good and easy and he wanted it back.

Alex tried to speak again—he had to tell Daniel to stop playing with him and say everything was all right—but his voice wouldn't follow his thoughts. The headache was like a huge vessel crushing his scalp.

If this wasn't a game, then he'd awakened to a nightmare—a mute nightmare with no house, no mother, and no job.

Whatever other bad news awaited him, he didn't want to listen.

He slid down into his bed and covered his face with the blanket. The old wool smelled of urine and sweat.

"I'm really sorry, Alex," he heard Daniel say.

"I'll pray for divine consolation," the old preacher said.

"A bad dream," Alex said silently with his lips as he closed his eyes.

3:13 P.M.

Painful chills woke Shaw from his delirium. He scratched his eyes and passed a palm over his face. The wound was cool. He grunted as if trying to blow away the dizziness. The chills passed. He wished he could grunt the eye pain away too.

The mirror and the basin with pus remained on the bed. He dropped the basin to the floor and held the mirror before his face. He gulped at the monstrous reflection: a black spot covered most of the right side of his face and his right eye was one stinking scab. He cursed Daniel. He should have killed him when he had the chance.

The longer he stared at his face, the more his hatred grew. He threw the mirror against the opposite wall—the shattered glass spread on the floor. He imagined plucking Daniel's eyes out and a thousand tortures more. His chest filled with air and he suddenly began to cough violently. *Water. I need water.*

Shaw looked frantically around him. He fell to his knees and opened his mouth to let out a mixture of mucus and vomit. What was happening to him? He stood quickly and dried his mouth with a towel. His chest hurt. Dread overcame him. Pneumonia? He couldn't die like this. He couldn't die without avenging his eye. He'd been spying on Daniel for more than a week, knew every place he went—until the day in the park when he stabbed him and left him for dead. How the hell had he survived?

His lungs felt raspy and Shaw feared another coughing spell. With trembling hands, he rushed to the wardrobe to gather scissors and an old red rag. He took them to the lone table in his flat and cut a round piece with a long strip of cloth emerging from both sides of the circle. Placing the cloth over his bad eye, he tied the strip around his head.

He walked over to the place where the broken mirror lay

and picked up the largest piece to look at his eye patch. It looked absurd. That made him angrier. And that's what he needed—anger to push him forward. And liquor to drown his fear.

3:55 P.M.

Susan leaned her head against the window of her almost empty room and stared out absently at the grass swaying in the wind. She had nothing else to do. She felt so lost in the new house. The beautiful, unfamiliar mansion had memories that weren't her own, sounds that strangers had grown up with, smells of unknown origin. It was also much smaller than her childhood residence—her father said it was the only house the insurance company could arrange at such short notice. That was about all she'd heard from her father lately.

He'd become more distant than ever, secluded in his study, apparently writing a speech that consumed all his thoughts. Poor Emily clung to her nanny as if she were her mother.

Knock.

Although eager to open the door and see someone, she was slumped in a state of lethargy she didn't want to abandon.

Thump, thump. "Miss Susan?"

"Yes, Mary?"

"Mr. Richard is here to see you."

Richard. Another gift? Oh, whatever it was, she needed a distraction.

"Miss Susan?"

"Yes, Mary, I'm coming."

She stood and passed her hands over her dress, then looked at her hair in the mirror and fixed it with her hands. She tried a polite smile for Richard, but it looked fake. There was no hiding her sadness. She walked out of the room and glanced up and down the hallway, trying to remember which way to go. Right. As she walked she thought of Daniel. Well, if Daniel didn't want to see her, she would scratch him out of her new life. Toss him away. The thought hurt dreadfully, but she breathed in deeply and walked down the stairs with the best fake smile she could manage.

Richard stood in the middle of the drawing room, yellow blooms spilling over his hands. Susan liked his hands—strong and clean, they had often touched her hand or shoulder these past few days. She looked at Richard's face and couldn't help but notice his resemblance to Daniel. She felt a lump in her throat. What would Daniel say if he knew she harbored these thoughts for his cousin?

"My dear Susan," Richard said, walking to her and kissing her hand. "I hope you're feeling better in these hard times. May these early spring flowers brighten your day."

"Thank you, Richard." Susan took the bouquet of daffodils.

"Is this a bad time, my dear?" Richard said.

"It's a good time. I enjoy the company."

Richard smiled, but perhaps too merrily, it seemed to her. She sat on a chair near the window—the drawing room was the only well-furnished room in the house so far—and crossed her hands in her lap.

"The house seems appropriate," Richard said. "Do you find it comfortable?"

Susan shrugged. "I guess I'll become accustomed to it with time. Life without my mother is hard to fathom."

Richard seemed distracted with something on his cuffs. Was he even paying attention to her?

"Bloody flowers," Richard murmured.

Susan frowned.

"I'm sorry," Richard said. "You were saying—"

"I was saying how difficult it is to imagine life without her."

293

Richard nodded, glancing back at his cuffs. "I can certainly relate to you, my dear Susan. My beloved uncle just passed away." He closed his mouth abruptly and his whole body stiffened. "A...very sad affair."

"Daniel's father died? When?"

Richard shifted in his chair.

"Richard?" Susan said. It sounded sharp, but she didn't care. "This is the first I've heard of it."

"Perhaps he didn't tell you because he didn't want to worry you," Richard said, shrugging.

Susan lowered her head and rubbed her forehead. She hadn't actually spoken to Daniel since the terrible attack at Hyde Park. Anything she knew about his doings came from Richard's mouth—a mouth that now twitched nervously.

"It must have happened very recently," Susan said. "Otherwise he would have told me."

"Well, yes—"

"Is that why he left London?"

His silence was maddening.

"But you led me to believe he was on a pleasure trip!" Her voice rose. "What else have you lied about?"

Richard seemed to shrink in his chair. "Susan, it's not what it seems—"

What a fool. Not just Richard but her, too. How could have she thought ill of Daniel?

Richard got up from his chair and knelt in front of her, grasping her hand.

"Forgive me, Susan. If I withheld anything it was only because of my deep...affection for you."

Susan winced and withdrew her hand. What was this cretin saying?

"The truth is, I'm not myself. My heart has been yours since the first time I saw you—"

Susan slapped his face so hard her hand hurt as if burned.

"You are despicable," she said. "You let me think the worst of Daniel. Your own cousin! Get away from me!"

4:05 P.M.

Daniel led Cole a few feet away from Alex's bed.

"I must say, Alex is in good enough health—despite his speech. What else can they do for him at the hospital?"

"I couldn't tell, my lad," Cole said. "But you may be right. He might be better off at home with his family."

"Can we just take him away?" Daniel said.

"I would prefer to ask. Wait until I speak to a doctor or a nurse."

Daniel nodded and walked back to his friend. "Would you like to go home, Alex?"

Alex's wide-eyed stare made the hairs on the back of Daniel's neck rise. He looked so afraid.

"You don't want to stay here," Daniel said, extending his arms. "Your father and sisters will be delighted to see you're alive and well. I mean, I still hardly believe it." Daniel smiled but Alex looked away.

He wished Alex could speak his thoughts. Daniel could only guess what his friend was feeling. It seemed Alex wasn't the same as he'd been twenty days ago. But he hadn't changed, surely. He was just entering new circumstances.

Daniel put a hand over Alex's shoulder and surprised himself with the words that came out of his lips.

"Don't be afraid, Alex. God will give you strength."

Alex reached for his hand and held it firmly. Daniel couldn't see his face but could tell his friend was crying. Cole's voice drowned out his sobs.

"All is arranged," Cole said. "Since I brought him in, I can take him out."

4:30 P.M.

"Are you sure you want to do this?" Daniel asked Alex once Cole had left and they were in the cab.

Alex pursed his lips and nodded.

"I guess you must see it, then," Daniel said.

The hansom rolled away from St. Bart's into more familiar areas of London, but Daniel's thoughts drifted north to Norwich. He thought about his father, how he now felt a desire to emulate him. The support Alex needed in this moment was the kind of support Daniel had seen his father provide to every parishioner in his church over the last twenty years.

What would his father do now? Probably utter some words of encouragement from his store of wisdom. But Daniel didn't know any of that, his memories were fragmentary. He tried to think of a Bible verse he could quote but none came to mind. He hadn't read the Bible in quite a while.

Alex stared at the sky. Perhaps he *had* changed. The extroverted, loquacious, mischievous Alex was no more.

The cab labored through congested streets as they neared their destination. Alex straightened and fixed his gaze on the end of the road. Daniel dreaded the moment they'd reach the path to the house, the spot where the plane trees no longer hid the blackened ruins.

When they arrived Daniel thought he heard Alex gasp, but it was him. His friend remained still, sitting in the cab, looking out at his old house.

Daniel shushed the cabby when he stuck his head in, demanding his fee. He didn't know what to do next. Would Alex want to walk through the remains or would he want to leave?

"So—it's tr—true." Alex sighed heavily.

And then, to Daniel's surprise, Alex turned to him with a new expression, one that despite the bruises and scars reminded him of the old Alex.

"Let's go—o."

Daniel smiled. "All right. I'll take you to my house and we'll find out where your family's living now."

5:17 P.M.

The darkness after sunset of the already gloomy day gave Shaw the confidence to seek a hiding place near Daniel's home.

He gulped down the last of the liquor, dropped the bottle on the ground, and crossed the street. He jumped the fence, trotted to a corner of the house, and crouched behind some bushes with his back against one side of the building. The street was visible through the leaves.

Shaw pulled back the cloak over his head and gripped the handle of his pocket knife. Turning the blade before his face, he imagined cutting through Daniel's stomach, making him whimper and cry like a dog.

Horses. Shaw peered through the bushes. A carriage pulled up. The lamppost nearer to the house was unlit, and he squinted to see who'd arrived.

5:21 P.M.

"We're here," Daniel said as the cab halted in front of his cousin's house.

Alex half-opened his eyes and closed them again.

"You look tired. Perhaps I should take you home right away. Stay here and I'll ask my cousin for directions."

Richard had better tell me where the Bolds are or I'll knock him sideways.

Daniel opened the door and asked the cabby to wait.

5:22 P.M.

Behind the bushes, Shaw waited. He heard steps and saw a black silhouette approaching.

Shaw rounded the bushes and positioned himself to attack Daniel from behind. This time he would not fail. No stupid rocks, just his reliable Barlow knife.

As he saw his victim coming closer, Shaw decided to finish him with one clean cut across the neck. He held the knife firmly and moved forward.

Shaw reached his prey in four steps and grabbed the figure. He pulled him close, immobilized his arms with a strong embrace, and raised his knife. Shaw could sense his fear and helplessness. He pressed the tip of the blade against his neck.

A hand pulled Shaw's wrist back and an elbow smashed into his wounded cheek, just below the eye patch. Confusion and pain filled his head. His victim spun away.

5:23 P.M.

Daniel squeezed Shaw's wrist with all his strength as he dragged him away from Richard. His arm curled around Shaw's neck, he pulled him down. Then he twisted the wrist and struck the forearm against his knee. The knife fell to the ground.

Shaw moaned as Daniel pushed him away.

Richard cried out as he looked back and forth between Daniel and his attacker. Daniel could see his cousin's knees trembling uncontrollably.

"Richard, get into the house." Daniel picked up the knife.

Richard seemed to hesitate but nodded when he saw Shaw stirring. He knocked on the door like a woodpecker until Mr. Welsh came out.

Daniel kept his gaze on Shaw. This had to end tonight. If he let him go, Shaw would come back to hunt him.

"Mr. Young! What's happening?" Daniel turned to see Thomas descending from the driver's seat of his cousin's coach.

Shaw jumped to his feet and ran toward the street. Daniel gasped. The librarian rushed to the back of Alex's hansom, grabbed the cabby by the shirt, and hurled him to the ground. With a quick movement, Shaw climbed to the driver's place and grabbed the reins over the cab's roof, whipping the horse forward.

Daniel's heart drummed in his chest. He ran to Richard's coach. "Thomas, hurry, we must catch them!"

Thomas nodded and climbed back up into the coach. The two horses neighed and surged forward at Thomas's command. Daniel's knuckles turned white as he gripped the edge of his seat and stuck his head out. Shaw was already turning east on Kensington road.

5:29 P.M.

Alex woke when the cab began throwing his body around. Had the driver gone mad?

He held tight and noticed Daniel wasn't at his side. Had Daniel sent him home alone? That didn't make sense.

Looking out the window he saw Hyde Park passing by fast on his left. The cab surged forward through Piccadilly. Something was really wrong. He wasn't supposed to be riding alone on Piccadilly. Unless his father had bought a house in—

The cab veered right without slowing down and Alex had to press his palms against the rooftop and clench his feet around his seat to avoid falling over—nonetheless, his head ended up out the window. He tried to yell to the cabby to slow down but speech was impossible.

He tensed his muscles and pulled himself up a little, but the bumping of the wheels brought him back down. He began to slide.

"He—elp!"

People recoiled from the path of the cab. Half his torso was now out of the cabin and the wheel brushed against his shirt.

The night shadows concealed the driver's face, but there was something eerie about him. It definitively wasn't the same cabby as before. Then a gas lamp gave Alex a brief glimpse of the man's face—a monstrous face.

The cab slowed, turned left, and picked up speed again. Alex took advantage of the momentum to pull himself back inside.

He gulped at the thought of the face he'd just seen. And shook when he realized who it was.

5:37 P.M.

Daniel slammed the seat with his fist. This coach was supposed to be faster than the cab they were chasing, but Shaw kept a good distance between them.

"They turned east on Pall Mall," Thomas shouted over his shoulder.

Daniel looked at the coachman and realized why they hadn't caught up with Shaw: Thomas was being careful while Shaw drove recklessly.

They reached the corner of St. James and Pall Mall.

The horses seemed to have been injected with a boost of energy as they gained on Shaw's cab. He could see the librarian turning his head back every few seconds to peer at them. Daniel still had the knife in his hand and would use it if Shaw tried to hurt Alex again.

"Overtake him," Daniel told Thomas. "Let's stop his horse."

"Hiya!" Thomas said and Daniel could picture him loosening his grip on the reins.

Daniel's heartbeat quickened along with the galloping horses as they drew almost parallel to the cab. Daniel saw the librarian less than two feet away to his right. Shaw gritted his teeth and cursed him over the sounds of the wind and pounding hooves.

The coach advanced until the tails of its horses were in line with the head of the cab's horse. Thomas pulled the reins to the right. The cab's horse whinnied and slowed, but Shaw whipped the beast hard with the reins and pulled it away from the other horses.

Daniel stared into the cab and saw Alex holding fast to his seat, then lost sight of his friend when a westbound carriage cut between the two vehicles. Suddenly, Daniel felt the horses slowing down. "Thomas, what—?"

Carriages everywhere, going north and south on Whitehall Street. Daniel frantically searched for Shaw's cab. "There!" Daniel pointed south.

"I see it," Thomas said.

Daniel's strength faltered as a half-dozen carriages trotted placidly between Shaw and them.

"Move out of the way!" he bellowed.

"He can't move very fast either, sir," Thomas said.

Something stirred inside Daniel. He felt like jumping from the coach and running after the cab, but he knew it was foolishness. A horse would trample him.

"Just don't lose them, Thomas!"

Somehow Thomas made it through the traffic until they were right behind the cab.

"Give up, Shaw," Daniel called.

Shaw recoiled and turned to face him. In the dim street-lights, the ugly eye patch seemed a natural part of Shaw's scarred face. The librarian growled and whipped the horse—his reins cracked and the horse bolted towards Westminster Bridge.

"His horse has gone wild!" Thomas shouted.

6:00 P.M.

Shaw jumped off the cab and rolled on the street. He felt his chest constrict and his whole body ached. Pneumonia, for sure.

He had to escape and seek a doctor.

Shaw looked down to the Thames and remembered the night he'd attacked the viper Sedgwick. He was near Westminster Hall. He knew the riverbank well. He stumbled to his feet and limped down to the gravel and rubbish at the water's edge.

6:01 P.M.

Alex gritted his teeth and looked out the window of the bouncing cab. *I have to get out.*

The wheels skidded through a mud pool and Alex felt his weight falling back. Then a cracking noise and a harsh shake rattled the cabin.

The world turned around on its axis and Alex bumped into the hard rooftop. He bounced off the window and saw the cab tumbling free from the horse and its wheels crashing against the stone balustrade.

He hit the ground.

6:03 P.M.

The coach came to a stop twenty feet away from the bridge, and Thomas ran down to where Alex lay still. Daniel jumped off the coach and glanced undecided between his friend and Shaw trailing down the slope to the riverbank. The fleeing librarian climbed down the wall separating the riverbank from the street. Daniel lost sight of him. With no lights down there, how would he find him?

The lamps on top of the bridge barely illuminated the water below, only the balustrade and the top of the arches beneath. Daniel peered down from the top of the wall. He could see the shapes of two boats stranded in the sand, hear the gurgle of the water, and smell the foul odor of the river—but no sign of Shaw.

"You should turn yourself in, Mr. Shaw," Daniel called. "You can't keep going like this."

He waited for an answer, any human sound, but nothing came. Daniel sighed, wondering if Shaw was already far from there. "God, please take control of this situation," he muttered, then decided to keep trying.

"You see, Mr. Shaw, Alex is alive as well as the superintendent. You haven't killed anybody. If you come out and denounce those who hired you, I'm sure you won't go to prison. Stop running and do what's right."

Dense fog moved in the current of the Thames. It seemed he was speaking to the air. Daniel felt the knife in his pocket, bit his upper lip, and jumped onto the gravel below. With his back against the wall, he studied the black shapes around him. If anything moved he'd stab it. He kept the knife ready by his side, but hoped he wouldn't have to use it.

A faint splash to his right, below the bridge, broke the monotony. Daniel moved south, keeping close to the wall until he reached the bridge, then followed the stone structure until he got to the first arch. He peered beneath the bridge and saw a figure turning at the opposite end of the arch, about forty feet away.

Daniel darted across the channel, stepping over the rubbish piled along the edge of the wall. He slid and splashed a few times before getting to the other side. He looked up and saw Shaw climbing the slope. He was going back to the street, probably to cross the bridge—but Alex was there.

6:10 P.M.

Alex had landed on his back. His lower back hurt and his right elbow had a small cut. Perched on a short column near the end of the bridge, he listened to the coachman tell his version of the wild chase and accident.

Where was Daniel?

The coachman didn't seem to understand what was happening, referring to Shaw as the "bandit" who attacked his master. Truth be told Alex himself didn't understand how they'd all ended up in this situation. All he knew for sure was that Shaw stole the cab with him inside and now Daniel was chasing Shaw down the riverbank. Alex felt chills under his skin just thinking of Shaw's disfigured face. It all made sense if he believed the stories Daniel told him at the hospital.

Alex shook his head. What an eventful day. Just this morning he was lost to the world, considered dead by everyone he knew. And now—

"Sir?" the coachman said. "If you feel better now, you can sit in the coach and wait for your friend there. I do hope he's all right."

Alex nodded as a sudden weakness took hold of his muscles. His stomach groaned. He'd hardly eaten all day. He looked over to where he'd seen the coach before, but the fog rising off the river enveloped everything, veiling whatever stood more than a few feet away.

He heard something behind him. The coachman glanced over Alex's shoulder. Alex turned to see a man climbing over the rail of the bridge and stepping on the balustrade.

Alex gasped as the librarian faced him for the first time that day. Shaw's eye widened. His lips trembled. "Impossible."

6:12 P.M.

Shaw blinked twice and considered removing his patch. Perhaps his uninjured eye was deceiving him. His hands began to sweat and his pulse surged. The apparition of Alexander Bold was a thin, pale figure with spiky hair floating in the fog. No, no, he must be seeing things.

The ghost opened his mouth, letting out unintelligible cries. All the hairs on Shaw's skin rose. He'd called this down on himself for all the crimes he'd committed. Death had come for him. He had to flee from death.

6:13 P.M.

In the diffuse light of the bridge lamps Daniel saw a balustrade emerging from the fog. A large shape stood there. It was Shaw, his back toward him.

He put the knife in his pocket and walked noiselessly toward the librarian. He attacked from behind, locking his hands across Shaw's abdomen. Daniel felt tiny besides the taller man he feared would overpower him easily. He pressed hard against the librarian's ribs. Shaw let out a scream of terror and Daniel felt his intertwined fingers separate as Shaw broke loose.

Shaw stormed forward, shrieking, along the footpath of the bridge. Daniel grunted and ran after him, but a barricade suddenly appeared in the fog, and Daniel had to recoil and change direction. They'd begun reconstructing the bridge. Daniel kept running, alert for more barricades. He saw Shaw's back less than ten feet away.

"Stop!"

The librarian turned his head back and a second later bumped against a barricade. His body slumped forward and to one side as he tried to regain his balance, but he tumbled over the rail.

Daniel heard a loud crack—as if something had broken—followed by a splash. He bent over the rail to look down at the water, but all he saw was the thick fog.

TWENTY-FIVE

LONDON - SATURDAY, 5 MARCH, 1836

8:03 A.M.

"Are you ready?" Daniel asked Alex as the coach halted in front of the Bold's new house.

Alex smiled and nodded. He looked happy after having collapsed exhausted into bed last night. Daniel grinned, remembering Richard's face when he'd explained who Alex was and what had happened to Shaw. There were no arguments. On the contrary, Richard was eager to spill the address of the Bold family and offer whatever was needed. He couldn't look Daniel in the eyes.

They came out of the coach and stared at the two-story house and the modest garden around it.

"It is smaller, but looks perfectly fitting for you," Daniel said.

Alex shrugged. "I don't—care. Let's—go."

Daniel was surprised. Although he paused after nearly every word, Alex's voice sounded stronger. "All right, let's go."

They walked to the door side by side. Alex was about to knock when Daniel put a hand over his shoulder.

"Wait." Daniel stepped back and to one side, out of view of whoever would open the door.

"Now you can knock," he said with a grin.

Alex knocked and the door opened thirty seconds later. Daniel held back a laugh at seeing the butler's consterned expression. The butler stared at Alex for a long time.

307

"Good—to see—you." Alex walked in past the butler. Daniel quickly followed suit.

Mary was crossing the foyer when they came in. The housekeeper let out a small cry and fainted. Daniel knelt beside her—good, she didn't hit her head. The butler came to help but kept staring at Alex.

"Where is Miss Susan?" Daniel said.

"Upstairs, sir," the butler said.

"And Lord Bold?"

"In the study, sir."

Daniel glanced at Alex. "They should see you all at once."

Alex nodded. "Yes."

Mary moaned and opened her eyes.

Daniel turned to the butler. "Call everybody to the drawing room but don't tell them about Alex yet."

"Yes, sir."

8:11 A.M.

Susan grumbled when someone knocked at her door. She had decided to seclude herself in bed until—well, she wasn't sure until when, but at least she wouldn't go out for a while. She rolled onto her stomach and buried her head under a pillow.

The knocking continued. "Miss Susan, you must wake up."

She wanted to tell the butler to go away but eventually he would without her being rude.

The knocking stopped and Susan sighed. Two minutes later, it resumed.

"Miss Susan?" This time it was Mary's voice.

They really wanted to wake her up. Something must have happened. She stuck her head out from under the pillow.

"What is it, Mary?"

"It's Mr. Young, miss," Mary said. "He has important news. He's waiting in the drawing room."

Daniel.

Susan had dreamed about him all night. He was here. But how was she going to look him in the face after her shameful behavior?

She sat up straight. "Come in, Mary."

The housekeeper opened the door and went straight to open the curtains. Light flooded the dark room.

"Help me get dressed," Susan said.

8:28 A.M.

Susan found the butler waiting right outside her room.

"Have you told his lordship?" Mary asked him.

"No," the butler said. "Mr. Young said they should all see him at the same time. I was waiting for Miss Susan."

"Well, go now," Mary said.

Susan wondered why Daniel was summoning her father. Mary had an odd smile. In fact, Mary had been jittery while helping her dress.

"What is happening, Mary?" Susan said.

The housekeeper gave a modest shrug. "You'll find out soon, miss."

This was all so strange. Susan rushed across the hallway and down the stairs.

When she entered the drawing room, Daniel stood from his chair with a huge smile that warmed her heart. Then she noticed a man with his back toward her, looking out the window. He looked so familiar.

The man turned around slowly. She gasped and put a hand over her mouth.

"It's really him, Susan," Daniel said.

Susan felt as if her chest was going to explode. Tears brimmed in her eyes.

"Hello—little—sister," Alex said.

Susan shouted in mixed disbelief, joy, and surprise. She ran to him and hugged his neck. "Oh, brother, my brother."

She felt her whole body trembling with happiness.

Soon her father, Emily, and even the servants were crowded into the drawing room, surrounding Alex with hugs and tears.

It seemed Alex had trouble talking, so Daniel told them how he'd found Alex, as well as amazing stories of fights and chases. After a while, her father dismissed the servants and only the family remained to listen to Daniel.

Susan didn't leave her brother's side but clung to his arm while listening to Daniel's story. His voice and demeanor were different—more confident and optimistic. Her hands tingled. She felt extremely attracted to this new Daniel. How wonderful it would be to—

"Well done, Daniel," Lord Bold said.

Susan looked at her father, whose face was actually smiling.

"It pleases me to know not only that my son lives but that Lloyd is in prison and the attacker is dead. I expect to deliver a speech tonight in the House of Lords that will crush any attempt to establish a republic in England."

Lord Bold observed Alex for a few seconds. "What about my son's speech? Is it a permanent damage?"

"I don't know, sir," Daniel said. "But I'm optimistic it's only temporary. I've seen a noticeable improvement between yesterday and today."

Alex nodded. "Yes—father. I am—doing—better—now."

Susan winced, seeing her brother gulp and close his eyes after a word.

"Does it hurt when you speak?"

Alex shook his head. "It's just—slow—co—ming."

"The blow to the head affected his speech," Daniel said. "Let's pray and hope he'll be rattling away at us in time."

"Thank you, Daniel," Lord Bold said. "You have proved to be a worthy man, and I welcome you as a friend of this family."

Susan could have overflowed with joy. Her father had never addressed anybody like that, much less Daniel. Perhaps now he would approve of their marriage. She could only hope.

10:00 A.M.

Scrope walked into Lyell's office at Somerset House and closed the door behind him.

"Where's Adam?" Lyell said. "I thought he was coming with you."

Scrope snorted. "He ran away to Cambridge as soon as he knew of Stephen's fate—I heard they took him to the Hulks. Anyway, Adam said he would come back to London in the winter."

"I see." Lyell crossed his arms over his chest and leaned back on his chair. "So it's up to you and me to salvage the society."

Scrope slumped into a chair and groaned. His body still hurt from the beating at Westminster Hall.

"Is it that bad?"

Lyell shrugged. "I'm not sure how the government's investigation will turn out. There's nothing they can find in our membership records that we should worry about. And it will probably be several months before we hear back from them."

"So it's business as usual in the Geological Society," Scrope said.

311

"As long as we don't do anything to call attention to ourselves, yes."

Scrope knew Lyell was right, though he hungered for revenge against Lord Bold. But without Lloyd and with the chief superintendent watching his every move, he had no choice.

"Don't worry," Lyell said. "We'll come back stronger. I have many plans to advance our cause. You take care of advancing the republic in Parliament and I'll give you the tools to defeat the Tories."

Scrope stared at Lyell. Behind that unremarkable face, there was a brilliant mind.

"I know you will, Charles."

2:35 P.M.

It was a fair afternoon and Daniel whistled as he entered Cole's chapel. He glanced around the empty pews and the narrow walkways. Cole, who was sweeping the floor near the pulpit, looked up and smiled.

"My lad, so good to see you. Do you bring good news about your friend?"

Daniel smiled. "I do, Mr. Cole."

"Excellent, for I also have good news about the superintendent. He will walk again, with a cane."

Oatts with a cane? That would slow him down, but it wouldn't stop him.

"Come sit and tell me everything." Cole leaned the broom against a pew on his left and sat down. Daniel sat next to him and told him everything that had happened since they parted ways at the hospital the day before.

Cole sighed. "I was hoping the sorry man would be redeemed."

"Shaw?"

"Indeed."

"Perhaps not every person can decide to be good," Daniel said. "It's just some's destiny to be evil."

Cole stared at him. "The work of redemption is for every man, my lad. There *is* no sin that the blood of Christ cannot cleanse. If Shaw had repented and sought the Lord, he would have found mercy and forgiveness. But that wasn't his decision."

Daniel nodded. Part of him felt sorry for Shaw.

"What now, Daniel?" Cole said with a more cheerful tone. "Have you decided what to do next?"

"I think so, yes. Next week I'm going back to Norwich to stay with my mother for the summer. I've thought about it and perhaps I should help with my father's congregation—make sure the parishioners have a leader."

"Goodness, lad, are you entering the ministry then?"

Daniel waved his hand. "I wouldn't say that, Mr. Cole. I'm not an ordained minister—"

"But you may serve the Lord in many ways."

Daniel cocked his head and glanced at the altar. "You know, Mr. Cole. I made a promise to my father many years ago that I would glorify God with science. Perhaps it's time I fulfill that promise."

"And how do you plan to do that?" Cole asked, leaning forward.

Daniel had thought about his talks with Andrew Ure.

"There are some geologists who remain faithful to the scriptures. I will try to study under them."

"What a wonderful idea! Perhaps you can teach me."

"Actually," Daniel said, "I was hoping you would teach *me*, about interpreting the scriptures. I'll need a solid biblical foundation before going back to geology."

Cole's smile beamed. "It would be a pleasure, my lad. Without a holy foundation to fight the war of ideas for the minds of men, you would either deny the Word or compromise your beliefs. As the gospel of truth says, 'For though we walk in the flesh, we do not war after the flesh: for the weapons of our warfare are not carnal, but mighty through God to the pulling down of strongholds; casting down imaginations, and every high thing that exalteth itself against the knowledge of God, and bringing into captivity every thought to the obedience of Christ; and having in a readiness to revenge all disobedience, when your obedience is fulfilled.'"

"But how do we bring captive the thoughts of science so they obey Christ?"

"That isn't the way," Cole said. "You must first obey Christ with your mind, with your thoughts. Then your researches in science will remain faithful to the truth."

"I don't understand," Daniel said.

"It's simple, lad. If your mind accepts the scriptures are true and inspired by God, then you'll interpret geological evidence according to that sacred thought. Hence, when the scriptures speak of a global flood in which the world perished, you interpret most geological formations and fossils as a result of that flood. If, on the contrary, your mind is not subject to Christ and your assumption is that the scriptures are irrelevant myths, then you may give the evidence any interpretation that suits your philosophy."

"What philosophy?"

"Any philosophy," Cole said. "Materialism, for example. Many so-called men of science are materialist philosophers who require every fact that comes before them to be interpreted without God. They will only accept material causes. Those men exalt themselves—and even nature—against the knowledge of God."

Daniel thought about many of his acquaintances at the Geological Society. They claimed to believe in God—but theirs was certainly a distant impersonal God. Not the Christ of the Bible.

"Now, then," Cole continued, "beware also of those who are deceived though well-intentioned, those who reinterpret the meaning of the scriptures to accommodate the thoughts fed to them by the materialist philosophers."

Daniel nodded. "Like the bishop at Oxford," he muttered.

"You must read my book, Daniel. There I refute the wicked doctrines of those who twist the eternal *veritas*."

"I'd love to read it," Daniel said as he stood. "Perhaps it will be published by the time I next visit London."

Cole smiled and embraced him. "Will you come often?"

"Of course, Mr. Cole, I must visit often. My future wife lives in London."

EPILOGUE

LONDON - SATURDAY, 29 OCTOBER, 1836

7:10 P.M.

"Are you sure you don't want to stay for dinner, George?" Lyell said.

Scrope glanced down the foyer into the drawing room.

"You know I dislike Sir Owen." He put on his hat, buttoned his coat, and walked to the door.

"Pity," Lyell said. "I really wanted you to meet my other guest—a man I'm sure will become a valuable asset to the society." He glanced at his watch. "He should be here very soon."

Scrope opened the door. "Perhaps some other time."

A strong wind almost blew Scrope's hat off as he stepped outside. "It feels as if a storm was coming, but I don't see many clouds in the sky."

"Oh, here he comes, George." Lyell sounded almost giddy. "Look down the street! I'm sure that's him."

Scrope saw a young man heading in their direction.

"Why are you so excited about this fellow?" Scrope said.

Lyell faced him with a big smile. "He's just returned from a long trip around South America. We've been in correspondence. His ideas are fascinating—and mind-boggling, let me tell you. This is the man we need in the society."

Scrope raised one brow. Lyell had made him curious enough to wait. The newcomer crossed the front yard and waved to them.

Lyell waved back. "Is it you, Charles?"

"Yes, Mr. Lyell," the man said and walked up to them.

"I'm glad to see you." Lyell shook the man's hand, then turned to Scrope. "This is my friend—and Member of Parliament—George Scrope."

Scrope extended his hand. "How do you do, Mr.—"

"Darwin, sir. Charles Darwin."

HISTORICAL NOTE

This is a work of fiction and does not pretend to be history. However, many of the people in the novel are real historical characters: Charles Lyell, Adam Sedgwick, William Buckland, George Scrope, Henry Cole, Andrew Ure, Georges-Louis Leclerc (Comte de Buffon), Jean-Jacques Rousseau, Jean-Pierre Laplace, James Hutton, Jean-Baptiste Lamarck, Jacques-Louis (Comte de Bournon), William Pepys, George Greenough, and other minor characters.

The author has tried to represent accurately the thoughts and beliefs of these historical characters as evidenced in their books and the historical accounts that we possess today. Although their scientific and theological thoughts—as described in the novel—are true, their internal motivations and the interactions between them are solely the imagination of the author.

The Askesian Society and the Geological Society of London are also real institutions. In fact, some of the members of the Askesian Society founded the Geological Society in 1807. There is no known connection between the Askesian Society and Comte de Buffon. However, there is evidence that the early Geological Society had strong political motivations and that these motivations framed the debate between uniformitarians and catastrophists in the 19th century. You may read more on this subject at *www.NickDanielsBooks.com*.